BLOODY SUMMER

Also by Robin Newbold

Vacuum-Packed

BLOODY SUMMER

Robin Newbold

WILKINSON HOUSE

FIRST EDITION
Wilkinson House Ltd
February 2012

ISBN 978-1-899713-13-4

Wilkinson House Ltd.,
145-157 St John Street,
London, EC1V 4PW
United Kingdom

www.wilkinsonhouse.com
info@wilkinsonhouse.com

Cover photo: © Moorefam/vm/istockphoto.com
Cover design: R. Evan/M. Sanchez

British Library Cataloguing-in-Publication Data
A catalogue record for this book is available from the British Library.

For Jun-Chan

"I had to touch you with my hands, I had to taste you with my tongue; one can't love and do nothing."

Graham Greene – *The End of the Affair*

CHAPTER ONE

"It's going to piss down," said Bill, standing up, his Mancunian baritone as heavy as the sky, his pot head's propensity to state the obvious heralding the first fat drops of rain.

"Are you just going to bloody sit there, Madam?" protested Sarah in her awfully Home Counties accent, riling her housemate with the childish nickname she had coined, and hastily tidying away the picnic in her annoyingly efficient way.

"Yeah, I am," snapped Adam, ignoring her and reducing her to background noise as he contemplated Bill, her boyfriend.

The blackest, most threatening of clouds were gathering. Just moments ago St James' Park had been bathed in early summer sunshine, and Adam had imagined Tony Blair sitting down just over the road at 10 Downing Street addressing his first meeting in that style over substance way that was now pervading all their lives.

By the time he actually made to get up and help, the lovers were already trudging off on ground that was rapidly becoming a quagmire. Rain fell violently from the opaque sky, split periodically by vicious shards of lightning, the booms of thunder making them tense.

"This wasn't in Alastair Campbell's script," said Bill as they finally reached the cover of Horse Guards Parade, shaking the water out of his shoulder-length black hair like some excitable dog. The lovingly tended hair that Adam longed to run his own fingers through.

"Whose bloody idea was it to have a picnic?" asked Adam, knowing full well it had been Sarah's and making a big show of pouring the water out of his expensively fashionable trainers.

"Out of a clear blue sky," replied Sarah, shrugging her pathetically skinny shoulders and brushing a hand nervously through her sopping-wet hair. Hair she liked to call blonde, though Adam always insisted it was mousy.

"We should have stayed in the pub," Adam said accusingly, feeling his head swim with the afternoon's concoction of beer and champagne, though as he looked at Sarah he was lucid enough to realise that one day he wouldn't be able to help himself as far as she was concerned. He despised her surface sheen of political correctness and her vegetarian-induced gauntness that the fashion rags dubbed "heroin chic". He couldn't help but clench and unclench his fists but hoped for all of their sakes she hadn't noticed.

The ensuing silence only seemed to increase the unbearable weight of his stare and as though sensing the power of his hatred, Bill put a large hand on his shoulder and Adam felt the inescapable stirrings of desire.

"Don't worry, mate," Bill whispered conspiratorially in his ear. "She can be a silly cow at times."

Adam could taste his friend's breath even as Bill finally moved away. He savoured his scent, but only wanted more.

He'd stayed out with the excuse of shopping but went into Soho and got wasted in some faceless gay pub instead. He'd feared no one would speak to him and he'd been right. It was like they could smell the fear, the desperation, but he hadn't wanted to sneer his way through another meaningless conversation before getting into some boy's pants anyway.

Emerging from the Underground at Hampstead, Adam elbowed his way past a gaggle of American tourists studying their Fodor's, no doubt bemused why so many shaven-headed men with little pooches were walking so purposefully along High Street. The crowd of people began to thin out as he headed for home and he felt a distinct nip in the air. There was an iciness in his own heart as he contemplated a night in with the two cooing lovebirds that Sarah and Bill had become.

"Faggot," came the cry from a group of kids running along behind him, jostling him on their way past and making him flinch. Like the losers in the pub who could sense his fear, he thought.

As he hurried his step he could still hear the teenagers' high, boisterous shouts in the distance and guessed they were on their way to hassle some of the desperadoes who cruised the heath for sex. He shivered, imagining the broad, dark expanse of common where, as he well knew, the rustling of the bushes gave way to far more human sounds after dark, particularly on clear summer evenings.

He hadn't been up there since before Easter when some geriatric queen had had his face mashed into oblivion by some excitable lad's baseball bat. He'd laughed at first when he saw the puréed face in the newspaper but soon stopped, mostly because he was worried it could have been his face confronting aghast readers over their cornflakes. He knew the good denizens of Hampstead were not overly concerned. Another bashing meant one less man soiling "their" heath.

It was odd to think all that was going on, all those sins of the flesh, as he walked down the manicured tree-lined avenues of Victorian houses, artfully subdued lighting and flickering TV sets offering a welcoming glow. He envied people their homes because he'd never really felt at home, never felt he'd belonged. He'd escaped his tyrant of a dad, furnished with a gold card to ensure he stayed away, only to find himself secondary to the two lovers in Hampstead.

He had a knack of unearthing new problems. Sarah's father, a family friend, owned the house and it was originally meant to be shared by just her and Adam until he realised he could make a bit more money by having another tenant. Adam had known Sarah since childhood, not that well, but well enough to have that little bit in common to enable them to become mates. Then Bill came along and added a powerful undercurrent to once still waters. Not that the oblivious Sarah really knew it, he thought, but Bill had irrevocably overturned all their lives when he walked in on their domestic north London bliss.

They all got on so well at first, after Bill answered the ad for a housemate on a university noticeboard. Adam had lusted after him in lectures but they'd never really spoken, not until the day he came to see the house for the first time and both Sarah and him sat giggly and totally in his thrall on the sofa. Sarah had scolded Adam afterwards for coming on to her "new vocation".

Even then he'd seen the desire in her eyes and that was the moment something as small and insignificant as a crush grew into something ugly and all-consuming for the three of them. Bill moved in the next day.

The imposing front of the century-old house seemed to swallow him in its shadows. He shivered as he walked through the overgrown garden, pungent with decay, the detritus of the building's old innards on the driveway after its recent makeover. It was all illuminated by light spilling from the living-room window, which far from welcoming was a horrible sign that they were in.

As he slid the key ever so delicately into the hefty front door and opened it, the usual smells of joss sticks, Bill's marijuana smoke and Sarah's veggie cooking wafted over him, but his senses were immediately attuned to the unusual sound of raised, near hysterical voices from upstairs. The shouts were audible above the cheesy chill-out music favoured by the couple that was coming from the living-room stereo.

He crept up the steep stairs he often feared might trip him up with devastating consequences one drunken night. It was a huge drop from top to bottom such were their grand Victorian dimensions. Perched outside their closed bedroom door plastered by a large *Meat is Murder* poster he listened harder, trying to decipher Sarah's infuriatingly practised middle-class accent, that had now risen to an uncharacteristic animal-like howl, from Bill's Mancunian basso. Then both came into sudden, frightening clarity.

"I want to know what you were doing whispering sweet nothings in his ear after our soaking at the park?" she yelled.

"For Christ's sake, you're totally paranoid."

"You start going on about how sexuality's a fluid thing and how you might fancy our housemate *if things were different*. Whatever that means," she screeched. "I'm fucking pregnant with your baby."

"What?"

"Pregnant. With. Your. Baby," she repeated, like she was speaking to a retard.

"Why didn't you say something?"

"Because you're never around," she wailed, breaking down

into sobs.

As the raised voices fell to a murmur, almost a hum, Adam just waited, hoping for another explosion, another disaster, some revelation that would break them apart, but all he heard were the muffled, placatory sounds of Bill.

"Don't worry, I'll ask Madam to move out soon, after this term," he said casually, like his housemate didn't matter.

To Adam the words felt like they were spearing him in the kneecaps, cutting right through to his marrow. He crept back down the stairs, past the portrait of the three of them taken a couple of days after Bill had moved in. They all wore wide smiles, but he noticed that even then they'd both been looking at Bill. Behind him came Sarah's newly confident laughter, like a final taunt as he slipped out the front door.

Shattered as he walked leaden-footed to the heath, he wondered if they'd known he'd been listening and contemplated finally ripping up the picture of Bill he'd so carefully placed in his wallet all those months ago.

The nip in the air began to chill him and he pulled his flimsy leather jacket tighter as he approached the bleak open ground that promised another snatched, desperate moment. It was disorientating in the dark but he could vaguely make out the silhouette of human shapes moving around just out of reach. He sought a more secluded spot and stumbled further into the common, though the image of the man who'd undergone a facelift with a baseball bat flickered uncomfortably in his mind.

Adam finally found a bench flanked by two large beech trees rustling edgily in the breeze. He lit a cigarette, tip flaring orange in the gloom, and waited. It didn't take long, it never did, as a human form loomed out of the night towards him.

"Got a light, mate?" said the voice out of the shadows as though this was a perfectly normal, everyday interaction.

"Yeah," Adam replied, feigning almost total disinterest, which he was absolutely great at, but eagerly scrutinising the guy's face as he briefly illuminated it with a cigarette lighter.

"Cheers," the man said, now puffing away and sitting right next to him on the bench, their knees touching.

Adam put his hands around his companion's shoulders. It was like he was holding on rather than hugging him. All puffer jacket no back, he thought sadly, but then he brought his lips to the guy's mouth, breathed in the manly allure of beer and cigarettes, and lust overrode everything else.

After they'd finished, the guy handed him a Kleenex, which seemed to appear from nowhere like in a magic trick and practically amounted to chivalry on the heath, but to Adam it was as uninspiring a gesture as the sex had been.

"Be careful, yeah?" said his brief encounter as he slid away back into the darkness like a guilty man.

The comment, which felt like a warning, only made Adam shiver as he walked off in the direction of Hampstead never feeling more desolate. The ring of his phone, *Can't Take My Eyes Off of You*, intended to be ironic, made him jump as he reached the edge of the heath.

"Yeah?" he said, irritated as he saw from caller ID it was Sarah.

"Oh babe, where are you?" she replied, concerned, cloying, but her soothing tone only betrayed how she'd made an art form out of being two-faced, he thought savagely.

"I've just been down the pub," Adam lied, fighting the primal urge just to confront her so they could bare their hatred for one another in the open and end the pretence, but instead he listened for a response, for a reason to her calling.

"We were hoping you'd come home for dinner," she said patronisingly. "You know Bill and I love having you around."

"Yeah, well ..." he stuttered, her duplicity leaving him speechless as he searched for an excuse not to go back to the house that was now as far from being a home as his parents' place.

"Don't worry. We had to throw away the nut roast as it got burnt," she said, laughing hollowly. "We're going to order pizza instead."

"Well, I might just stay out."

"Come on, pick up a couple of bottles of wine while you're at it," she said brightly, expert as she was at glossing over the darkest of truths, another middle-class trait of hers Adam hated, but only because he saw it in himself too.

"Okay," he replied for the sake of keeping up appearances. He knew everything was about how things looked, not how they really were.

"What pizza do you want, love?"

"Meat feast," he snapped in a final attempt to rile her, knowing it would upset her vegetarian manifesto. The line went dead.

He tentatively unlocked the front door. There was a fresh pall of marijuana smoke coming from the living room, and the chill-out had been replaced by the bland wailing of the Cranberries – like Britpop had never happened, he thought – obviously all was right with their little world.

"All right, mate?" said Bill, getting up from the sofa, a joint burning in his right hand as he grabbed Adam with his left to give him a peck on the cheek, an act that had progressed from a one-time joke to an almost customary greeting.

"Yeah, Billy Boy, I am," replied Adam, using the affectionate nickname for his friend that he'd hijacked from Sarah. He averted his gaze, reeling from the electric thrill of Bill's stubble having brushed his smooth, hairless cheek, but he couldn't escape the lingering fear that it was all coming to an apocalyptic end with his expulsion from the house. It was the reason they were both being so nice, he guessed.

"Pizza's here, boys," cried Sarah, poking her head around the living-room door, mastering that motherly expression of delight and disapproval as her gaze fell on Bill's hand, still affixed to Adam's shoulder. She coughed nervously as she went to pay the delivery boy.

"Everything all right with you?"

"Yeah," said Bill sheepishly, recoiling from Adam's eye contact.

"Sure?"

"Nothing that a bottle of wine won't cure," Bill said, laughing a little too loudly, nodding at the carrier bag of wine that Adam had in his hand.

"Yeah, I'll go and open it," he said, for the first time that day feeling a little more optimistic as he slung down his jacket on the sofa and headed for the kitchen.

He was fiddling with the bottle opener when he heard Sarah's footsteps uncomfortably close behind him.

"Hi," she said, so near in the confines of the kitchen that he could taste her chewing-gum tainted breath, feel its heat on the back of his neck.

"Hi," he said, spinning around agitatedly to face her as half the cork broke off in his hand. "Cheap shit wine."

"A bad workman always blames his tools."

"Whatever."

"Here," she said, adopting a more conciliatory tone, though as usual the damage had been done, placing the pizza boxes on the counter. "Give it to me."

He tried to resist her with an elbow but as they struggled for the bottle he lost his grip. It crashed to the tiled floor, red splashing excitedly over Sarah's white T-shirt and oozing out over the kitchen like an artery had been severed.

"What the fuck are you doing?" he shouted, eyes blazing accusingly as he clenched and unclenched his fists, uncaring this time whether she noticed or not.

"Sorry," she replied curtly, looking faintly ridiculous with her top stained crimson, a drop of wine on the end of her long nose.

"At least make it sound like you mean it," he said, throwing the corkscrew uselessly on the counter as the liquid puddled over his trainers.

"What do you want me to do?" she wailed, her normally pale features grotesquely flushed. "Get down on my fucking knees?"

"No, what I want you to do is clean up and then I want us to forget this ever happened," he said slowly, like he was addressing a child, a final attempt to restrain his boiling temper as he bit ferociously into his lip feeling the metallic taste of blood in his mouth. "Deal?"

"Deal," she murmured, turning away from him and snatching up a tea towel.

"We'll be in the other room," he uttered as though it was an order.

"You're taking your time," said Bill, sprawled back on the sofa with the BBC's Nine O'clock News flickering on the huge television in the corner, the "mega" TV Bill had insisted on to watch his beloved football, the audio drowned out by the Cranberries on permanent loop on the stereo.

"Just a little accident, isn't that right?" said Adam, nodding at Sarah who'd just entered with pizza boxes and plates.

"What the hell?" said Bill, pointing at her blood-red T-shirt. "If Adam wasn't sitting here, I'd think you'd chopped him up and buried him under the patio."

"You'd both love that," he said with a strained laugh, knowing it was too close to home. As Sarah left the room, an unusually uncomfortable silence descended between him and Bill.

The hush was broken when Sarah re-emerged, freshly changed, the stained shirt no longer blotting her carefully cultivated image, bearing the other bottle of wine. Bill seized it and poured out three characteristically large glasses.

"I have an announcement to make," he said, raising his glass theatrically.

"Bill ... I ... er ..."

"I'm going to be a father," he continued, rudely cutting his girlfriend off.

"For fuck's sake, Bill, I told you not to tell anyone until ..."

"Until what?" he shouted. "Until you have an abortion."

"I haven't decided anything yet," she replied unconvincingly.

"Well, congratulations you guys," Adam cut in, raising his glass and revelling in their argument as he watched the pizza go cold, congealed, unwanted like the baby.

"Thanks," she grunted.

"I thought you believed in the sanctity of life and all that stuff?" he added, mischievously addressing Sarah as he picked up a slice of pizza from the cardboard box the TV had come in – so big, it not only doubled as a table but also as a hiding place from where Bill would jump out and scare them. He looked around as he chewed on his pizza and saw he was the only one eating, presumably the only one who still had an appetite.

"Nobody believes in anything any more, that's the fucking problem. Just look at him on the telly," said Bill acidly.

Adam looked over at the TV and watched the animated but mute image of Tony Blair, frighteningly larger than life on the gargantuan screen, then back at the deflated figure of Sarah and he couldn't help smiling. "Yeah, so says Bill the card-carrying member of the Labour Party." His mocking laughter filled the void accompanied only by Sarah's sobs.

CHAPTER TWO

"But we're the beautiful ones," protested Adam in response to his tutor's assertion that the young think they're immortal.

"Yes, well I expect you've got three decomposing self portraits in your attic, dear boy," chortled Mike Smale archly, fingering a Polaroid of the previous afternoon's picnic in St James' Park, a picture of the three disparate housemates smiling.

"Don't quote your Wildean bollocks at me and it's a cellar we have, not an attic," Adam replied as the dank concrete stairwell of the basement came to mind. Way out of reach of the interior designers, it had been so dusty, dimly lit and full of the decaying junk of several generations of Sarah's family the day his curiosity had got the better of him that he'd never been back down there. The fact that it still existed made him shudder.

"Well, we're all in the gutter but some of us are looking at the stars," said Smale, continuing with the Oscar Wilde theme and throwing his head back in laughter, his perfectly tended mane of grey hair quivering. "And don't you quote your bland Britpop nonsense at me re the *Beautiful Ones* by Shade."

"Just because you read the lifestyle section of *The Guardian* doesn't make you hip, old man," said Adam cruelly, meaning to hurt. "And it's Suede not Shade!"

"What a very lovely ménage à trois," shot back Smale, studiously ignoring Adam's jibe as he stared at the photograph on his desk, poring over it like it was some failing student's summer exam paper.

"Yes, but three's a crowd," he replied, unable to keep the foreboding out of his voice.

"Whatever happened to the summer of love," said Smale, tapping a forefinger thoughtfully against his chin, faint smile on his lips.

"Everything has a cost nowadays."

"Hmm ... but he is just edible, isn't he?" said Smale,

dismissing Adam's comment and running a finger around the imprint of Bill's face like he just didn't want to deal with anything that would impinge on his comfortable, cosseted life in academia. "So of the moment too."

"Yeah," he said, finally smiling at his tutor's ability to put into words what he was thinking. Their relationship had progressed to more, much more, but for Adam it was bound by necessity. "What about my grades this year?"

"Always when you fucking want something," the professor muttered agitatedly under his breath, taking a long drag from his cigarette, even though he'd forbidden Adam to smoke in his office, fixing him with an intimidating, well-practised stare over half-moon glasses. "Your grades are shit."

"I already knew that," mumbled Adam, cowed by the professor's gaze, discomfited being in the shadow of the shelves lining his office, warped with the weight of books, a weight like the one he felt pressing on his shoulders. He wanted to run but he knew it would mean giving up everything. He needed Smale, at least to pass the first year.

"Well," said Smale, "let's discuss how to proceed tomorrow night, my place for dinner, bring your toothbrush."

"But I have plans ..."

"Bugger your plans if you want to start your second year here, young man," the professor said, rudely cutting him off and giving him another schoolmasterly stare. "You're too busy chasing that boy to think about studying, that's your bloody problem."

"What can I do?" Adam replied, helpless as he looked back at the towers of books as though the assembled tomes of English literature could provide an answer.

"That's where I might be able to help," said Smale, chuckling his most self-satisfied and menacing chuckle. "I've been thinking of conducting a little experiment."

"What kind of experiment?" he questioned but sounding far more interested than he knew he should.

"Well it seems you're intent on seducing Bill, Mr Laws, I should say, and I want to see, in the current parlance, if he's on message."

"You mean if he's gay?"

"My dear, you don't need to be *gay* to sleep with another

man."

"But Billy Boy's always fucking around," Adam insisted. "With other women."

"Maybe he doth protest too much. And, if you're so convinced he's straight, why are you so infatuated? You've even given him a pet name, for goodness sake," said the professor. "Anything happen between you and, er, *Billy Boy*?"

"He's just different, sensitive, I guess," replied Adam. "And we did sleep in the same bed once, when we were drunk, nothing really happened, just touching. We were both fully clothed."

"I happen to know his grades are not up to scratch and as his tutor I can offer him, shall we say, counselling, with a promise to discuss his, er, mitigating circumstances with the dean of the school."

"I'm really not sure," Adam said hesitantly, worried the professor's concern was only another bid to manipulate him, to manipulate them all.

"Let's put it this way then, his grades are worse than yours and if he continues in this vein he certainly won't be strutting his handsome stuff at this institution next year," replied Smale, taking another long drag on yet another cigarette and smiling almost triumphantly, his crooked teeth the same colour as the late afternoon sunshine which was barely visible through the dusty blinds. "The dean is a highly principled man but as he's having a little tête-à-tête with one of my young female students I'll see what we can do. He shouldn't be a problem but we still have to sell this to Bill Laws."

"Anyway, I've got to run," said Adam, anxious to get away, distance himself from the professor's warped plan.

"You youngsters, it's all busy, busy, busy," said Smale, sighing and aggressively adding another dog end to the overflowing ashtray sat among the papers strewn across his desk.

"Yeah, well I've really got to go," reiterated Adam tetchily, standing up.

"You don't get out of it that easily," growled Smale in his accentless drawl that seemed purposely hard to place, pinpoint, pin down. Leaving his glasses on the desk, he made his now customary lunge.

"Nice to see you," Adam lied but barely got the words out

before he was pinned back by the groping, everywhere hands, felt the professor's tongue slithering around at the back of his throat.

"Don't forget tomorrow night," said Smale, finally disengaging and walking back to his desk, crooked smile at the corners of his mouth.

As he unlocked the always locked office door, Adam tried to blot the last half an hour from his mind. He tried to forget the bitter taste of Smale on his tongue, the all too familiar reek of cigarettes and an old man's staleness. He did what he knew he shouldn't and taking the now time-worn photo of Bill out of his wallet stared at it longingly, like nothing else mattered, but of course it all mattered very much.

Bill thrust his hand into the darkness of his departmental pigeonhole and was pleasantly surprised when his hand brushed up against stiff paper. Unusual, he thought, but it could have been from one of the Athletic Union girls he was always, as he put it, "knocking off" – being chairman had its privileges. The envelope however felt far too weighty to be a perfumed love note. Nevertheless, he looked guiltily left and right for any sign of activity, but no one was around. It was way too early for first years, except him of course. After a sleepless night following Sarah's revelation that she was pregnant, he'd gone for one of his early morning jogs around the campus – something he'd done every other day until he discovered pot. But he never really did get a good night's sleep, there was always something on his mind. Some part of him wanted the baby, the right-on, idealistic part, but he felt the more mercenary, more mature part, thought Sarah was right to be doubtful. He certainly feared anything that might put a brake on his promiscuity that had flourished like a bad case of VD since he began university. It was like he couldn't help himself.

He heard coughing behind him, but it only announced the passing of another faceless lecturer, breezing by in a cloud of perfume. Probably sociology, he thought, as he finally let his eyes fall on the crisp white envelope in his hand with "*Mr Laws*" scrawled formally across the front. Bill looked furtively left and right again, drew it to his nostrils and breathed in a smell of cigarettes so strong that it almost made a marijuana smoker like himself cough. Getting impatient, he aggressively ripped off the top of the envelope, pulled the card-like paper out and unfolded it.

Ominously his attention was drawn to the embossed university crest at the top of the scrawled missive and he began to read:

Mr Laws,

As your tutor, it has come to my attention that your grades are not going to come up to scratch this year.

The welfare of my students, I can assure you, is my very first priority and I'm willing to take up the baton for you with the dean. From what I've seen in your group tutorials you're an able, enthusiastic student.

I realise some first years find it difficult, shall we say, adjusting to the rigours of academia and I'm hedging that the dean will accept you onto the second-year programme if you submit to a weekly individual tutoring session with yours truly. We can discuss your academic concerns and any other problems you may have in an informal counselling environment.

I am free to address the matter this afternoon between 1-3pm. I anticipate your attendance.

Yours,
Smale

He carefully folded the letter, tucked it back in the envelope and put it in his pocket. It felt bulky there, as though it didn't belong, full of its own self-importance like the professor, he thought. He caught a whiff of the scent Smale always wore. It seemed to taint his fingers. Even the lingering stench of stale tobacco couldn't quite mask it. He punched the wall and felt the impact zigzag all the way up his arm.

Lighting a cigarette in the "strictly no smoking" area, he thought of Adam and the way he swore by Smale, but he hated the professor with his theatrical flourishes, how his whole personality seemed to advertise he was gay. Bill feared it was a side of Adam he hated too, at times wanting to strangle it out of him, but he knew, deep down, it wasn't just hate, he felt threatened.

As he threw the cigarette to the ground, he moved to stare out of a window which was vibrating to the sad tune of summertime rain when he felt a hand rest lightly on his shoulder. The flowery aroma of a woman's fragrance swept over him and he resignedly turned around to acknowledge, what he guessed, was another drunken mistake.

"Hi, Bill."

"Hello," he replied gruffly, turning to face the girl whose name he'd forgotten, impassively taking in the dark, frighteningly androgynous looks that had seemed so appealing when he first spotted her across the bar one night, unsure then whether it was a boy or girl. "What are you doing up so early on a Friday?"

"Handing in an assignment for my sociology module," she replied, brushing the rain out of her short boyish hair and waving the plastic work folder in her hand. "Been burning the midnight oil. And you?"

"Couldn't sleep," he said, gratefully acknowledging the name "*Helen Tidy*" typed across the front of the assignment in her hand.

"Wanna go for coffee or something?" Helen said brightly, smiling shyly up at him as she dropped the folder in a professor's pigeonhole.

"Yeah," he said unenthusiastically, watching as the smile faded from her features like it had never been there, like she wished she hadn't bothered, and he really wished she hadn't. Sleeping around had come to rival his drinking and smoking in its frequency, but sadly he knew the girls performed almost the same function, a quick pick me up that made him feel like shit the next morning.

"You're a bit of a morbid one, aren't you?" said the unnervingly cheerful Helen, fixing him with her piercing blue eyes, exotically at odds with her swarthy features.

"I'm fine," he replied darkly as they headed to the cafeteria but he wasn't really listening, Bill was still fixated on Smale's letter, the bulk of which he could feel in his pocket and he knew it wasn't going to go away.

"Did you have fun the other night?" she said, gently brushing the back of his large hand.

"Oh yeah ... course," he replied, pulling his hand away, feeling embarrassed and wondering why she was putting them through this charade. His mates all talked about womanising with such glee but it was as though he was still frantically looking for that missing component. It always ended up like now, he thought, just numbness.

"You don't like girls, do you?"

"What?" he snapped back, shocked out of his apathy as they sat at a table in the near-empty refectory. "What's that meant to mean?"

"I mean you don't respect women. You don't even remember my name, do you?"

"Look, Helen," he blustered, taking her in fully for the first time that morning, the tears in her eyes. "I have a girlfriend."

"Jesus," she said, throwing her hands up in the air as though that underlined everything.

"Sorry," he said, reaching out and uncharacteristically patting her hand, recognising her cheerfulness to be a facade for some deep-seated hurt only because it was how he felt himself.

"No, no it's me," she replied quickly, regaining her composure. "Just having a hard time with boys."

"Yeah?" he said, concentrating not on her but on the torrential rain outside the window, wary of getting too close.

"I'll get those coffees. Cappuccino?"

"Hot chocolate, please," he said absently, his thoughts muddled by the closeness of Smale's claustrophobic office and the fear Helen had been right about him not liking women.

"Chocolate," she said, breaking his train of thought, placing a paper cup in front of him.

"Cheers," he replied, looking away from the window and finally across at her, feeling like he had to make a huge effort just to be civil. "Look, I'm sorry I'm not that talkative, I've got a lot on my mind."

"That makes two of us," she said and they both laughed, breaking the tension.

"Damn weather too," he said, swigging back his chocolate, preparing to leave.

"Yeah," she said thoughtfully, looking out of the window. "I know you said you live in Hampstead, you can come back to mine at least till the rain stops. You know it's just around the corner."

"Well, I shouldn't but ..." he let his voice trail off as a grin sprang to his lips. He really didn't remember where she lived because he'd been so drunk that night and it worried him. It worried him even more that she remembered he lived in Hampstead.

As they left the cover of the campus, they broke into a trot because Helen's umbrella was totally inadequate for the summer storm. When Bill saw Adam it was already too late. He was marching towards them, snug under his golf umbrella, with an inquisitive look that his smile failed to mask.

"Hey," he said. "I didn't know you two knew each other."

"There's a lot you don't know," Helen replied.

"And I didn't know you two *knew* each other," added Bill, his usually flawless olive skin reddening under Adam's intrusive gaze, the uncomfortable urge to lash out at his housemate gripping him again.

"Yeah, we're good friends," he replied. "We're on the same sociology module but how are you two acquainted, pray tell?"

"Now that would be telling," said Helen answering for Bill. "See you."

Bill's illogical ire subsided as he felt the girl's arm loop through his and allowed himself to be guided up the street, away from his friend's prying eyes. As they turned into the halls of residence he guessed Adam would still be watching them and he was, a wicked smile on his lips.

She was all embarrassed bustle when they got into the room and rushed around getting him a towel. Bill though grabbed not for the proffered towel but for Helen. "I know what you really want," he said as she continued to dab at his wet hair, but when he brought the boyish face to his and tasted the full lips, he couldn't get Adam out of his head.

It was late afternoon but it could have been any time in the gloomy, windowless corridor. Bill had left his appointment with Smale as long as he could and felt resigned as he knocked on the heavy office door, a sliver of light spilling uninvitingly from the gap at the bottom.

"Just a minute," came a rather strangled cry from the other side.

It was as though, thought Bill, the professor was doing something he really shouldn't have been and he breathed out nervously when the key finally turned in the lock. Smale stood in front of him, supercilious grin firmly in place by way of a greeting, his surprisingly bulky frame blocking Bill's entrance.

He'd never experienced the professor up this close, he'd always been a comfortingly distant figure even in group tutorials or a blip waving his arms around at the front of a lecture theatre. It was that voice, Bill thought, the booming, resonant voice that lent him a certain gravitas, like he was a trained actor or something, the way he cajoled, admonished and intimidated his students simply by his tone.

"Ah, Mr Laws," Smale exclaimed, peering over his glasses as though examining a precious artefact, excitedly wafting a cigarette around with his right hand. "So nice of you to join us."

Bill felt himself reddening under Smale's scrutiny but he stood his ground. "Sorry I'm late," he mumbled morosely.

"Nonsense, nonsense," cried the professor, accommodating as ever, although his cold eyes said otherwise. "Come in."

Instead of the formal wooden chairs reserved for tutorials, Smale waved him to one of two armchairs side by side, adjacent to his untidy desk where a large computer hummed, the screen facing away from them.

"Sit," he commanded as though addressing a recalcitrant dog.

Bill did as he was told but felt lightheaded as the stuffy, smoke-filled room affected him, Smale's sickly sweet perfume only added to his nausea, the towering bookshelves closed in on him, and he longed to be outside in the fresh air but the windows were shut, blinds drawn as though the rest of the world didn't exist.

"Cigarette?" said the professor chummily as he sat down in the adjacent chair, making Bill flush by placing a hand ever so lightly on his arm.

"No thank you."

"Don't tell me you don't smoke," Smale said, laughing, discarding his glasses but still peering at Bill like he was a specimen. "I've seen you puffing away like a chimney."

"Trying to give up," said Bill, shaken at the thought of being observed.

"Yes, well you'd be surprised at what I don't see," said Smale as though feeling Bill's discomfort, wrenching the blinds aside and rapping loudly on the windowpane. "I can watch the whole bloody campus from up here. And you'd be surprised by what some of my students divulge."

"Yeah?" questioned Bill but really not wanting to know as the professor's amused laughter filled his ears, wanting to get out in the afternoon sunshine on the other side of the fastened windows.

"Now, Mr Laws, let's get down to business, shall we?" said Smale, sitting down again and rearranging his ridiculously out of place cravat, all sound of laughter wrung from his voice. "Tell me what the problem is and we can see about you being readmitted to do your second year."

"Problems?"

"Girlfriend trouble, boyfriend trouble, parents divorcing, your dog died, what?" growled Smale.

"Well if I may say so, I don't think it's any of ..."

"Hush," said the professor, rudely interjecting and placing a hand on Bill's arm again. "You don't think it's my business, fair enough. There's the door Mr Laws and if you walk out of it now we won't be seeing you again after the end of term. Do I make myself clear?"

"Yes," murmured Bill resignedly, feeling the sweat spring to his forehead in the cloying, overheated room.

"Good," replied Smale, smiling and revealing his array of nicotine-stained teeth.

"Well, my girlfriend's pregnant," he blurted out, quivering with the baldness of the statement, realising how far he was from where he wanted to be in his life.

"I see," said the professor thoughtfully. "Now we're getting somewhere."

"She wants to get rid ... I mean she wants an abortion but I don't ..."

"Mr Laws, just take your time. This won't go any further. Promise."

"Well she wants to get rid of it, our baby, but I want a child," said Bill, anxious to find the right combination of words that could get him out of Smale's office, the right combination to convince *himself* that he was happy. "I'm under a lot of pressure."

"My dear boy," he replied breezily, "I've never been in your position before but I can sympathise with what you're going through."

"Thanks," said Bill, though he sensed from the professor's tone that he wasn't the slightest bit interested in empathy.

"I know that you live with Adam, have you tried speaking to him?" said Smale, quickly snatching up his glasses and perching them on the end of his nose.

"I love Adam ..."

"Love?" questioned Smale, like he was an interrogator unearthing a vital clue.

"Yes, I mean love as a friend," said Bill, colouring under his questioner's glare. "But I don't think he'd understand about Sarah and me."

"Sarah and I, it's Sarah and I, Mr Laws," said Smale pedantically, tapping his chin. "But I think you'd be surprised. He's very bright."

"Well I think he's a bit jealous of Sarah and *I*."

"And are you jealous of him?" shot back the professor.

"What the hell are you trying to say?" Bill said, viciously gripping the side of his armchair, using all his resolve to stop himself running out of the office, running away from his university life for good.

"Oh come Mr Laws, even I can see he's a very attractive boy, angelic even," Smale said deadpan. "When we're young we often like to have, how can I put it, a finger in as many pies as we can."

"I'm not gay," said Bill with such hostility it made him wonder just who he was trying to convince. He rose an inch or two from his chair, the urge to run even stronger, but he slumped back again as the professor fixed him with his jewel eyes.

"Not saying you are Mr Laws but things aren't always black and white," he said, sighing dramatically.

"Look, I really think you've got the wrong idea about me and Adam."

"It's Adam and I, Mr Laws, Adam and I, but that's quite enough for this week anyway," said Smale dismissively as he got up and threw open the windows. "I'll talk to the dean and we can probably come to some kind of arrangement. As long as you agree to these weekly counselling sessions, of course."

"Thank you," said Bill, flushed and uncertain as he shivered in the uncomfortably cool breeze now coursing through the office.

Smale shooed him out of the chair and towards the door, like he'd suddenly become an unwanted guest.

"See you next week, Mr Laws."

It was the last thing he heard as he slipped quietly out of the office, panting for breath in the dim corridor, glad of the shadows to mask his insecurities.

CHAPTER THREE

"When I saw Billy Boy with Helen, even though I was jealous, it made me feel great to see him cheating on Sarah and made me think maybe I do have a chance. He's more of a slut than any gay boy I know."

Adam typed in the password-protected journal that he knew would be incendiary if anyone else were to read it, particularly his housemates.

"Adam," he heard her shouting through the door.

It broke his concentration but he listened as the handle turned and was relieved that he'd locked it. "Just a minute," he said, disguising the irritation in his voice as he carefully, almost fanatically, saved what he'd written and began shutting down the computer. "Coming."

"Ooh, er," said Sarah, sarcasm rumbling through the door, above the CD playing on his stereo.

As he unlocked it, a smile imprinted on his features, Adam felt riled before he'd even laid eyes on her. But taking her in, the anorexic blonde (she insisted on being called blonde) that used to be his friend, he couldn't believe she actually had a baby growing inside her. Maybe it would munch its way out of her pathetically skinny tummy like that creature from *Alien* and then finish her off, he thought hatefully.

"How are you, honey?" she said finally, breaking the edgy silence where they'd simply looked at one another as though in mourning for what they'd lost. They hadn't really spoken since the incident with the wine.

"Come in," he replied coldly, ignoring her meaningless pleasantry and motioning her to sit on the edge of his bed, the only uncluttered surface such was the chaos of his life.

"This looks like the Third World War," she said, looking around with mock disapproval and they both laughed.

"Yeah, well, I'm not used to visitors," he said. It came out more pointedly than he'd intended, revealing his bitterness, and he looked up just in time to see her flinching, like she'd developed a nervous tic.

"It can be tough, first year at university and all."

"Yeah," he said in agreement but it was like she was reading her lines from a script, there was no emotion there, no feeling, no empathy, he thought.

"I'm lucky I've got Bill," said Sarah, smiling.

"I'm so rude," he said, blotting out her last comment and moving to turn down the volume of the CD playing on the stereo, the *Wild Ones* by Suede, which he guiltily imagined as the soundtrack to his *relationship*, for want of a better word, with Bill.

"Oh no, leave it," she said. "I love Suede."

"Yeah?"

"You don't remember?" Sarah said like she was hurt. "We used to listen to their albums together. In my bedroom."

"Of course," he said, forcing a thin smile, momentarily sad at feeling so little for the friendship they'd once shared, actually finding it difficult to recall how close they'd been. She'd even made a move on him before she found out he was gay. They laughed about it afterwards, a carefree laughter like nothing mattered. A laughter he feared never experiencing again.

"Have you seen Bill?" Sarah shrilled, finally betraying the reason for her sociable visit to his room, indicating the status of their so-called friendship.

But it was the question Adam had been willing her to ask. "Well ..." he demurred.

"Well, what?" she snapped.

"Well, he was with Helen Tidy earlier," he replied with a barely concealed smirk, knowing she had no idea who Helen was.

"Helen *who*?"

"Helen Tidy," he repeated triumphantly. "She's on our course, they were having coffee."

"You're so incestuous all you bloody Literature students, I'm glad I'm doing Law."

"Just a coffee, take it easy. Anyway I think he's with Smale this afternoon," he said, picturing Bill seated uncomfortably in the armchair where *he* usually sat as the lecturer hungrily devoured his friend's handsome features with his eyes.

"Smale?" she said, warming to this new horror. "What that bloody lecherous old professor?"

"The very same."

"How do you know?"

"I was walking by the department and saw him go into Smale's office," he lied but cursed himself for the slip which he hoped wouldn't give away the fact he'd helped engineer the whole thing – Bill would never talk if he knew.

"What do you think that's about?"

"Oh, probably nothing," he blustered. "Smale often sees his students to enquire after their welfare."

"Oh," she said lightly, suddenly unconcerned about the professor. "But what about this Helen?"

"Don't worry about her, she's not a supermodel like you," Adam replied sickeningly sweetly, running the hand he'd just unclenched from a fist over Sarah's porcelain-fine features. "They were just discussing course work."

"Yeah," she said, getting up. "Well, I hope he comes back soon, I've got some news for him."

"What?" he said anxiously as she headed for the door, her back to him.

"I'm going to have the baby, me and Bill's, our baby," she said, turning around and beaming at Adam as she edged out of the room.

"Fuck, fuck, fuck," he said under his breath as the door clicked shut, alone again, all alone with Bill further away than ever.

As he walked down the stairs he could hear Sarah singing contentedly in the kitchen, probably rustling up a celebratory nut roast for three, he thought. He wasn't about to tell her he wouldn't be home tonight to play gooseberry over the scented candles once again. He grabbed his coat from the hanger and slammed the front door. Edgily turning the car keys over in his pocket, mind elsewhere, he was surprised by Bill on the pathway.

"Hey, where you been?"

"What's it to you?" said Bill, unusually blunt and looking to move past his friend and into the house.

"Just that 'er indoors was asking," replied Adam, grabbing Bill by the arm to slow him down.

"Yeah? Well just keep your nose out."

"She knows about Helen," he said smugly.

"You told her?" shouted Bill, snatching Adam up by his collar, lifting him off his feet. "What the fuck did you say?"

"I just said you were friends on the same course," Adam managed to blurt out as a large hand closed around his throat.

"You just keep out of my business," hissed Bill, tightening the pressure, hot breath in Adam's face. "Little queer."

The heavy push that sent him reeling backwards down the path and onto his back hurt but it was the hatefulness behind his words and the sight of Bill walking away which filled him with an aching emptiness. Even as the front door slammed, it took him a few moments to get back to his feet.

Tears were streaming down his cheeks, hot with anger and humiliation as he made it to the MG. He turned the engine over, relieved that it started first time, but as he drove to Helen's, Adam feared that through his selfishness he'd just alienated the one person he actually cared about. He couldn't get Bill's face, so twisted with anger and hatred, out of his mind.

He turned the stereo up, *"...and if you stay well I'll chase the rainbow fields away, we'll shine in the morning and sin in the sun, oh if you stay we'll be the wild ones."* He sobbed along but was broken out of his trance by the explosive sound of impact. He looked up out of the windscreen, wondered how he hadn't seen it. Somehow he'd hit a parked car.

"Shit," he shouted over the steering wheel, coming to and quickly reversing out of the wing he'd careered into. Luckily the roads were pretty free of traffic and with a spin of the wheels he slammed the car forward again on the slippery tarmac, sluiced by what seemed like the endless rain.

He brightened after the little accident, like it had focused his mind, but he hoped he hadn't damaged his car, although it hardly mattered on such a rust bucket. Adam delighted in his little bit of Englishness on wheels which had been in the family for years. He loved it down to the St George's cross that Sarah had lovingly stencilled on the boot in happier, less complicated times.

He'd had enough of Brett Anderson's caterwauling, ejected the tape, chucked it with the mass of others on the passenger seat, stuck in Blur's *Parklife* and couldn't help singing along. He and Bill had been to see them a couple of weeks before at the Shepherd's Bush Empire. Sarah hadn't come along as she deemed the band "way too blokeish", which was almost as big a crime for her as eating sausage sandwiches. Damon had implored the fans to have a "luvverly summer" but it had been far from lovely so far, thought Adam, cracking open the window and taking a long drag of his cigarette. Just thinking about the two of them at the concert, together, alone, sweating on each other in a sea of strangers made him feel euphoric, high like he was on ecstasy.

"All the people, so many people ..." he sang along, full of energy again but the words spluttered to a stop as he saw her in her über cool white Harrington jacket, standing out from the garish anoraks and sportswear. He beeped three times on the horn and skidded to a stop just a few feet ahead of Helen, who he now noticed was weighed down with a couple of bags of shopping, face tight against the rain. He gallantly threw open the passenger door and scooped up the mound of cassettes as she scurried over through the shower.

"Hop in," he said, throwing his cigarette out of the window and grabbing her bags to put on the back seat.

"Thank God for you," she said, leaning over to give him a kiss. "I forgot my umbrella."

"You're too busy trying to look like an It Girl," he said, laughing unkindly as she ran a hand through her bedraggled bob, a hair-cut that he knew cost more than most student's weekly budgets thanks to the generous allowance from her architect father. "And you know what?"

"What?"

"I'm not going to give you a lift unless you promise to tell me what's up between you and Bill *and* make me a cup of tea when we get to yours."

"Well, I promised ..."

"Well, I'm not joking," he said gruffly, rudely reaching across her and flinging the passenger door open as the rain cascaded down, bouncing off of the pavement. "Up to you."

"Okay, babe, as long as it won't go any further."

"Scout's honour," he said, raising his hand though he'd never even been near a Scout hut, as he finally started the engine and pulled away.

"Blur, this is a bit old innit?"

"I do have the new album but I like the old stuff and what's all this *innit*, do you have to sound so street?"

"Well Bill's not exactly a gentleman," she said, laughing.

"No, he's a real working-class lad."

"Yeah, I heard you liked rough trade," Helen replied, giggling.

"You're one to talk, missy," he said as he ejected Blur and rooted around for something to impress his passenger. "Will The Prodigy do?"

"That's so last year," Helen said disparagingly. "They're being used in TV commercials now."

"Sorry, everything's become mainstream, Pulp are in the Top 30 and we have a Labour government."

"Everything's mainstream because everything's becoming so bland. Look at Tony Blair."

"Oh no, you're beginning to sound like Bill, the angry young man," he said, sighing dramatically. "Too much marijuana I'd say."

"What do you believe in then?" Helen shot back as they made eye contact for the first time.

"Grant Mitchell from *EastEnders* and a good shag," Adam said and they both cracked up with laughter as he drew the car into the halls of residence. Though above the giggles, he actually wondered whether he did believe in anything other than his obsession with Bill.

After running around to inspect the damage to the car from the earlier crash – a buckled wing and shattered headlight – he hurried down the path behind Helen.

"What about your roommate?" he said as she let him in.

"She's met some rugby player from the Athletic Union and they've been loved up for days in his place," she said, looking down at her shoes, like she was ashamed to catch his eye.

"Don't worry, you'll get yours girl," he replied, smiling. "Which reminds me about my demand."

"I need something in return. I'm a journalist, remember?"

"You're a journalist, if you call being editor of the student rag journalism," Adam said, cackling.

"Well?"

"Look, I can give you a story on a professor having an, er, inappropriate relationship with a student, but not for a few weeks," he said, grinning mischievously but concerned at what he'd do in his all-consuming attempt to get Bill, to have him.

"Why the delay?" she said dubiously.

"I need time to gather the evidence, speak to people."

"Is it you?" she asked, running her eyes over him with a journalist's instinct for scrutiny. "Are you the student?"

"No," he insisted but he knew the crimson flush that had risen to his cheeks had given him away.

"Okay, I can wait," she said, thoughtfully tapping a finger against her chin.

"Now about Bill ..."

"Let me make you that cup of tea first," she said as she left the room for the communal kitchen. The intensity of student life seemed to negate any form of privacy where even making beans on toast garnered an audience.

He wandered around the room restlessly, picking up things and putting them down again just as carefully. Adam hesitantly sat on the edge of Helen's bed, wondering if this was where Bill had gently peeled her clothes off before drawing her to him. Maybe they hadn't even been able to wait till they reached the bed. Maybe he'd fucked her on the sofa by the door, the one with the cheap printed throw, he thought jealously.

"Tea," she said and he turned to face her, momentarily startled.

"Thanks," he replied, regaining his composure and moving from the bed to that very sofa. She sat in the armchair opposite. "So?"

"So, what?" she said, taking a gulp of her tea.

"So, what happened?"

"Nothing much to tell," she said, sighing. "I really like him, we've had sex, *twice*, but he has a girlfriend. Plus my ex in Cambridge has just told me he wants to get back together, he's talking marriage and everything, but I don't know, I'm so over him really."

"Oh," he spluttered, doubly peeved at the way she'd emphasised the fact they'd slept together more than once, but ignoring what he thought was a red herring about a pushy ex as she'd never talked about him before with anything but derision.

"You look pissed off," Helen said. "I know you all live together but I've got nothing against ..."

"Sarah," he said, finishing the sentence for her and desperately trying to conceal his anguish. He hated imagining anyone else with Bill but he needed the whole story. "No, I'm not pissed off, I'm just surprised."

"Surprised?" she said sounding exasperated. "What, surprised that your frigid friend Helen can actually get a guy to find her attractive?"

"No, Helen, just surprised at your choice," he said hatefully, goading her, knowing he shouldn't, but unable to help himself. It was like he was willing to lose everything, if he could only get Bill.

"Well, I don't think my *choice* is actually any of your fucking business," she said, standing up and facing the window. He could hear her sobbing.

"Look, I know women find him attractive," he said to her back, desperately trying to sound sincere, hiding behind words as he always did, a lifetime of secrets and lies had made him good. "He's just a bit of a slut that's all, I don't want you to get hurt."

"No, I know," said Helen finally, turning to face her friend, tears glistening off her angular cheeks. "You're right."

"Will you see him again?" he said as he moved to cradle Helen's head in his hands but feeling nothing but jealousy. It was sickening to him that he actually envied and not pitied her.

"He said he'd call," she said, words still thick with emotion. "But he won't."

"There are plenty more fish in the sea," he said, guiding her to the sofa and only wishing the cliché was true but his want told him that wasn't possible, he couldn't just turn his feelings on and off like he was flipping a switch. To Adam, only one person mattered, apart from himself of course.

"It looks like Dowdy's stepping down as head of the

department," said Smale, a smile revealing his weathered teeth, jumbled and leaning like old tombstones – the only real imperfection on his otherwise smooth, unreadable features.

"You mean the one knocking off one of his students?" Adam questioned.

"Allegedly," said Smale, laughing heartily, "but it means the dean's vacancy finally becomes free."

"Oh," he replied with a smile, his ever-alert mind seeing where the professor was headed with this piece of news. The emailed love notes he'd kept in his inbox – completely damning as they were sent from Smale's university account – had just doubled in value.

"I'm obviously going to apply and I'd make an excellent choice, don't you think?"

"Of course," he replied on cue, desperate to disguise the fact his earlier thoughts had now flowered grotesquely into a fully fledged plan.

"Let's have a drink to celebrate my good fortune, dear," said the professor as he got up and kissed Adam on the forehead, making him flinch and not for the first time. "Whisky and soda?"

"Please."

As he listened to Smale banging around in the kitchen and imagined him fussily mixing the industrial-strength drinks, Adam snooped about the cluttered living room that was as elegantly untidy as the professor's office. He was most taken by the big glass paperweight on the coffee table that sat majestically atop a mass of documents. Adam picked it up and looked at the miniature of the Star Ferry, "a cheap souvenir from Hong Kong", according to the professor but one he wouldn't let him have, even though he'd already asked more than once. Adam possessed a childlike wonder for travel and as he looked at the little green boat behind the glass, he knew where he wanted to go in the summer and hoped he could persuade Bill to join him, with or without Sarah.

"Oh put that bloody thing down," Smale boomed as he came back into the room carrying two brimming glasses.

"Can I have it?" said Adam, naughtily palming the surprisingly heavy paperweight between each hand.

"We'll see," replied the professor, waiting for him to replace the souvenir before handing the drink over.

Adam swigged it back, the cool liquid welcome in the uncomfortably warm and airless room, though Smale's icy stare made him shift around in his armchair. He'd rationed his visits as the relationship had evolved obscenely. The professor had become more and more demanding, and thoughts of him panting and flushed during sex were enough to make him almost retch now.

"What's on your mind?" he snapped, rudely breaking the silence.

"Nothing really," Adam mumbled, hoping the professor wasn't a mind reader but fearing he probably was. The truth was he didn't think he could bear any more intimacy with the man, this drunken man in tweeds lasciviously licking his lips, just inches away.

Initially it had been flattering, thrilling even, to have an older, supposedly respected academic lavishing attention on him. Now Adam found it just disgusted him. He'd only agreed to the house call because he wanted the lowdown on Bill. There was also the small matter of his own grades to be attended to by the liberal marking pen of his tutor. Though tutor was a word he could no longer use without an involuntary shudder.

"Speak up boy!" bellowed the professor, face reddening.

"Nothing to worry yourself about," Adam replied arrogantly, no longer in awe of Smale's outbursts like he'd once been. It was the one positive aspect of the desperate downward spiral of their relationship. The more Smale had plumbed the depths of human behaviour, the more he had lost all respect for the professor's authority. Adam wasn't cowed by his tantrums but bored by them, which he knew only agitated him further.

"What worries you, worries me," said Smale taking a more conciliatory tone, but the forced tenderness in his voice, the dishonesty, chilled Adam.

"I'm thinking about Bill."

"Yes, well that's where I can help you," said the professor, scrambling to his feet so athletically it belied his age. He rustled around in one of the drawers of a large wooden bureau in the bay window then, like he'd known exactly what he'd been looking for, triumphantly held a Dictaphone aloft. Smale placed it on the table between them and they listened as Bill's shaky testimony unfolded.

"Well?" said Adam when it was all over, underwhelmed.

"Well I think he doth protest too much," said Smale through a smile, taking a big swig from yet another glass of whisky and clicking the tape off. "From what I can discern he comes from a very traditional working-class family and we're not going to get out of him at his first meeting that he has feelings for other men."

"I suppose."

"Look Adam, he says he loves you, that's a pretty big admission to make for starters."

"Yeah," he replied absently, staring off into space. He wouldn't be convinced until the Mancunian was wrapped around him in his bedroom; with Sarah in the adjoining room if need be.

"You've had something from me this evening," slurred Smale, slamming his now empty glass on the table and rising menacingly to his feet, swaying slightly with the alcohol. "Now I want something back."

"I really think this should stop," Adam protested but felt pinned to his armchair as the professor hovered just above him, so close he could taste the whisky on his breath.

"Stop?" said Smale, laughing dementedly, moving his face to within an inch of his student's. "How do you propose we stop?"

"Like this," Adam shouted, pushing the professor as he got down on his haunches, reptilian-like tongue poised to caress him. He fell backwards almost comically onto the floor.

"What the fuck do you think you're doing?" wailed the professor as he got back to his feet unerringly quickly, fists raised, but Adam was up too as they faced each other again.

"I'm standing up for myself, which is what I should have done long ago."

"I'll have you thrown out of the school for this," said Smale, his strangled cry sounding hollow and desperate. "Thrown out I say!"

"Don't threaten me," Adam shouted but not quick enough as the professor awkwardly swung an arm which caught him just beneath the right eye, knocking him slightly off balance. He felt it swelling, blurring his vision, but managed to grab Smale by the collar before he could wind up another punch. The cravat came free and a couple of buttons popped loose from the professor's shirt as Adam dragged him towards his face.

"Let me go," he spluttered, choking from the pressure around his throat.

"I'll fucking let you go," Adam spat as he shoved Smale as hard as he could and watched him fall. The professor thumped his head heavily against one of the wooden bookcases lining the room before crumpling pathetically into a ball.

"What have you done?" Smale croaked, finally uncovering the hands from his face, turning to look up at Adam.

"It's over," he said, standing triumphantly over the professor who was propping himself up on his elbows, face lined in anguish, looking his age for once, thought Adam. He fixed his eyes on the small gash at the back of the professor's head which was leaking blood, turning the garish canary-yellow shirt a more fashionable crimson.

"It's over," Smale repeated like a child upbraided by an angry parent and then he started to cry.

Adam felt the beating of his heart pulsing in his ears. Still thinking clearly and familiar as he was with the old house he ran to the bathroom where he fetched a towel.

"I still have those emailed love letters you sent me from your university account," said Adam, voice contorted by revulsion, regaining the professor's attention as he threw the towel at him. "So don't even think about reneging on the deal regarding my grades or your meetings with Bill. That's if you want to end up dean of the school rather than on the streets."

"Bastard."

"No more of a bastard than you," Adam replied as he watched the professor still hunched up pathetically on the floor, frantically dabbing at the gash, the towel turning a sickening red.

"I can't believe this has happened," he said, his resplendent mane of hair becoming matted as the blood slowly coagulated.

"I can't believe you thought you could abuse your power in the way you have. I'll be back to see you next week, in your office. No more house visits," said Adam as he turned his back and headed for the front door, putting a hand up and feeling the egg-shaped swelling around his eye.

"Fuck you."

"Oh and you might need stitches," Adam called behind him, slamming the front door with a satisfying crash.

CHAPTER FOUR

He was still breathing hard as he trotted through the evening drizzle to the MG. Studying himself in the rear-view mirror he was unsettled by the discolouration around his eye, which had gone a tell-tale yellowy black. It was an unwelcome flaw on his downy features and he couldn't help feeling marked, somehow soiled, by the whole tawdry affair with the professor as he brushed a hand thoughtfully over the bruise.

On starting the engine he afforded the house one last glance and watched as the light in the bathroom burst into life, illuminating the thick bushes, indicating Smale was already up and about. Accelerating away with the furious squeal of burning rubber in his ears, he knew it was all far from over.

He stopped off at Cullens at the top of Hampstead High Street and Bill and the horrible confrontation they'd had on the pathway came into focus in his mind. He'd almost forgotten but minutes from home his object of desire and his lap dog girlfriend loomed awkwardly. As he scanned the well-stocked shelves of the fashionable mini-market, he pulled out one bottle of sparkling wine and then another. They weren't impressed by much, at least not where he was concerned, but Adam knew his housemates would be impressed by the relatively cheap wine in the Cullens bag plus the small wrap of cocaine he had in the car's glove box.

This time of year the last summery shafts of sunlight should have still been shining but the evening gloom had already descended when he pulled up beside the house. The tall trees and overgrown hedges meant it was almost permanently shrouded in impenetrable shadow but from the street he saw the living-room light throwing out an ominous but predictable glow. He could already picture them curled up together on the sofa, candles aglow, anaesthetised in front of some supposedly zany, so-called sitcom on BBC2 laughing at all the worst jokes. Opening the front door, the reek of stewing vegetables hit him – the smell of domesticity – and he was confronted by the conundrum of their oneness again.

"Hi, guys," he said, but when he poked his head around the living-room door, concerned at exposing the black eye, disgusted by the prospect of having to explain it away, he was surprised to see Bill stretched out on the sofa alone, TV chattering away inanely in the corner. Adam knew as soon as their eyes met that the storm clouds of earlier had passed as quickly as they'd blown in.

"Look I'm sorry about earlier, mate," said Bill languidly but as he sat up from the sofa he looked at Adam harder, like he was studying him. "What the bloody hell happened to your eye?"

"Oh, it's nothing," he said, waving away the concern with his hand but turning from his friend's now burning gaze. "Walked into a door, you know how it is. And don't call me mate."

"Would you prefer honey?" Bill shot back, face clouded by hostility again.

"Just take a chill pill," Adam replied, unperturbed by his friend's spiky behaviour, wielding the new-found confidence that came with the knowledge that Bill supposedly "loved" him, though in the other ear he could hear Smale's diatribe "What is love anyway?"

"But seriously, what happened to that eye?" he said, insistent, concerned. "It looks nasty. Did you go to that bloody heath again?"

"Something like that. But why are you so interested in my nocturnal activities?" said Adam, laughing it off, indicating he wasn't going to elaborate, but drinking in Bill's sudden concern, warmed by it.

"Well?"

"It was great sex, though," said Adam, laughing hysterically, though he knew it was a nervous reaction, an attempt to conceal. He placed the wine on the coffee table like it was a strategic manoeuvre, anything to distract attention away from himself.

"Okay, that's enough," said Bill, raising his hands as though in surrender, like he didn't want to hear any more. "Put that wine in the fridge, there's a good boy."

As instructed, he went to the kitchen, stomping off in his DM boots, on which he'd even considered painting Union Jacks now that London was the "most swinging city on Earth" and they were all "Cool Britannians" according to *Vanity Fair*. Sarah hated him wearing the boots on account of their perceived links to fascism and of course because they were leather. For so long he'd been hurt by her disapproving sneers, while he had listened to anything she said with at least a modicum of respect. Now he delighted in upsetting the Sarah he faced. The Sarah banging and crashing around the kitchen, the domestic, dull follower of Bill, that he could not care less for. Hunched over the sink as she was, Adam couldn't even look at her without wanting to laugh cruelly and deride her for the doormat she'd become.

"Hi, love," she said, sensing his presence as she turned away from the sink, but she may as well have said nothing. She enunciated it in such a way that the greeting was neither here nor there, meaningless, and the eyes were cold, blank.

"Hi," he replied, incredulous that she'd not even looked at him closely enough to register his black eye. She'd hardly looked at him at all. "Nut roast again today, is it?"

"Noooo," she said as if hurt. "It's pasta bake and there's enough for three."

"Count me in then," he said as he quickly dispatched the bottles in the fridge, eager to get out of the kitchen and away from her.

"Thanks for the wine," she said, placing a hand lightly on his shoulder, finally laying her eyes on him but only a cursory glance that missed his glaring bruise.

"No problem," he muttered and left her alone. It was like she didn't want to know about his life, he thought. She never dared ask him any awkward questions seemingly out of fear it would upset her ordered little world, but Adam was absolutely intent on doing just that.

"Uh, Billy Boy, you're not watching football are you?" Adam whined on entering the living room.

"It's Manchester United."

"Well, you hate Manchester United," he replied, a little uncertainly as he was totally illiterate when it came to football, although he had been with an ex to see a Crystal Palace match once, enough to put him off for life.

"Listen, sonny," said Bill, finally rising from his slouched position on the sofa in an apparent attempt at gravitas. "I'm a Manchester City fan, which means I have a vested interest in seeing Man U fail."

"Oh."

"Yeah, oh," said Bill, turning back to the TV and returning to his slouched position on the sofa. The Neanderthal-like chants spewing from the set filling the room.

"Cool," said Sarah cheerily as she came in bearing a tray of food. "Footie."

"No one calls it footie, apart from middle-class Chelsea fans like David Mellor," shouted Bill testily, still fixated by the images on the screen, not even deeming to look at his pregnant girlfriend, who'd just brought him dinner.

As Adam watched Sarah redden, he couldn't help but smirk. "I thought you loathed *footie*," he commented, goading her, knowing that before she'd met Bill she had declared her all-consuming hate for the sport.

"What's wrong with women liking sport?" she replied defensively, banging down the tray of food on the coffee table.

"Don't you mean footie?"

"Fuck off, Madam," she hissed.

"Hey, come on you two," said Bill, at last turning away from the screen and glaring at them both, his two admirers.

"I'll get the wine," Adam sniffed as he marched agitatedly out of the room.

"Well done," Sarah called after him sarcastically, still not finished.

"Fuck off, bitch," he mouthed as he wrestled angrily with the cork before calming down enough to pour three glasses and place them on a tray. As a finishing touch he spat in the flute he intended to give Sarah, dispersing the phlegm floating on top of the wine with a finger.

Adam was smiling as he re-entered the living room and handed her the drink. She even smiled back, much to his enjoyment.

"Okay, let's eat," she said.

"Let's raise a toast first. To the best housemates in the world, ever," said Adam, barely concealing a giggle. As their glasses clinked and he watched Sarah drink his sputum, part of him wished the statement was true, rather than just another attempt at the mocking irony which had become his staple.

"Yeah," chimed Bill and Sarah hesitantly, like they were waiting for him to burst out laughing, betray the fact he was taking the piss.

As he forked some food into his mouth, Adam was irritated by the sound of the football match reverberating around the room but he knew Bill was the undisputed king of the remote control and Sarah certainly wasn't going to voice any displeasure. Besides he just couldn't face another fight.

"We've got some good news," said Bill after they'd done eating, putting his plate on the floor presumably for Sarah to clear away. "We've won two pairs of tickets for a weekend break in Barcelona and wondered if you'd like to come."

"You don't have any other friends?" he replied, laughing nervously and looking at Sarah to see if she actually approved but she was staring off into the distance, unreadable as ever.

"We've all had a tough time lately, mate," Bill went on. "We're going next weekend and would like you to join us."

"Can I bring a friend?"

"Who?" asked Sarah with a pained look, finally returning to the conversation.

"Helen," he said but as soon as it had left his lips, Adam knew it was like some dark, terrible thought that should never have been voiced aloud.

"I don't see why not," said Sarah. "Do you Bill?"

"Er, no," he mumbled but Adam watched rapt as Bill's demeanour visibly darkened. The two men's eyes locked like boxers sizing one another up, before Bill's gaze returned to the football, mercifully saving whatever it was for later.

In the ensuing silence, aside from the TV, Sarah busied herself clearing the plates, but as she headed to the kitchen to fetch the homemade dessert fit for a vegan, Adam feared being alone with Bill – a position he normally pined for.

"What the fuck?"

"What?"

"You know what," said Bill, moving menacingly into a sitting position. "Why the fuck did you invite Helen?"

"I know there's nothing going on between you," Adam

squeaked, lying, doing what he did best. "She'll be a good laugh and it'll be fun for us to go away together, two couples. I don't want to play gooseberry."

"Yeah?" said Bill, still sounding sceptical but reclining on the sofa as though satisfied Helen hadn't revealed anything.

"She's a great fag hag, too."

"Whatever," grunted Bill, turning back to the television.

"Key lime pie," cooed Sarah, laden down with bowls this time.

"And coke," said Adam, casually tossing the sizeable wrap of cocaine on the cardboard box cum table.

"Good boy," she squealed.

"Nice one, mate."

"One premise," said Adam, looking intently at both his housemates, hoping to draw them further into his deceitful web. "You've got to come to Popstarz with me tonight."

"I'm not going to any gay club," said Bill indignantly, face darkening again.

"Homophobe," charged Adam, holding the bag of cocaine invitingly under his friend's nose.

"Oh, come on Billy it's mixed. And anyway, I won't let go of your hand the whole time we're there," pleaded Sarah like a little girl, using the grating, squeaky voice she used when she wanted something. "Even Liam Gallagher's been there for God's sake and he's not exactly gay friendly."

"Just this once then, now hand over the charlie."

"So easily bought," said Adam, laughing, though it was his own private joke, because he happened to know that a certain Helen would be at the club, the Helen he sometimes looked at and wished he was straight. She was so world weary and resigned about life, with none of the dark ambition of the place he mostly inhabited – the decadent, duplicitous lifestyle gay men excelled at, he thought. But now she'd just become another tool in Adam's attempt to wrench Bill and Sarah's relationship apart, smash it to pieces.

"Hey, what happened to your eye?" said Sarah, looking at Adam accusingly after he switched the main light on to ensure they didn't miss any coke. It was like she was looking at him for the first time as she continued to stare.

"Just a scratch," he said, amazed that it had taken her this long to notice, to take an interest. "Nothing to worry yourself about."

"As I was saying earlier, he likes a bit of rough," joked Bill.

"Piss off," he replied but they were all laughing, heads thrown back, like a scene at the end of a feel-good movie. Adam, slightly buzzing from the wine, enjoyed the sound and hoped in that moment that nothing would change. But as he held a line of the slightly off-white powder under Bill's nose and looked hungrily into his eyes, he knew everything had to.

"Don't look so worried," said Adam as they approached the club, the long line snaking down the street. "No one's going to grab that manly arse of yours."

"If they do, I'll break their bloody nose."

"I thought you were Channel 4 watching, Labour supporting Mr Politically Correct, but you're so threatened by it all," he said pedantically, pinching Bill's behind, unprepared for the lightning-quick slap that left his face red and stinging in the cool evening air.

"Bill!" said Sarah admonishing her boyfriend, who'd stridden off slightly ahead of them.

"What the fuck did you do that for?" said Adam calling after him, still holding his hand up to his cheek, pain and frustration impinging on his cocaine high, but his words were left unanswered, foundering on the pavement.

The straggly group walked in silence the last few metres to the entrance of the club and just as Adam was about to nod and wink his way past the doorman, Bill drew him close and kissed him very lightly on the cheek that only moments ago he'd hit. As his friend pulled away wordlessly, the feeling that flooded through his body beat any drug high and he could only smile as he caught Sarah's most matronly of stares, disapproval etched on her every feature.

He dragged both housemates to him, refocused his grin on the doorman and they breezed into the club. Adam looked back as if to mock the long line of people queuing and they slipped down the stairs to the soundtrack of *Champagne Supernova*. It couldn't be more apt, he thought, and as he looked across even Bill was smiling the widest of coke smiles. Self-confidence radiated from the threesome.

They almost slung their coats, vintage leather jacket, Harrington and Adidas track top (Bill's of course) at the poor cloakroom attendant and passed through double doors reverberating excitedly to the intro of Jarvis Cocker's acid-tongued *Common People*. It was loved by Adam but loathed by Sarah. He knew she hated the sentiment of the song about a "posh bird" slumming it at university. It was obviously too close to home, too close to their Hampstead home. In her less infuriatingly PC moments she even referred to Bill as "my Manchester bit of rough", like he was some kind of trophy.

As they danced away, the three of them together, Sarah gyrating awkwardly to a song she apparently hated with the most contented of smiles on her face, something pricked Adam's contented bubble. Thrown back into the complexities of his life he scanned the crowd frantically, not for a shag, like he guessed everyone else was doing, but for Helen. He knew he had to get to her before Bill managed to talk her out of Barcelona. He didn't want to contemplate a trip to Spain with just the three of them, with him outnumbered, cowed by their so-called love.

As the first incendiary bars of Blur's *Song 2* resounded across the dance floor he saw her, picked out in silhouette by the strobes, looking deliciously oblivious as she swayed to what seemed like her own rhythm. He knew it was partly an act but she did seem to bumble through life leaving things to fate. Adam couldn't and realised his obsession to go out and get exactly what he wanted would get him into trouble, big trouble. He made his way dismissively through the crowd of narcissists, realising he was no different with his gym-toned body, obscenely expensive hair-cut, clothes straight off the pages of a glossy and an almost rote-learnt stream of ironic one-liners.

"Hi," he said, shouting above the music as she pogoed up and down looking radiantly androgynous, accentuated by her boots, jeans and vintage Adidas T-shirt ensemble.

"Hello, babe," she said, flinging her arms around him.

He saw her brow prickled with a light sheen of sweat, the sweat of what he guessed was an ecstasy high. Ecstasy in an indie club was totally inappropriate, he thought, like wearing sandals with socks, but still he knew she was a babe.

"You're coming to Barcelona with me next weekend," he said leaning seductively into her ear, pulling her away from the dance floor, wanting her total attention. "For free."

"What?"

"We've got free tickets."

"Who's we?" she said sceptically, wide eyes scrutinising him.

"Sarah and Bill," he said, almost giving away a sigh of defeat. "But they want you to come."

"Oh, I don't know."

"Please," he insisted, childlike, desperate.

"I don't even know this Sarah and I'd feel awkward."

"Look, it's a way of putting this whole thing to rest. You still feel bad about it, right?" Adam said conspiratorially. "You come, we go out, have a laugh and find you a hung Spanish guy."

"Yeah?" she questioned but she was giggling, acquiescent.

"Cheers," he said, handing her a can of Red Stripe from the bar, knowing he'd hooked her. "To Spain."

"To Spain," she repeated as they touched cans and another piece of Adam's distorted jigsaw fell into place.

"Come on, let's go and tell Bill and Sarah the good news," he said, dragging her roughly back across the dance floor to his housemates, one of whom they both had dangerous designs on. The threesome was about to become four.

CHAPTER FIVE

The daylight seeped into the room, clashing with his hangover like some tragic collision. It took all his energy just to raise his throbbing head from the pillow. He almost wished he hadn't bothered when he saw the rain cascading out of the sky, bouncing violently off of the pavement. But above the white noise of the mesmerising torrent – it was heading into the record books as one of the wettest summers on record – something else had become discernible, something unmistakably human. He felt a chill run through his body as he realised it was Sarah, her sudden shrieks and moans vibrating through the wall. He buried his head under the duvet but could still hear her squealing disgustingly like a pig.

Adam was quickly up on his feet, swaying, about to retch, cocaine and beer pulsing in his temples. He flicked on his stereo. As if gauging his mood, The Smiths' *How Soon is Now* flooded the room, drowning out Sarah, replacing it with Morrissey's morbid vocals. He'd never felt more alone as he lay back, thinking of them bundled up as one in the room next door. The aggressive banging on the wall, presumably Bill's way of warning him to turn the music down, only served to remind him they were more estranged than ever despite being just feet from one another. Still, he dutifully turned down the stereo to a murmur and lit his first cigarette of the day.

Watching the smoke crawl to the ceiling, he regretted that his life had become stuck on a permanent loop. He'd go to the gym this afternoon for the must-have accoutrement of the gay scene, *disco tits*. He'd then do a few hours work at the frighteningly trendy and oh so ironically named Mars Bar in Covent Garden where he'd gob in the most annoying customers' drinks and try, but fail to get into the pants of Ronaldo, his drop-dead-gorgeous Brazilian colleague. They'd end up going clubbing together anyway taking two or three pills, *candy*, as Ronaldo so beguilingly called it, and get *off their tits*. The evening, well morning by the time they were done, would finish one of two ways, either he'd go home alone or he'd end up with some equally drug-fucked disco bunny. Yeah, just another weekend, thought Adam sadly, but no matter what he did, how frenetic his lifestyle, he still couldn't bury the raging desire for his housemate.

Despite all Bill and Sarah's right-on protestations, there was an almost unspoken rule that he could get as fucked up as possible on these weekend jaunts provided he didn't bring anyone home. As far as they were concerned it seemed preferable for him to end the night in intensive care after a binge, rather than bringing a piece of rough back and rucking up the carpets. But he was rapidly passing the point where he actually cared about the sensitivities of his housemates, being more intent now on shocking them out of their smug coupledom.

Listening to them moving around next door, sex obviously over and an intimate post-coital breakfast of muesli to follow, he stubbed out his cigarette dejectedly behind one of the wooden bed legs. He enjoyed his guilty pleasure of smoking even more because Sarah forbade it in the house. She'd achieved the near impossible by convincing Bill to become almost 100 per cent vegetarian, but her jibes about the "grill smelling of death" when Adam cooked his dinner only made him more determined to keep aggravating her, as testified by the "family pack" of bacon in the fridge.

He stumbled back over to the stereo and turned it off. Switching on the adjacent TV he almost had to shield his eyes from the garish set of *The Jerry Springer Show*. Adam watched as the trailer-trash American crowd tried to prove how normal they were by partaking in this human freak show. It was as if even problems had to be sensational, had to be a little bit showbiz to seem real these days, he thought. A particularly grotesque transsexual, once Adrian, now Adrienne, was guided onto the stage by the ghoulish, ever-grinning Springer to hoots and hollers from the audience. Adam imagined himself being there, his love for his housemate cruelly exposed as Bill and Sarah confronted him, the mob roaring them on, baying for his blood.

He turned the volume down low because he didn't really want to hear but he also didn't want to be alone with the sound of the rain and the noise of the young lovers going about their weekend business. Turning away from the screen, he looked in the dressing-table mirror at the bruise around his eye and thought back to the night at Smale's. He felt a dangerous rage well up inside him again and wished he'd pummelled the old professor's head in. He punched the mattress, punched and punched it until the sweat seeped down his brow.

Drawing up outside the Soho Athletic Club, the large rainbow flag seemed to cast a shadow over him as he turned the engine off and sat tentatively in the driver's seat. An all-gay gym had been an uncomfortable step. He couldn't abide the sickly self-adulation in stretched Lycra, but membership was subsidised by Mars Bar whose gay owner wanted his waiters to "look the part". Or according to Ronaldo, so that the disgustingly obese millionaire could "slobber over our tight little buns".

In the end, Adam hadn't been able to say no because he wanted the disco tits and the bubble butt that seemed to feature on every other page of the gay press, as though they were off-the-peg items to be acquired for a successful life. He was prepared, literally, to do anything to get them and had even ripped out a profile of the so-called "perfect body" from *Men's Health*, the semi-pornographic magazine laughably targeted at straight men. He'd stuck the picture on his wall together with a collage of other body beautifuls, their fading smiles like a constant reminder to Adam that his time was limited. He didn't have that far to go to reach his goal of being simply to die for though, judging by the attention he got from some of the frighteningly attired old dinosaurs, held together by the modern miracles of moisturiser and man-made fibres, that used the gym.

Adam happened to catch some guy's eye, the "built-like-a-brick-shithouse-I'm-not-on-steroids-but-what-the-fuck-are-you-looking-at?" type of guy. He lifted a weight in his left hand, naturally a pretty hefty one, and carried on a conversation into his mobile gripped in the other. He also managed a scowl that surprised Adam because he thought it was so unusual for a "Muscle Mary" to be able to do two things at once, let alone three.

"Fuck head," he whispered, moving behind a strategically placed potted plant and out of the bodybuilder's sight.

But he felt desperate because he actually found the guy attractive, always desiring the seemingly unattainable. Smale had surmised at one of his so-called counselling sessions that because he'd received no love from his parents (he knew his dad hated him not just from the verbal abuse but from the look of terrible disappointment in his eyes and though his mum had smothered him with a suffocating kind of affection it was the superficial type lavished on pet dogs) he always went after what he couldn't get because he didn't want to be "disappointed" again. Adam had dismissed it as "cod psychological bollocks". Disappointed didn't come close to what he felt about the two people who called themselves his parents but he was beginning to think the professor might actually be right.

"You could always be a miserable old spinster like Kenneth Williams and perfect the art of the hand shandy," Smale had said, laughing cruelly the day Adam had told the professor more than he'd ever told anyone. That coldness and the thought of those clammy white hands moving all over him made him shudder. The professor lurked in the same dark recesses of his mind as his disapproving, abusive father.

He approached the bench press, obviously the gym's most popular item as it involved pectorals but arrived marginally behind "steroid man".

"I'm using this, love," he lisped.

"Okay," said Adam, turning away and bursting into a fit of giggles behind a bank of running machines. The squeaked utterance had sounded so comical and limp coming from such a big guy that any attraction had been replaced by an all-consuming hatred.

Still bristling with homophobia, or "self-loathing" as Smale termed it, he began a light jog. He knew, doused as he was in CK One, that he was hardly one to challenge stereotypes. He ran faster, trying to burn off the angst as the poison he'd ingested last night oozed out of his every pore. It was a life of excess even in the gym and doing a couple more rounds on the equipment equated to a couple more pills or another line as a reward. Deep down he feared that his lifestyle, so lovingly promoted by fashionable sections of the media, was all wrong. It was a means of escape but he was so aware of what he was escaping from that it was no escape at all.

He watched himself intently in the mirror as he jogged on and on, a modern-day Narcissus surrounded by so many clones of himself. Adam feared their personalities, for want of a better word, hardly differed either, which made Bill even more attractive. With the pumping house music threatening to obliterate his thoughts, he held onto the one that told him his friend was an individualist, which in a world of Bacardi Breezer-sipping, pill-popping, Diesel-shopping, self-styled sophisticates was almost heroic and incredibly sexy.

Still, he couldn't resist winking back at the perfectly white smile offered by the tanned and toned guy in the halter-top panting elegantly on the exercise bike just a few feet away. They'd held eye contact for a full 10 seconds, which in London normally only happened as a prelude to a psychotic attack by some "care in the community" nutter. Adam was about to make up the short distance between them when he felt the urgent vibration of the phone in his pocket, so of course the pose value that someone actually cared enough to call became the new priority.

"Hi," he said evenly, looking over to watch the guy's reaction to his new ring tone (some Ibiza "dance anthem" he didn't know the name of) but was dismayed to see from caller ID that it was Smale.

"Thanks for your message," the professor hissed. "And no thanks to you, yes I am all right. How's your eye? Bruised I hope."

"It's gone yellow, actually," he replied, studying his newly flawed features in the mirror.

"Sorry, dear boy, but one has to protect oneself," said Smale with a chilling laugh that stunned Adam with the promise that the professor was his old combative self again. "You might want something from our little arrangement but I also want something from you."

"What?"

"Well, I used to enjoy shall we say, liberally marking your work," he said slowly, deliberately, "and if you want that to continue then it's not all one-way traffic like you seem to suggest."

"Listen," he replied angrily in a half whisper, no longer wanting to be the centre of attention, "I'm not having sex with you again, ever. Understood?"

"Oh, dear boy, no! Whatever gave you that idea, that I wanted sex again? I do have rather a big pool of talent to choose from," Smale said, his sickening laugh reverberating down the line. "I'd just like you to continue our weekly chit-chats at my place, that's if you also want me to look on Billy Boy's pathetic grades as favourably as yours. Does smiler have *anything* between his ears?"

He listened as Smale's clipped tones tailed off and the line flooded with an uncomfortable silence. "See you next week," Adam said finally, picturing the professor's triumphant smile as the line went dead, sensing the balance of power subtly shifting away from him.

He was aware his hands were trembling and swiftly thrust them in the totally inadequate pockets of his exceptionally tight shorts as the guy who'd caught his eye sauntered over, checking Adam out with every closing step.

"Another one of your admirers?" he said in a rather soft Australian accent, laughing just a little too nervously, unsure of himself as he looked into Adam's flustered face.

"Yeah, I can't help being such a star," he replied almost seamlessly, surprised at himself for recovering so quickly from another unpleasantly close encounter with Smale. His power to deceive was shocking even to him, though he knew that being on the scene was all about being something you weren't.

"We should go out for a drink or something sometime," the guy continued as ambiguous and non-committal as possible but betraying the all-consuming fear of rejection.

"Yeah," Adam said just as artfully but gazing into his beautiful face, checking out all the bulges in the right places, giving himself away. Not that he actually liked the guy, he just looked so edible.

"What's your number?" he said as though sensing his chance.

"I'll only give you my number if we can meet tomorrow night. Busy, busy."

"It's Sunday."

"So?" Adam shot back. "Sunday's the new black."

"All right, where and when?" he said, laughing, hardly taking much convincing.

"The Box at 8pm. You know it, right?" said Adam, wincing at the pretentiousness of his choice of venue, enthralled at his ability to ensnare.

"See you there," he replied as he programmed his name and number into Adam's proffered phone. "Jason" Adam suspected, would only be a temporary entry, a short-lived imprint on his mobile's memory.

"Oh fuck this," said Adam, sighing, feeling a migraine coming on. His boss insisted they play *Massive Attack* because it was "edgy" even though it was being used on *Top Gear* now. "I hate *Massive Attack*. I mean how much more mainstream can you get than Jeremy bloody Clarkson?"

"Yeah," said Ronaldo, nodding in agreement though Adam guessed Clarkson was as foreign to his friend as the Brazilian president was to him. Ronaldo didn't have a TV and only caught snatches of Aussie soaps and daytime chat shows at tricks' houses. "Fuck what anyway?"

"See, I knew you didn't know what I was going on about," he said as he aggressively banged another ashtray against the side of the bin. "I mean fuck this Massive Attack crap and fuck washing up. We're not slaves."

"Yeah," said Ronaldo again, shrugging his shoulders Latino style but sponging even more vigorously at a row of dirty glasses. Unlike Adam, he appeared to have a conscience.

"Didn't you hear what I was saying," Adam continued as he banged down a full ashtray on the bar top, sending a mountain of dog ends spilling messily over the counter. "Let's go."

"What?"

"Jabba the Hutt is away in Paris with one of his fuck toys this weekend," said Adam, laughing at his own joke, referring to his obese boss as the grotesquely fat creature from *Star Wars*. "Let tomorrow's shift worry about the mess."

"Jabba the Hutt?" pondered Ronaldo, still not getting it. "Hold on, *I'm on tomorrow's shift.*"

"This can wait then," said Adam dismissively, throwing down his tea towel. "I'm going to get rid of these bastards, then we can go."

He approached the bar's last remaining table of customers. Their Carhartt T-shirts, industrial denim and multiple piercings suggested they were trying way too hard and he couldn't wait to throw them out into the dreary night.

"Time to go people," he said, hovering above them, clapping his hands in an attempt to shoo them away like stray dogs, not making eye contact.

"Mate, it's only eleven-fifteen," pleaded one, taking an infinitesimal swig of his designer beer.

"Yeah and last orders was eleven," said Adam, hands on hips, hating them all. "Let's go."

"No worries, man," piped up another of the drinkers, the one with the dreadlocks, *a white guy with dreads.*

"No, I'm not worried," Adam replied, patience having evaporated. "Because you're leaving right now."

"Keep your hair on, queenie," shot back the one with the NHS-style specs perched on his fat nose, fingering his beer, putting it to his lips and putting it down again.

"I've had enough of this shit!" Adam shouted, surprised at how loud his voice sounded in the intimate bar as it resounded above the drum and bass. Enraged, he grabbed the bespectacled one around his wangy 1970s-style shirt collar. "Now fuck off."

As he finally let go, the guy with the glasses turned meekly away from Adam's brutal gaze, got up and urged his friends to follow.

"Shit bar anyway, mate," screeched the dreadlocked one from a safe distance as they all piled out of the door.

"Yeah, yeah, yeah," Adam said as the door slammed and he couldn't help smiling when Ronaldo – who'd been busy polishing the chromium bar top throughout – broke into spontaneous applause.

"You go, girl."

"Yeah, thanks for all your help," Adam replied sarcastically. "Cinderella it's time to drop your sponge. Let's go party, we need candy tonight."

"Well, if you put it like that," said Ronaldo, finally won over. "What happened to the eye, by the way?"

"Not you as well?" he replied, turning away. "I walked into a door, all right?"

"Was it that hunky flatmate of yours?" he said, laughing. "You're always going on about him."

"Oh, fuck off," he replied angrily, picking up a heavy glass ashtray from the table just vacated, using every shred of willpower to stop himself hurling it across the room as Bill and Smale flared discomfortingly in his mind. His housemate had met Ronaldo at Mars Bar just the once and Adam suspected once had been enough, for Bill at least. "And we live in a house, not a flat."

"Take it easy, man," said Ronaldo, moving across the bar to put a hand on his friend's shoulder, an attempt to calm him.

"Don't take the piss," he said, spitting the words out into the Brazilian's face just inches from his. "All right?"

"All right."

"Now, let's go and find ourselves some stimulants and some men," said Adam, aware that he was flitting almost psychotically between sheer anger and lightheartedness – it was as though the incident with Smale had only stoked what Bill had already stirred up in him: inner rage, jealousy, envy. He looked at himself hopefully in the mirror but in the flushed, angry face saw only his father about to destroy him for some ridiculously minor infringement. His dad had never been physically abusive to him (his mother wasn't so lucky). It was what he said.

"Ready then?" said Ronaldo, hesitant as though nervous of having broken the silence.

"Okay," said Adam, moving across to the CD player where he ejected the album and threw it in the bin with laughter that was all surface. "I fucking hate Massive Attack."

"Yeah?" questioned Ronaldo, more uncertain than ever.

"Yeah," Adam said, laughing hysterically, not really sure why but he didn't want to stop for fear of breaking down. "Britpop, mate, that's the future."

"Yeah?"

"Yeah," he said as they left the bar, locking the door behind them and "woohooing" the opening lines of Blur's *Song 2* on entering the street, sending it echoing around Covent Garden, but knowing where he'd rather be, *who he'd rather be with*, as he rubbed a twitchy hand over his still swollen eye.

"Do you know where to score?"

"Course I know where to bloody shop," said Adam, amazed Ronaldo should question his powers when it came to scoring drugs. "I'm an account holder with these guys."

"All right."

"Very all right," he replied, feeling anything but as they headed past England's youth, waving a B&H in front of him as if staving them off. It was chucking out time and morose young men were bustling by looking for violence to escape the monotony of their lives, while their girlfriends invariably followed at a distance shrieking. "Watch out for the bridge and tunnel crowd."

"Disgusting," said Ronaldo, giving another Latino shrug as the boisterous shouts erupted around them.

"So much for Blair's 'New Britain'. Fucking breeders," spat Adam with such bitterness that the words almost stuck in his throat, Sarah and Bill coming to mind. "We'll never hate them as much as they hate us."

"Have you thought about counselling?" said Ronaldo, goading his friend, both quickening their pace as they passed The Strand's shadowy, piss-stained doorways. "You have anger management issues."

"Whatever," Adam replied, laughing a little too hard as they reached Villiers Street and sashayed past the snaking queue for Heaven.

"Hello, babe," said the doorman, a man Adam had slept with so many men ago that the intimate moment had disintegrated to nothing. Well, to nothing more than free entry into the nightclub.

"Fine, fine," he replied, blowing an air kiss towards the lump in the puffer jacket whose name he'd forgotten, assuming they'd swapped names.

They descended the steps into the club, past yet more people queuing obediently, Adam anxious to buy a pill so he could actually start to enjoy himself. Once they'd had access to the hallowed "VIP" room until he'd felt compelled to throw a paper plateful of French fries over a C-list celebrity. The guy had been in *The Bill* – just the one episode. More shockingly, he'd once seen the supposedly squeaky-clean king, or rather queen, of daytime TV, later the doyen of the National Lottery show, with a snowstorm of coke falling out of his nose, writhing around like an eel on one of the lounge's sofas, pawing some slip of a thing who should have been at home studying for his GCSEs.

"You know you say this place is like a supermarket," shouted Ronaldo above the music, grinning hesitantly as though building up to one of his jokes that Adam always derided him for. "Well, it has to be Tesco, so down-market, ugh."

"Actually, it's a meat market, I call it a meat market," shouted back Adam, rolling his eyes as the first few bars of Kylie's *Better the Devil You Know* spewed from the sound system.

"Oh, yeah," Ronaldo replied but looking confused as ever by his friend. He'd only been in London a little while and it was as though he still couldn't quite get a handle on English culture.

"Yeah," said Adam, slightly bored by his friend's obliviousness, which others would probably find sweet. Ronaldo was *beautiful* even if he was totally unattainable, and Adam knew all too well what unattainable felt like.

He supposed they looked good together and Adam knew that appearances were all that mattered on the scene. As he glanced around the sweaty, heaving dance floor, inane grins fixed to the faces of those bobbing around to the shallowest of pop trash, he felt the now familiar wave of desperation smother him. He scanned the crowd for his dealer, craving his first pill.

"Bandits at 12 o'clock," he said to his friend, pointing, discreetly of course, across the dance floor.

"Hey?"

"Never mind," he replied to his bemused friend.

"Now be a good boy, get me a drink and meet me back here in a minute."

"What do you want?" said Ronaldo, shrugging.

"Do you have to bloody ask?" he shouted over his shoulder. "I'll have a Breezer."

As he approached the Burberry-clad dealer, outfit complemented by what looked like the cheapest of high-street gold, Adam couldn't help but laugh at the club's so-called anti-drugs policy when the dealers were so obvious they were virtual caricatures. Any venue that stayed open past 4am knew it wasn't the alcopops keeping the kiddies awake.

"All right, man?" he said through a mouthful of cigarette, looking so conspicuous he could have been awaiting arrest as he waved Adam over to a darker corner, beady eyes flashing in the half-light.

"Yeah," Adam replied, smiling, intimidated and aroused all at once. Always the straight guys, he thought.

"What you 'avin?"

"Make it two."

"'Kin 'ell, I'll be out of business at this rate," he said, eyes darting this way and that but never, Adam noticed, landing on him. "That'll be twenty quid."

"Cheers," he said, cocky now, handing over two £10 notes and smiling again.

"Don't fucking look at me like that, batty boy," hissed the dealer, snatching the notes with one hand and imitating the cocking of a gun with the other, finally looking Adam in the eye. "I'll be waiting for you outside otherwise."

"Yeah?" Adam managed to blurt out questioningly but grabbing the proffered pills from the black palm and turning away. If only he'd looked back, he would have seen the dealer guiltily staring at his taut back tapering to reveal his beautifully curvaceous arse.

"Fucking dealer," he said as he returned to his friend, who was obediently holding a Bacardi Breezer – cranberry – in each hand.

"I thought you said he was your best man?"

"Best mate, not best man, and no he's not my best mate," said Adam exasperatedly.

"Well what 'appened?" continued Ronaldo, throwing his hands up despairingly.

He'd taken to dropping his aitches, Adam noticed, since everyone wanted to be "street", but it sounded even more ridiculous coming from a foreigner than some middle-class kid from Carshalton Beeches.

"Nothing *'appened*," he said. "I got the pills, the guy's just a bit of a wanker, that's all."

"Oh," said Ronaldo, beaming as he held out his hand.

"Greedy bitch," replied Adam, laughing and placing a pill in his friend's palm. "It's going to be a bumpy ride."

"Yeah," he said, still grinning as he brought the pill to his wonderfully full lips – lips Adam couldn't help eyeing. "How many did you get?"

"Two."

"Two?" questioned Ronaldo, sounding disappointed.

"Hey, you can't expect me to keep funding your drug habit," he replied, rolling the ecstasy around on his tongue, fearing his generosity in that department was one of the reasons they were so close, a generosity that had virtually wiped out this term's student loan. "I know you're skint but daddy isn't going to bank roll me forever."

"No?"

"No," he replied, wary that his dad's generous allowance, primarily to keep him away, would eventually be cut off, just another way his old man could exhibit power, manipulate him.

Adam tried to forget the negative thoughts as he waited to come up. The music didn't really help as a slew of cheesy pop anthems reverberated monotonously across the dance floor. He couldn't understand why almost everyone at university nodded sagely about gays being style arbiters, apart from the token right-wing homophobes who thought Hitler had the right idea, as testified by the graffiti in the library toilets. Saying every gay boy was cool, was like saying every one of them was camp. It was so sickeningly crawly, like reverse homophobia, he thought.

No matter how bad the music was (someone had even made the *Magic Roundabout* theme into a "tune") the advent, or should that be ascent, of ecstasy made everything sound great, Adam thought as he felt the embarrassing urge to dance to a Spice Girls track.

He watched Ronaldo's body artfully silhouetted by the strobe lights, a modern-day Michelangelo's David. Adam cringed, the concept sounded so tacky. They'd kissed once but he'd felt nothing, no spark. Still, he'd been upset that the Brazilian had been the first to recoil from their awkward embrace with the words, "Friends don't do each other." For once he'd been accurate, Adam reserved friends for having a laugh with.

Anything else was out of bounds. He didn't want anyone getting too close. He certainly didn't want anyone to know what was on his mind, though he knew, and Smale had concurred, his penchant for unattainable men and his unwillingness to open up was a product of his loveless upbringing.

Adam also knew his charm, like his father's, was all surface and he didn't want anyone penetrating that veneer, though Sarah had come worryingly close once or twice. No, his dad was a respected history professor of many years standing, loyally church-going, fanatically *Telegraph* reading, unfortunately wife beating and an unrelenting bigot, but he crucially managed to do it all with a smile on his face.

The dark thoughts finally melted away as the ecstasy began to course frantically through him and he looked back across at Ronaldo. The Brazilian already had his arms around some equally bulky, shirtless mass of muscle. It caused Adam's druggy smile to turn sour on his lips and he could only turn away. He was disgusted that his so-called friend could abandon him so quickly but the etiquette of the scene did say a shag came before friendship, and getting high came before everything.

He looked out into the sea of waving arms. Normally he'd bitch to Ronaldo about someone else's facile expression or their dance action or their need to have an infusion of Botox for Christmas rather than *that* sex-tourist holiday in Morocco, but all he could see tonight were dozens of himself: the generic hair, the identikit bodies, hungry and unsmiling lips curled edgily around designer beers. It wasn't the first time he'd felt revulsion. His crazy dream was that being with Bill could somehow take him away from the bars and clubs, the drugs and drink, the one-night stands and those that didn't even make it that far. But as someone grabbed his hand and he looked into brown eyes he dismissed it all for another quick fix and smiled right back, his sexiest of smiles.

"What's your name?" he said, moving coolly to Adam's ear, gently kissing the lobe.

"Adam," he said and while the once-well-built-but-going-to-fat black guy in the flimsy suit and tie didn't really measure up, he desperately didn't want to be alone. "What's your name?"

He shouted something into his ear, probably a name, but

Adam couldn't hear above the bass beat and what did it matter anyway, he thought, as he began gnawing at the guy's lips, more in hope that he'd shut up than out of any desire.

"I'm a city analyst," he shouted like it was all that mattered, this time making himself heard.

"I love anal," Adam replied, bursting out laughing but his new companion just looked at him.

"Really, I am," he said, slapping Adam's arse a little too hard. "I'm good, too."

"Good in bed?" Adam murmured, losing interest fast but unwilling to make the effort to seek out someone else, go through the same meaningless conversation just so he could walk out of the club with something on his arm, something that back in the real world would be termed a person.

"What do you do?"

"Out of work model," he replied, lighting up a B&H as casually as he'd lied.

"I'm bisexual," said the black guy unconvincingly, moving his hand down and furiously groping Adam's behind.

"Hey, I'm Catholic," he said. "Don't worry about it, we've all got our crosses to bear. Wanna do an E?"

"No, you're all right," he said. "I've already done some charlie. You know, that's what we do in the City."

"Yeah?" Adam replied dubiously.

"Yeah," he stuttered, thumbing his large nose for effect but looking away.

"You gonna take me back to your City penthouse then, out east?"

"Well, actually I still live with my mum," he said, looking down at his shoes, cheap brogues, Adam noted.

"Your mum?" He would have laughed had it not been so depressing.

"It's close to where I work."

"Look, you can come back to mine," he said, regretting every word that tripped off his tongue, spurred on by the thought of facing the loving couple over the breakfast table in Hampstead with his new friend in tow. "As long as your mum doesn't mind you staying out all night."

"Noooo," he said, desperate to sound convincing.

"Get your coat, you've pulled," said Adam, laughing uproariously at his attempt at irony, his companion looking totally lost.

"You want to leave now?"

"Yeah," said Adam. "You coming?"

"Yeah," he replied. "I like you, you know."

"Oh, bless," said Adam as they walked to the coat check, ridiculously hand in hand.

Being high was no insulation from the detritus of The Strand, empty beer bottles, dog ends and staggering drunks – just another Saturday night, Sunday morning, Adam thought miserably.

"Where are you going?" he shouted after his companion who was heading for Trafalgar Square.

"I thought you said Hampstead?" he replied, shrugging his shoulders, momentarily blocked from view as a drunken mob weaved past him like he was an obstacle course. "It's the N42 night bus, isn't it?"

"Night bus? No I only take cabs, darling," Adam said as he approached a battered Japanese heap that had parked up, it didn't take long for the cabbie to wind down his window letting out an unwelcome stream of Celine Dion from the stereo.

"Where you off to, man?" he shouted from the driver's seat, making no attempt to turn the music down, presumably thinking it was a unique selling point.

"Hampstead."

"Thirty quid, man."

"Twenty quid, mate, and turn that crap off," Adam said, opening the door and sliding across the shiny backseat as his nostrils were hit by a noxious mixture of cheap pine air freshener and body odour.

"How much?" asked his new friend, sliding in beside him and awkwardly slamming the door.

"Twenty, only a tenner each," he said, smiling lustfully at the guy he didn't even know the name of, sure he'd detest him the morning after.

"Yeah, fine," he replied as the cab finally moved off. "Look, I'm not really an analyst."

"Shush, baby," said Adam, not interested in the truth, wanting to pretend a little longer, aware that was all he was ever doing as he tapped the driver on the shoulder. "Don't you have anything else apart from Celine *bloody* Dion?"

"I've got a cassette of Gregorian chants, man, real relaxing, chilled vibe," he said, turning around and flashing a worryingly lopsided smile. "Hackney, right?"

"Hampstead and Celine Dion is fine," said Adam as he looked out of the window at the brittle light of early morning, monochrome and lifeless. And even though a hand was working its way up his inner thigh, he felt numb.

"Hampstead, got you," said the driver finally, like he was looking for some acknowledgement but no one was really listening.

"Tenner each, okay?" said Adam, prodding his companion awake as they drew to a stop.

Bleary eyed, he rooted around in his pockets, finally shaking his head sheepishly. "Actually, I only have five pounds," he said, bringing out the crumpled note.

"That'll do," Adam huffed, handing the driver a £20 note and snatching the proffered fiver.

He'd told the driver to stop at the end of the street because he didn't want the rattling car engine to alert the sleeping lovers. As they approached the house Adam was relieved to see the front room was in darkness. Sometimes Bill got so stoned he'd be up all night watching cartoons. He really wanted to get him into ecstasy but the Mancunian claimed he was scared of "losing control", which is exactly what Adam wanted, of course. It had even been a battle to get Bill to snort coke, though now he couldn't get enough, as long as someone else was paying.

He flinched at the sound of a passing car as they walked up the path but realised it was only the taxi they'd just exited.

"Nice place."

"Shhh," he hissed as he slid the key into the front door, the sound filling his ears.

Reaching quickly for the hall light, he waved his acquaintance over the threshold. Adam regretted he looked somehow bigger, more awkward inside the house, an encumbrance that he'd have to get rid of the next morning after the usual ritual of shower, breakfast, and the expectation they'd swap numbers.

"This way," he whispered, not so gently grabbing his arm and guiding him up the steep stairs and past Bill and Sarah's room where a light glowed menacingly from under the door, the sound of a stereo turned down low offering an unwelcome promise of what was going on inside.

Adam finally breathed out as they reached the confines of his bedroom but didn't switch the light on till he'd locked the door. He could still hear the music vibrating through the wall, *their music*, and it was then that he was delighted to have a six-foot-tall black man in his room. He wrestled him onto the bed but he wasn't the insatiable groper he'd been in the club. Moodily shrugging Adam off, he sat back up, edged away, tears in his big doleful eyes.

"I'm not really an analyst," he sobbed.

"Shut up," said Adam rudely, not wanting to know, moving for the guy's zip, only to be pushed away.

"I'm not what you think," he said, tears rolling down his cheeks.

"Look, it's a one-night stand," Adam cried, suddenly unconcerned whether they could be heard in the other room. "I don't give a fuck what you do."

"But I've got a problem."

"What kind of bloody problem?"

"Erectile dysfunction," he said, collapsing in a heap on the bed like he'd been gunned down, mortally wounded.

"What the hell are you doing here then?" shot back Adam.

"I thought it would be different with you, you looked so cute in the club but I'm still, you know ... totally soft," he whined.

"Don't worry," said Adam as feelingly as he could, unzipping his trousers, he had another plan. "Suck me."

"Suck you?"

"Yeah, you know, blow job," he commanded.

"Okay," said the guy pathetically, drying his eyes on a tissue, eyes he couldn't bring to meet Adam's, eyes that didn't remain at eye level for long.

"Hey, I've gotta go."

It was the first thing Adam heard as the vague memory of the night before came painfully back to him. "Yeah?" he said raising himself from the pillow to look at the clock (it was eleven) rather than at the unwelcome lump next to him in bed. "Have a bit of breakfast first."

"Cheers, Adam."

"Hey, don't mention it, my housemates keep a full fridge," he said, laughing but concerned the guy had actually remembered his name. It wasn't as if the sex had been stunning. It was all quiet in the room next door so he guessed post-coital muesli was on the menu in the dining room.

"Will they mind?" his guest asked, hurriedly putting his clothes on, seemingly anxious to get away from another embarrassment, not realising he *was* the embarrassment.

"No they won't," Adam lied. They'd mind very much and while he hated having this big lanky thing cluttering up his room, he was looking forward to seeing what kind of impact he'd have on their cosy, domesticated world. "They're students, *they're educated*."

"Yeah, I saw a copy of *The Times* on the hall table."

"Actually, that was mine, Bill normally reads *The Mirror*, lefty that he is."

"Oh."

"Yeah, oh," Adam said hastily, all shred of humility gone from his voice, drained by another disappointment as he quickly dressed and they headed down the stairs. "But they don't bite."

"Hi, guys," he said cheerfully, poking his head around the dining-room door to be faced by the two of them, Bill with his head in *The Mirror*, Sarah reading *The Daily Mail*, which only betrayed the shallowness of her so-called political correctness. He began his subtle attack. "Room for two more?"

"You have company?" said Sarah in an almost strangulated cry, dropping the paper on the table and glaring over Adam's shoulder to try and make out who he could possibly be with.

"Bill, Sarah meet ..." he spluttered, leading his companion into the room and working out his next move. "This is Bill and Sarah."

"Steve," he said, giggling nervously as he held out a ridiculously large hand that Sarah daintily took in hers. Bill only nodded curtly before going back to reading his paper and rudely munching his cereal.

"Sit yourself down, Steve," said Adam, feeling like a total fraud using his name for the first time.

"Cheers."

"Just got to get some more bowls. Orange juice, Steve?" he said, overcompensating madly for the name faux pas, hating himself for leaving *Steve* alone with the two of them while he went to the kitchen but overwhelmed at the point he was making to the supposedly loving couple, the six-foot-tall point at the table.

"Yeah, please."

As he headed to get the bowls he was relieved to hear Sarah making conversation, though at the same time he loathed her middle-class trait of always managing to keep up appearances no matter how disapproving she was. It was the voice that gave her away. The vocal equivalent of a raised eyebrow, Adam thought, having heard it once too often.

"Okay, dig in," he said on his return, pricking the horrible silence that had quickly settled after the niceties had dried up, handing Steve a bowl. "It's muesli or muesli, I'm afraid."

"Muesli it is," Steve said, his pathetic giggle followed by a polite little chuckle from Sarah, like one of those false laughs people perfect for use in theatres and a snort from Bill.

"I'm actually off to the library," said Sarah, scraping her chair back suddenly, clearing her throat edgily as she stood up. "Very nice to meet you, Steve."

"Yeah, likewise, love."

"Bye, Bill," said Sarah, feebly kissing her boyfriend on the cheek, even though he was still engrossed in his paper.

"So Steve, any plans for the rest of the day?" Adam said against the background of Bill noisily rustling the pages of the newspaper and huffing out great clouds of cigarette smoke, having lit up as soon as Sarah had left the room.

"Yeah, I'm in a bit of a hurry actually," he replied, mouth partially full, trying intently to finish his cereal and uncomfortably batting away the cigarette smoke that was coming right at him from across the table.

"You're done? That was quick," said Adam, watching as

Steve dropped his spoon in the bowl with a triumphant tinkle before swigging back his orange juice in one gulp. "Anything else?"

"No, better be going," Steve replied, already up on his feet, coughing from the residue of cigarette smoke, nerves or both.

"Okay, I'll show you out."

"Bye, er, Bill."

"Later, mate," he replied, barely looking up.

Adam puffed out his cheeks as he ushered Steve from the room, cringing with the unbearable ordeal breakfast had been, finally feeling sorry for his guest.

"Turn left, walk down the end of the road and left again and you'll be at the Tube," he said as he opened the door, determined not to swap numbers, not to be civil, killing any possibility of a sequel. "See you around."

"Bye," he said as he headed out of the house. Adam would have seen Steve turning around to offer a sheepish smile from the path but he'd already slammed the door on their brief liaison.

He coughed to announce himself on re-entering the dining room to finish his breakfast.

"What the fuck?" said Bill, no longer interested in his paper, instead sat glaring at Adam at the other end of the lengthy table. "You know Sarah doesn't like you bringing strangers back, you've abused her trust, *our trust*."

"Actually, he's not a stranger and I pay rent and have as much right to bring friends back home as you or Sarah," Adam shouted, pushing his bowl away, suddenly losing his appetite.

"I heard voices in your room last night and it disgusts me to think about you being fucked by another guy while I'm in the room next door," said Bill, rising aggressively to his feet, face crimson.

"Why? Because you're jealous?" spat Adam. "Wish you were fucking me?"

"You just don't get it, do you?" Bill yelled, snatching up a breakfast bowl, Adam helpless as it flew just past him and smashed into smithereens, milk and muesli inelegantly sliding down the wall.

"Get what?" he replied, trembling but Bill had stomped out of the room. Adam had sensed the jealousy and fear in his friend's voice, and knew it was a good thing even as the front door crashed shut sending anger reverberating through the old house again.

"I thought you were going to the library?" Adam said as he came face to face with Sarah on the stairs.

"It was an excuse, I felt uncomfortable in the dining room."

"You're so right-on when it comes to vegetarianism and politics," he said, barring her way, thinking how easy it would be to send her skinny frame tumbling head first, "but when I bring someone home who's black *and* gay that's just a bit more than you can stand, isn't it?"

"Let me past," she yelled, tears welling in her eyes.

"I'm not letting you off that easy," he replied, enjoying her helplessness, clenching and unclenching his fists.

"Look, I don't like strange men in the house."

"He's not a strange man," he cried. "He's a friend."

"Friend?" she said, shuffling edgily from side to side on the stair. "You couldn't even remember his name."

"You're so fucking righteous," he shouted, leaning right into her face, knowing he'd already lost and that he couldn't go to war with both of them or it really would be over. "You should ask yourself why your boyfriend's so upset though. Take a look at the dining-room wall."

"I'll clear it up," she said. Adam finally moved aside to allow her to squeeze past and watched hatefully as she bounced down every step before turning in disgust back to his room.

CHAPTER SIX

Bill knocked on the heavy wooden door tentatively. It was so substantial, he thought, murders could be committed on the inside and no one would be any the wiser. He rapped louder on the thick hardwood, guessing his first knock had been barely audible in the office and had probably not distracted the professor from whatever was consuming his time, or from whomever he was consuming. He shuddered.

He was about to walk away and light up a celebratory cigarette in a "no-smoking area" when he heard the muffled turning of the lock from the other side of the door. Bill knew he still had time to bolt for the end of the corridor and out of sight but he waited, rooted to the spot by the mix of fear and obedience that Smale seemed to instil in most. Finally the professor yanked open the door.

"Oh, dear boy, how considerate of you to reschedule," he said standing in the doorway, ushering him in with the usual infuriatingly affected flourish.

"No problem," replied Bill in his flat Mancunian monotone, so at odds with the professor's theatrical inflections. "We're off to Barcelona, Spain, so I wouldn't have been able to make Friday."

"Mr Laws, I may be an English Literature professor but I am aware Barcelona is in Spain, though some would disagree, hmm, and who's *we*?" said Smale over his shoulder as he headed for the armchairs.

It was then Bill noticed it, the shaved patch laying bare the flaky scalp that was usually buried beneath the thick mane of hair, the blemish partially covered by a large plaster. Almost simultaneously the bruised eye on Adam's delicate face came to mind and he wondered.

"What happened to your head?"

"It needn't concern you," the professor said hurriedly, the familiarity of his measured tone absent.

"Come on." Bill blustered, finding confidence in Smale's apparent wariness.

"Look," he said, grabbing agitatedly for the packet of cigarettes on the table in front of him. "I fell over in the bathroom, very slippery those tiles you know."

"Oh."

"Yes, oh," snapped Smale. "Look Mr Laws, that's the first and last time we discuss me at these sessions or I call time on your university career, got it?"

"Yes," Bill replied, cowed by the professor's rising anger.

"Now I'm intrigued about you and whoever in the glorious city of Antoni Gaudi," he said, sinking back into his chair and sucking on a cigarette like the storm had passed, though the summer rain splattered the windows incessantly.

"We won free tickets in some competition."

"For Christ's sake," Smale roared, his usually placid features crimson, mood swinging wildly, "this is like getting blood from a stone."

"I mean my girlfriend, Adam and his friend," he said finally, intimidated into giving an answer.

"Thank you," replied Smale, putting his hands together as if in prayer. "Strange Adam never, er … oh it doesn't matter."

"Adam what?" probed Bill, concerned at just how well the professor knew Adam, at how well they knew one another.

"Look, Adam and I were friends," sighed Smale, taking another snatched puff of yet another cigarette. "Once."

"Yeah?"

"Yeah, Mr Laws," Smale parroted back irritably. "Friends, no more, no less, but we had a disagreement some time ago over some of his work. You know how impetuous he can be."

"Yes," said Bill, nodding vigorously but unsettled by the answer, the thought of the two of them together, united as though in some evil cult, the young man and his Svengali, made his stomach muscles painfully contract. The yawning silence that followed was broken mercifully by the ringing of the professor's old-fashioned telephone and Bill, finally distracted from the rain's depressing pitter-patter, breathed out.

"Not now," he growled into the phone. "Don't you know I'm busy?"

Bill cleared his throat nervously as Smale listened briefly to what the person had to say before slamming the phone clattering into its cradle, unaware his housemate had just got an earful.

"Don't worry," the professor continued but with an air of resignation Bill had never seen before, "the relationship between Adam and I is purely professional now and, of course, our discussions will not leave these four walls. You have my word."

"Good," said Bill. For once he wanted to believe Smale's words as they absolved him of the need to challenge anything, to challenge Adam later about how intimately he knew the professor, to challenge himself about what he thought of any of this or how it actually made him feel.

"Well, enjoy your trip to Spain," he said, rising to his feet, leaving a cigarette burning absently in the overflowing ashtray.

"That's it?" Bill said questioningly, shifting uncomfortably in his armchair before standing up.

"I've got far more important things to do than this Mr Laws," said Smale as he gently took Bill's arm and guided him to the door, unlocking it and flinging it open. "Besides, I haven't got the stomach for this today, we'll discuss your *problems* next week."

"That injury on your head," he said, pausing nervously, "did Adam do it?"

"Yes, Bill, he did," Smale replied, staring off into the corridor as though trying to forget himself for a moment. "Be careful of him, please, he's got the devil inside."

As the professor let the door shut, his words resonated out in the dimly lit corridor but Bill didn't feel deterred by them like the professor had obviously intended, he only felt the stabbing pain of jealousy that the two had been intimate together, that someone else had been with Adam. He'd felt the same the other day when he'd set eyes on Steve in his own dining room, like his own feelings were being mocked by the unwelcome presence of the stranger sat opposite him.

Bill dialled Helen knowing he shouldn't, knowing it was wrong. As soon as he pressed the dial button he regretted it but he was desperate to suppress the feelings Smale had stirred up in him.

"Hello, Billy Boy," she said, answering on the third ring.

Her croaky voice suggested to him that she was still in bed, maybe with a man, certainly with a hangover.

"Hi," he replied vaguely, it was him who'd called but he didn't really know why, couldn't admit to himself why, panicked at not feeling the slightest hint of attraction. "Can I come over?"

"Do you think that's a good idea, babe?"

"Yes," he said lying, wishing he really couldn't wait to see her but mortified that he didn't actually care. "Of course."

"Even though you're seeing that girlfriend of yours?"

"Don't worry," he replied. "Are you in bed?"

"Yeah."

"Naked?"

"Yessss," she said, laughing. "Why? Does it turn you on?"

"Can I come over?" he said, ignoring her question, his voice tinged with revulsion at her low, breathy voice he knew was a put-on, an attempt to seduce him.

"Later, around five o'clock," she said. "Bill?"

"Yes," he replied, fearing what was coming next.

"How much do you like me?"

"See you at five," he said, hanging up, ignoring her again. He didn't want to get caught in a lie about his feelings for Helen but he realised he was living one.

CHAPTER SEVEN

"The seat's still warm," said Smale breathily into the phone.

"What?"

"What is it with the youth of today?" the professor replied haughtily.

"What is it with these abstract references?" asked Adam.

"When you called just now," he said sounding exasperated, "I was with Mr Laws. He just left."

"Oh."

"I told him about us," he said triumphantly.

"You did what?" cried Adam, anger rising worryingly fast again. "What the fuck are you playing at?"

"I told him our *friendship* was over and that our relationship's purely professional now," he replied evenly as though robbing Adam of the shock value of his so-called kiss-and-tell tale.

"You're unbelievable," Adam shouted, looking at the crumpled picture of Bill he'd just pulled from his wallet but fearing he was further away than ever. "This is a nightmare."

"A nightmare of your own creation, Dr Frankenstein," chuckled Smale. "Did you really think I was going to sit back impotently and let you walk all over me?"

"Remember I've still got those emails," he spat, opening his bedroom door a crack to make sure Sarah wasn't within earshot, eavesdropping like he'd caught her once before. Adam knew Bill would love to tell her about Smale's revelation if he wasn't so concerned about what his own meetings with the professor said about himself. He could imagine his two housemates laughing cruelly about him being with a man old enough to be his grandfather.

"And you remember that your university career is in my hands, Adam," said Smale, eerily calm, "whether I get to be departmental head or not."

"I'm planning to meet my friend this afternoon, she's editor of the university newspaper," he replied but in the deafening silence that followed, which said more about their brief affair than words ever could, Adam feared his hold over the professor was slipping away.

"Don't do anything you're likely to regret," growled Smale, rapid-fire words cutting through the hush. "We need to meet on Wednesday night, my place, okay?"

"Yes," said Adam resignedly, intimidated by the professor and going back on his word about no more house calls.

"Usual time," replied Smale not even waiting for a reply as the phone went dead.

Adam had tried Helen's line a few minutes before but she hadn't answered. She always answered his calls.

"Hello, darling," she said after he tried again, answering after the tenth laborious ring. She sounded terrible.

"Were you still sleeping?" Adam replied incredulously.

"Went out with a few of my journo colleagues last night," she croaked. "You know how us hacks like a drink."

"Helen, for Christ's sake, working on the university rag and studying Media does not make you a fully fledged journalist," he replied, piqued that she'd not answered her phone the first time and enjoying winding her up. "Media whore, maybe, journalist, no."

"Speaking of which, I'm still waiting to hear more on this steamy relationship between a student and a lecturer."

"Student and lech you mean," Adam said laughing uncomfortably. "I can give you another titbit this afternoon when I come over."

"Who said you're coming over?"

"Come on," he said, disappointed, suspicious. She'd never refused to see him before.

"I've got a monster hangover."

"Hair of the dog is what you need, girlfriend," he said. "I'll bring over a bottle of wine."

"Ugh, Adam I couldn't think of another drink right now."

"Can I come or not?"

"All right but only for a little while, I'm meeting ... I've got an appointment later."

"Appointment?"

"I'm meeting someone," she said hurriedly.

"A guy?"

"Look, it's none of your business really," Helen replied, disappointing him again because she never normally kept secrets. "An old friend if you must know."

"Oh," Adam said but really suspected it was Bill.

"See you," she said with an uncharacteristic air of irritation.

"See you later."

He went downstairs with an overwhelming dread, knowing Sarah would be bustling around like a contented housewife and that he'd have to make polite conversation, force a smile here, a laugh there, while using all his willpower to prevent some acid comment slipping out, to stop himself setting about that fragile porcelain-looking doll's face of hers, the one with the vacant eyes and almost perennially pursed lips he'd like to smash to pieces.

"Hello there," she said breezily from the dining-room table. He looked at her almost disbelieving since only yesterday he'd sat there with Steve and felt her horribly calculated coldness. Were they now back to pleasantries?

"Hello," he said, offering a tight smile as he poured a bowl of cereal.

There was silence, apart from the stilted tones of Radio 4's *Woman's Hour* coming from the stereo. Her devotion to the BBC was another Home Counties trait that Adam hated. It was as though she used it, like the newspaper she now had her head buried in, to save herself from actually engaging in what was going on around her, but he wasn't about to let that happen, he wanted to prod her just a bit for a reaction.

"Look, about yesterday," he said and almost burst out laughing as her head shot up from the paper, "I didn't mean to upset you."

"No?" she said, staring at him now like some accusatory school ma'am.

"It won't happen again," he said in spite of the boiling anger he felt inside. "I didn't mean to embarrass you and Bill."

"You only embarrassed yourself," she said stuffily, returning to her paper.

"Yeah, well we can't all be perfect," he said as he rose from the table, breakfast not even half eaten and headed for the door knowing things were irreconcilable. It was like they'd crossed a line and nothing could reverse the direction the three of them were headed, he thought.

Reaching the welcome confines of his bedroom he had to resist the urge to slam the door, instead he wearily nudged it closed and turned the key gently in the lock. His attention was drawn to the garish photo montage on the wall that stood out against the greyness of the morning. Far from instilling happiness, he often imagined the inanely smiling models ripped from style bibles getting withered and wrinkled as they reached the wasteland of their thirties and beyond.

He couldn't imagine being a thirtysomething, let alone dying. An inexplicable chill ran through him as he listened to the uncharacteristically fierce wind ripping through the shadowy eaves of the old house. A relative had committed suicide in the bathroom and the house had lain dormant for years until Sarah needed somewhere to stay in London. Despite the artful minimalism the place had recently been decked out in, Adam found an almost unbearable sense of melancholy that track lighting and Artex couldn't disguise. It was a feeling characterised by the cellar. He'd only been down there once, but the hazy recollection of its existence made him feel uneasy in much the same way as the inevitable forthcoming showdown with his housemates. But instead of dwelling on another morning he wished hadn't dawned, he batted the "on" switch of his laptop, ready to pour out some more vitriol into his diary. Adam hoped it would provide him with an outlet for his anger because he didn't have many others apart from being destructive, like the way he'd destroyed the relationship that Smale had so carefully cultivated.

He tapped his fingers on the desk impatiently as the seemingly reluctant computer booted up. Adam entered the password "Billyboy" now unfortunately seared into his brain like the unwanted phone number of an ex with all its negative connotations. Deciding against typing more hate into his diary, he clicked his "images" folder and was almost instantaneously assaulted by an array of Bills and Sarahs, holiday snaps he'd filched from their bedroom one desperate day. He remembered anxiously looking over his shoulder in the university's computer room as he'd frantically scanned each one. Looking at the pictures on the screen staring back at him now, he didn't feel guilt, only pride at the enhanced, perfectly cropped pictures of Bill and the obscene distortions he'd performed on Sarah. He especially liked the one of her with a noose around her neck, innards spilling from a slashed open gut. He gently moved his hand to his flies.

"Hi," he said as she stood at the door, elegant as ever in a white skinny-rib T-shirt and a pair of faded jeans.

"That eye of yours hasn't got any better, has it?"

"It was Bill."

"Bill?"

"Yeah, Billy Boy," he said, giving himself breathing space to elaborate another lie, pull someone else into his web of deceit that was growing like the most virulent of cancers. "He gets jealous sometimes."

"What?" Helen said, still perched in the doorway as though unsure she wanted Adam in her room, maybe fearing his bad news cluttering up her life, turning another opportunity into disappointment.

"I brought someone home, a guy," he said with a supercilious smirk, "and Bill got jealous, lost his temper. We got into a fight."

"Now you're telling me he's gay?" she said incredulously, gnawing into her lower lip as she did when she was upset.

"Look, are you going to make me stand out here all day?" he replied as though oblivious to the strength of the toxic lie he'd just concocted and lobbed into her life.

"Is he gay?" she said belligerently, ignoring her friend's pleas, tears welling in her big eyes.

"Make your own mind up, babe, but don't you dare tell him I told you about the fight," he said, meeting her eyes and not so gently squeezing one of her beautifully slender arms.

"Ouch," she cried, stepping back and he let go. "I guess guys experiment at his age."

"What about girls?"

"I already went through my lesbian phase," she said, laughing, her mood lightening at last, "in high school."

"You're saying he's just going through a phase?" he replied, ignoring her joke, getting more caught up in his own deceit. "How fucking condescending is that?"

"Sorry," Helen said, moving aside so Adam could finally get into the room. "I think some guys just *are* and some want to experiment out of curiosity."

"Curiosity killed the cat," snorted Adam as he sat down on the old sofa, the only concession to homeliness in that depressing space.

"What's that meant to mean?"

"I'm saying he's juggling people's emotions and even if it's in the name of so-called experimentation," he said, pausing for effect, "he's going to lose his timing sooner or later and everything's going to come crashing down."

"Are you telling me I'm competing with you *and Sarah* for his affections?" asked Helen, dexterously rolling a joint with her long fingers.

"I'm saying he's trying to seduce me but I'm not interested," he said, shocked by his own duplicity, pulling the battered picture of Bill out of his wallet and laying it on the sofa between them. "He gave that to me."

"Ugh," she said, turning away in disgust.

"Helen, you don't like the idea of two men being together? That repulses you?"

"It's not that," she said breathlessly, lighting up the joint with trembling hands and turning to face him again. "It's just that men are such fucking liars."

"Yeah," he said in agreement, taking a large toke on the joint she'd offered him and as he blew out a cloud of smoke he was overwhelmed by the truth of what she'd said, overwhelmed at how he was deluding his one true friend in his ruthless pursuit of Bill. He returned the joint to her and discreetly slipped the picture back into his wallet.

"I know it's a cliché but you don't mind if I put on some Massive Attack, do you?"

"You're a walking cliché, babe," he said, giggling, taking

another welcome drag on the joint.

"Yeah?"

"Yeah," he said cruelly, leaving out the trace of irony he guessed she was looking for, still bitter at how into Bill she was.

"You taking the piss?" she replied through a druggy smile as the first few bars of *Protection* filled the room.

"Babe, your choice in music, like your choice in friends, is absolutely first class," he said, laughing as he flopped back on the sofa, feeling unusually relaxed.

"Like my choice in men," she replied sarcastically, stubbing out the dwindling roll-up and immediately reaching for her stash.

"You all right?' he asked, but rather than waiting for an answer he snapped on the television, unwilling to listen to someone else's problems.

"Not really," she said, head bent down, rolling another joint with almost fanatic precision, but her comment was lost, drowned out by a clash of Massive Attack and canned laughter from the inanity of daytime TV.

"Yeah?" he replied, hedging his bets, unsure what she'd said.

"Yeah," Helen said, lighting up.

"You go, girl," he said and laughed uproariously as the perma-tanned, horribly camp presenter lisped another one-liner.

"I'm still not sure about Barcelona," she said, snapping the stereo off, her words forcing him to turn away from the screen.

"Babe, you've got to come," he implored, gently squeezing her leg, fingers splayed desperately across vintage denim. "It's Billy Boy's birthday and you're his present."

"I'm third in the pecking order," she said, eyes downcast as right on cue the laughter from the TV filled the room again.

"Nonsense," he said, now running his hands through her hair, "it depends on how much you want him."

"I don't know but I've just replied to my ex and told him I'm not interested in getting back together. It's all so easily done via email. So that's one down."

"Helen, honey," he said, desperately trying to appear sincere, realising his gambit of painting Bill as the torn bisexual had only made him more attractive. "Sarah and I are just flotsam. If you really want the boy next door, go and get him."

"Adam, I've been thinking about this for days," she said,

chewing her lip nervously, joint burning low in her hand. "I really, really like him and I don't know what I'm going to do."

"Listen, we're kids really. He's not married. He's got no responsibilities," said Adam as upbeat as ever but feeling the horrible pain of jealousy flood through him. Far from a tool to split Bill and Sarah apart, it was as though Helen had just become another obstacle to getting his hands on what he really wanted. "Go for it."

"I don't know," Helen repeated, looking as lost as he felt.

"Let's watch a film," he said, not wanting to discuss it, *him*, anymore, the image of Sarah, pregnant, coming to the fore as the deception weighed heavily.

"Okay," she said meekly, like she knew her feelings had no currency with Adam.

"*Naked Lunch*?" Adam asked as he rifled half-heartedly through the pile of videos on the floor, obviously Helen's idea of a filing system.

"Again?" she said, laughing. "Why not."

Adam was wrapped around his friend, delighting in her body's gentle warmth, engrossed in both her and the film, when the knock at the door shocked him out of his comfort zone, a stoned paranoia kicking in at the prospect of who could be at the door. He never had someone to himself, he thought sadly, watching Helen lazily untangle herself from him as the knocking on the door started again, more urgent this time.

"Shit," she said, squinting at the clock. "I didn't realise the time."

"Expecting someone?"

"Yes, actually," she snapped. "I told you I was meeting a friend. Hold on."

As she opened the front door a crack, he could only make out a mumbled conversation but then it swung open fully and Adam was confronted by Bill. He reeked of cologne and his hair was fanatically gelled into the style he always wore to Athletic Union parties.

"Fancy seeing you here," he managed to say but wanted to run as Helen stood lovingly over Bill's right shoulder, planting a hand there as though it was the most natural thing in the world.

"Yeah," Bill grunted, like Adam didn't exist, like their friendship meant nothing as he turned around and pecked Helen on the cheek.

"I'm off, I've got a date tonight," he said as though seeing them together didn't hurt, like he didn't care, but as he brushed rudely past them, slamming the door and out into the corridor he convulsed into sobs. Running blindly out of the main entrance he was glad of the enveloping evening gloom.

As he lay on the sofa, Bill felt the pain of emptiness in his stomach collide with his guilt and still part of him wished he could be by Adam's side, consoling him. He could picture his friend's face, his beautiful face, blighted by angst, but he forced himself to open his eyes, forced himself off Helen's shoulder so he could shake the image of Adam from his mind. Finally looking at her, even though it wasn't *Helen's* face he wanted to devour, he took in the angular features and bobbed hair which invitingly made her look more boy than girl. He moved his hands across the roughness of vintage denim to her flies, past the point of no return as he fiddled with the cold metal and ground her roughly, angrily back into the sofa. Angry with himself, angry with Helen, he ripped at her clothes, tearing them right off as fear flickered in her eyes, her mouth forming into a pout, the word "no" on her lips, but he wasn't taking no for an answer as he agitatedly pulled off his own clothes. He held tightly to her arms, which turned a fierce red where he refused to let go, Bill's own muscles flexed as he prepared to penetrate her.

"I love Adam," he muttered, sickened as the words slipped out, emotion clouding his eyes, but he knew she hadn't heard as he entered her, they never did, he thought, repulsed by Helen's laboured moans in his ears. Her hungry mouth glistened with saliva but as she tried to clamp it on his he glanced away, concentrated on keeping up the mechanical rhythm of fucking her.

After he finally came he pulled out, pulled away from her, grabbed for the pack of cigarettes on the coffee table and standing up, looked sadly at the discarded clothes scattered all over the floor. Helen was still curled up on the sofa, tears in her eyes, a delicate hand strategically placed in a pathetic attempt to hide her nakedness, her vulnerability.

"I love you," she said, each word ripping through the silence, hanging in the air like fallout.

Bill stood smoking his cigarette impassively, feeling anything but. His silence betraying far more about how he felt than he could ever actually admit to her. Helen covered herself with the ugly floral-print throw of the sofa and drew it up under her knees as he got dressed.

Snapping on the television after returning from the toilet where he'd seriously debated whether to come back or not, Bill finally eased back on the sofa next to her, reached out and held Helen's hand hoping she wouldn't feel the cold clamminess, hoping it wouldn't give him away, hoping she wouldn't think he was a filthy faggot due to his ridiculous utterance. He couldn't be gay, he thought, but felt a hatred, a horrible self-loathing, creep back into his mind.

"I love you too," he said feebly as he turned to her and he knew in that moment, in the flicker of her ridiculously hopeful smile, things had to change.

CHAPTER EIGHT

Adam snatched up the vibrating phone from the passenger seat, hopeful then amazed that it actually was Bill calling him.

"What do you want?" he asked, disguising the delight he felt by adopting his most pissed-off tone. It was an extremely rare occurrence for his friend to call and usually carried the weight of some depressing motive like the whereabouts of Sarah.

"Nothing really," Bill said, morose as ever, Manchester monotone giving nothing away. "Just wondering how you are?"

"How I am?" he replied, amazed Bill actually wanted to know, admitted to caring. "On a scale of one to ten, I'm about four and a half, but I was about a three yesterday."

"Really?" said Bill, his carefree, infectious giggle coursing down the line.

"Well, now you've called, honey, you've nudged me up half a point to five," he said, smitten all over again, a smile on his face as he fought through the London traffic, phone in one hand, steering wheel in the other, seemingly endless rain battering the windscreen.

"You can be such a faggot sometimes," Bill replied coldly, laughter having evaporated.

"Sometimes?" said Adam, trying to make a joke of his friend's jibe but his good mood crumbled because he knew from Bill's hateful tone he was far from joking. "Make that all the time."

"Whatever. Just don't mention this evening to Sarah, okay?"

"What? So that's why you fucking called," he shouted, the sound of his voice, his anger, filling the small car as he opened the window, rain and air flooding in, reviving him. "It's always to do with you, isn't it?"

"Adam," said Bill softly. "I was calling to see how you are. You looked upset when you saw us together, me and Helen, this evening."

"I'm fine," he lied, drinking in Bill's concern, feeling his body swell with optimism again.

"You're not fine," persisted his friend. "I, er, I'm sorry Adam but things are going to get better."

"Sorry?" he repeated but he was smiling. "Sorry about what Bill?"

But there was no reply, his friend had already hung up leaving him with only the comforting riddle of his words. "Things are going to get better," Adam parroted back to himself and even though he was no closer to what Bill actually meant, he felt strangely reassured as he drew into the gloomy confines of a multi-storey car park in Covent Garden.

Switching off the ignition he did his customary check in the rear-view mirror and was relieved to see the bruise around his eye fading, though thoughts of Smale were never far away and he was edgy about their coming meeting. Running his fingers through his freshly sheared hair (his lovingly teased tresses had cost 40 quid in some Soho salon) he took one last look in the mirror and then got out, slamming the car door with characteristic brashness. Walking around to the exit and past the passenger side of the MG he noticed the graze down the side from where he'd ploughed into a parked car, it was already rusting. Like most things, he figured, running a hand across the ragged metal, there was always something rotten just under the surface.

It was Sunday night and Covent Garden was evidently still recovering from the collective weekend hangover. Setting off down the depressingly empty street he was irritated by the impatient ringing of the phone in his pocket. Hope briefly flickered it was Bill but he knew it would be his date. He checked caller ID to remind himself that tonight's lucky guy was called Jason, or that's what he'd said anyway.

"Jason, Jason, Jason," he answered coolly, pretentiously. "I'll be there in five, darling."

Adam didn't even wait for a reply as he slipped the phone back into his pocket with some difficulty as his jeans were virtually painted on. He smiled, picturing his date cast adrift in the über cool surroundings of *The Box* cursing because Adam wasn't fashionably late, he was "obnoxiously" so, as Smale always said of his reckless timekeeping. Finally entering the bar he looked frantically around, terrified that his date had got fed up with the wait and left him to face the horrible humiliation of drinking alone in such a place, a humiliation that could be multiplied by a hundred if, God forbid, Jason had *met someone else*. A panicked raspberry flush had already risen to Adam's cheeks by the time he spotted him, his back arched athletically over the bar where he was in animated conversation with the obscenely attractive barman.

"Well, I don't mean to disturb you," he said, putting his hand on Jason's shoulders to announce his breathless-with-rage arrival at the bar.

"Oh, you made it," his date replied in that succinct, nonchalant, pissed-off way that Australians have made an art form out of. "This is my friend, Hernando."

"Pleased to meet you Fernando," Adam replied, deliberately mangling the barman's name as he held a limp hand across the counter for him to shake, all the while staring at Jason. "There's a table for two in the window, highly sought after. *Shall we?*"

"Laters, Hernando," Jason said, kissing the Mediterranean-looking hunk on both cheeks, Adam's anger rising with each little peck.

"A gin and tonic for me," he barked, on the verge of clicking his fingers at the barman, now not so much a rival as someone he'd like to see dead.

Adam watched as Jason obediently made his way to the table, Bacardi Breezer in hand. Sipping his drink, he waited for Hernando to hand his change back on the regulation silver platter and delighted in leaving 10p. He watched the barman scoop up the coin and literally throw it into a big bowl of change behind the counter like it was the ultimate insult to have received so little for looking so good.

As he headed towards Jason, who was already sucking ever so elegantly on a cigarette, he shuddered at the mix of the almost edible and the grotesque. His designer clothing, the sunbed tan, the perfect teeth, the glossed lips that had been twisted with neurotic laughter at the barman's every quip, Adam detested it all but only because that's what he had become.

"Hi," he said, swallowing back the hatred with a sip of gin that flared viciously at the back of his throat, burned down to his stomach.

"Hey," replied Jason lazily, finally turning to face Adam after obviously eyeing Hernando all the way across the bar.

"Did I piss you off?"

"Oh, no, no, everything's just fine, going swimmingly," Jason said, at last looking into his companion's eyes but Adam was now only interested in humiliating the Australian, making him feel like he had when he'd entered the bar. "Don't worry about Hernando, he's married to the owner of this place."

"As if I'd worry about him. Brain the size of a pea and dick to match," Adam shot back, laughing uproariously like he'd just cracked the funniest joke ever. Jason joined in, it would have been rude not to. Adam felt an unwelcome spark of attraction again and was worried he wouldn't be able to fight it. "So what do you do exactly?"

"What do I do?" he replied, looking back aghast. "You mean you don't know? *I didn't tell you before?*"

"No, you didn't tell me before," he replied, looking forward to erasing Jason from his phone, which was as good as wiping him from the face of the Earth.

"Dolce & Gabbana, Armani, Alexander McQueen, Galiano," rapped Jason as though he was ordering extravagant items on a menu and so loudly other patrons in the bar were turning around to glare. "Still don't know?"

"You're a fashion designer?" said Adam, already bored by his date, looking out of the window into the darkness wishing he was anywhere but opposite Jason.

"Not a designer, silly," he replied, breathing out as though prolonging the suspense but only increasing the agony. "Better than that. I'm a model."

"Australia's answer to Kate Moss," said Adam drolly.

"No, darling, I've got better legs," Jason said deadpan, bringing out a bottle of lip balm and vainly glossing his lips.

"Who's your favourite designer?"

"Alexander McQueen," he piped up excruciatingly loudly. "His latest collection based on the homeless was just so edgy. He's just so street."

"Yeah?" said Adam, taking a large swig of his drink, surveying the bottom of his glass, wishing he hadn't asked.

"He's a great laugh too."

"Want to eat?"

"Eat?" said Jason, looking at his companion as though he was mad.

"Yeah, you know, that thing called food which helps keep us alive."

"Oh," replied the Australian, like he'd finally got it, laughing just a little too enthusiastically. "I'm not that keen."

"On food?"

"I don't eat much, it's mostly salad and high-fibre milkshakes but I'm still getting fat," he said as he patted ridiculously at his non-existent waistline and puffed out his gaunt, what would be termed in the industry as "angular" cheeks. "I get the muscle tone from the milkshakes and, of course, the steroids. But I read an interview with Kate the other day and she said she survives on coffee and cigarettes."

"Look, fuck Kate," said Adam, finding it painful just to stop himself rolling his eyes, having already bitten the inside of his lip raw. "It's all fusion food here, Asia-Pacific cuisine, very healthy."

"Oh, Asia-Pacific cuisine," Jason said, eyes sparkling. "I love couscous."

And I'd love to kick your fucking head in, Adam thought, barely suppressing a smirk as he waved across a waiter who looked mortified to have been requested to do anything other than stand around and look pretty.

"Can I see the menu?" he said as he looked into the requisite doleful brown eyes, took in the beautiful face, olive skin perfectly tanned by a childhood under the Mediterranean sun, no doubt.

"Sure," he hissed like a cornered cat, attitude straight from London. Adam recognised the trait immediately because he was so adept at dishing it out too.

The uncomfortable silence the pair had made for themselves was only pricked by the waiter's return and his slapping down on the table of two fashionably unwieldy menus.

"Today's specials are Thai green curry lasagne, vegetarian bangers and mash or tofu satay," he said uninterested, looking out of the window.

"Hmm," said Adam, laughing quietly to himself at the unbelievable naffness of the specials as he looked at the inside of the huge menu, embarrassingly large considering the paucity of items on offer. He had already decided that he wouldn't actually be hanging around to *eat* dinner, so it wasn't worth getting too agitated about. "I'm ordering for both of us, okay?"

"Okay," Jason replied, fiddling nervously with another cigarette.

"The tofu satay, the green curry *lasagne*, the spaghetti bolognaise in Thai red curry, the devilled chicken wings and pineapple, the Indonesian spring rolls, though not sure what makes them Indonesian and the curried Quorn samosas," he said, breathing out, hoping he'd ordered just enough so it'd be piled under Jason's nose, a variety of smells to play havoc with his borderline anorexia.

"That's the satay, lasagne, spag bol, chicken wings, *Indonesian* spring rolls and the samosas," said the waiter, unnecessarily enunciating each dish as though their request was highly suspect and spoke volumes for their lack of sophistication.

"Can you serve everything at once?" Adam requested.

"Pardon?"

"Before it's all come in bits and pieces, just bring everything together," Adam said, a smile playing at his lips, imagining Jason sat there with platefuls of food and a newly vacated place at the table yawning in front of him to feed his many insecurities.

"That's a lot of food."

"I'm hungry but don't worry the tofu satay is just for you," Adam replied, winking cheekily.

"My favourite, it's 100 per cent fat free," said Jason, smiling.

"Great."

"What do you do, by the way?" said Jason, obviously having no interest in the answer as he studied his polished nails like some kind of beauty queen.

"I'm a student."

"Oh," he replied, mouth forming into a pout as though nothing could possibly match what he was doing.

"When's your next show?"

"I'm on twenty-four-hour standby. Whenever the agency call, drag a comb through my hair and I'm there."

"Yeah?"

"Yeah, I'm a total professional, bloody good at what I do,"

said Jason, running a hand affectedly through his fashionable skinhead. "Not many can sashay down the catwalk like I can, especially after a gram of coke."

"Yeah, I'm sure you're just a genius with that nose of yours. Practice makes perfect," replied Adam, unable to stop some of his viciousness finally slipping out but keeping it civil enough to make Jason's humiliation complete. "Just a little joke."

"Thought so," the Australian said but there were tears in eyes that didn't look unfamiliar with sorrow.

"I'm sorry," replied Adam, reaching a hand across and trying to touch Jason's but he'd already twisted away, body language speaking volumes.

"Don't be."

"Got to go to the toilet," he said hastily as he spotted the waiter coming through the kitchen door with two trays groaning with food. Jason was too busy making eyes at Hernando to notice him slipping a £20 note partially under a table mat before he headed not for the toilet but for the exit.

"Hey," said a guy, barring his way.

"What?" replied Adam, recognising the person who had been sat at the adjoining table.

"He's not really a model, well not one that makes any money."

"No?" he replied flustered, wanting to get away, looking over to see if Jason could see him, but he was fixated by the array of food being laid before him, plate by steaming plate.

"I've been trying to pull him for ages," said the guy, smiling. "He works in a gay pub in Kings Cross."

Adam could barely stop laughing as he bowled out onto the dark street. The phone rang incessantly in his pocket on his way to the car and he couldn't help but erupt into more giggles every time he thought of the so-called model sat there alone facing his ultimate nemesis – food.

CHAPTER NINE

Bill hated birthdays, not just because it meant he was another year older but because it usually involved having to spend time with his bitch of a mother. She was bound up in religious dogma – Catholicism to be precise. Like most fanatics she couldn't help but taint her whole family. Her indoctrination had driven his father away, not into the arms of another woman but into a drying-out clinic. It had driven Bill away too but he was still intimidated into submission by her weekly phone calls where she breathed fire and brimstone down the line. Her latest topic was gay priests. Oh, how she despised them.

"Dolores, these are my friends Sarah and Adam," he said quietly, worried about the very sound of his accent in the pretentious Soho "brasserie". Noel Gallagher's Manchester drawl would probably be the only Mancunian thing welcome within a six-mile radius, he thought, angry with Adam for having gone so chichi with his choice of venue. Bill wished he'd coached his housemates on Dolores' prejudices but he'd been too ashamed to let them know what they were in for. Sarah though, had agreed to pose as "just a friend" for the purposes of the evening as he had told her his mother was "sensitive". He could have added she was a sociopath.

"Hello, pleased to meet you, Mrs ..."

"Dolores, just call me Dolores, please," she said, voice resonating as she unsmilingly scrutinised Sarah, Manchester accent almost as brutal as Bill's but with the slight trace of Irish brogue.

"Hiya," said Adam breezily, seemingly unfazed.

Though Bill saw an odd look in his friend's eyes, something like fear, as Adam took in all 17-stone of his mother. She dominated the table, huge earrings hanging from her ears like Christmas tree decorations, pallid face brightened only by a slash of violently red lipstick. As they sat in silence, the chatter of other enthusiastic diners in their ears, four people with everything to say to one another and yet nothing, he felt what he disgustingly admitted to himself was a spark of attraction as a pretty-boy waiter approached.

"Drinks for you guys?" he lisped.

Bill reddened and studied the table rather than looking up to face his shame.

"What would the birthday boy like?" Adam cooed, camp as ever, looking conspiratorially at the waiter like they were involved in a game no one else knew the rules to. "It's got to be champers, hasn't it, sweetie?"

Bill winced as he looked up and saw Dolores' eyes boring into Adam. He could have punched his friend for his stupid faggot mannerisms, his sickeningly obvious flirtation with the waiter. He probably would have if he hadn't been so cowed by the horribly affected cool of the brasserie.

"I'm not really a birthday boy, it's my actual birthday on Friday when we'll be in Spain. And I can't afford champagne, not on a student budget," he replied finally, a chorus of nervous laughter filling the void.

"But I'm paying," Dolores boomed, her deep voice almost masculine in quality, a light film of sweat on her forehead.

"Dolores!" Bill protested. It had to be Dolores, never Mother. This had been a barrier to intimacy from the day he had begun to pronounce his first words, but he knew it was pointless. He didn't want her getting drunk (it was her one vice, "a wee dram" she called it) because when she'd been drinking she was even more outspoken and righteous. However, due to the belligerent mood she was obviously in, he feared nothing could alter the disastrous course of this night, drink or no drink.

"If my son wants champagne, he can have champagne," she shouted, ignoring his wishes completely.

"Bill?" said Sarah, gently touching his arm. He'd been so absorbed in the waiter's every provocative move, he flinched, reddening again as though caught out. "What's wrong with you?"

"Er ... yeah," he said distractedly, his girlfriend's words in his ear while he caught another sly glance at the waiter, "champagne's fine."

"Any particular bottle, sir?"

"A reasonably priced one," snapped Dolores, answering for Bill as though she sensed the distraction, the temptation hovering at the head of the table and wanted rid of it.

"A bottle of champagne coming up, oh and er, happy birthday," said the waiter, bowing down as he backed away from the table so he was eye level with Bill.

"Cheers, yeah," he mumbled, fiddling with the pack of cigarettes he'd just retrieved from his pocket rather than looking up, rather than watching the waiter's perfectly rendered arse, so obvious in scarily tight hipsters, disappearing off into the kitchen.

"He's friendly," said Sarah, sounding totally exasperated.

"Yeah," Adam chimed in, shooting Bill a hateful glance, "and I think he's got the hots for our Billy Boy."

"Whatever," he blustered, lighting a cigarette, for once uncaring about Dolores' reaction, needing a cigarette more.

"I didn't know you smoked," she said aghast as soon as he raised the cigarette to his lips, her chins wobbling with indignation, a flush rising to her cheeks.

"Why, want one?" he said, struggling to stop the bitterness, nurtured over years, spilling out to engulf them all, but he was scared, scared of her.

"Don't you take that tone with me, young man," she said, Bill watching his two housemates caught in the crossfire, sat in rapt silence like they were awaiting an inevitable casualty.

"What?" he said, playing for time, though he knew it was futile and didn't dare return the burning cigarette to his lips despite the hurried efforts of the waiter to provide him with an ashtray.

"Put. It. Out. This. Minute," she said, labouring every word, bright red in the face with the effort.

As he stubbed it out, ground it into the ashtray, disgusted with himself, capitulating in front of his incredulous friends, it all came back. The times she'd taken a belt to him and the times she'd locked him in his room without food. The time, worst of all, when he was just five years old, a little boy cowering in her shadow as she loomed over him and triumphantly hung a crucifix around his neck and told him God was always watching. Involuntarily he put his hand up and felt it there now, felt it like the weight of her stare and was forced to turn away.

"Champagne, guys," said the waiter, his cheerful campness clashing horribly with the silence.

Bill didn't look up. Instead he listened to the wine sloshing into the glasses and the carefree buzz of conversation coming from other tables that seemed to mock their stilted efforts. Out of the corner of his eye he saw Adam smoking a cigarette opposite, aiming a stream of smoke at Dolores sat directly to his right.

"So what do you do?" she said, turning to face the direction of the smoke, peering at Adam like she was studying an animal in a zoo, presumably wanting to draw a line under the embarrassing incident she'd caused with Bill. She put on a pair of wire-rimmed John Lennon glasses as if to get a better look, which would have seemed comical if she hadn't appeared so scary. "By the way, I don't mind you smoking but I don't want my son getting lung cancer."

"What do I do?" he repeated back facetiously. Bill recognised Adam's stock response to this type of question. He admired his friend, the free spirit, the refusal to be intimidated. "I'm a male prostitute."

Dolores laughed so hard into her flute of champagne it looked as though she might burst a blood vessel. Her face reddened to the extent that she was almost unrecognisable from the pale ghost who'd sat in her place earlier. Even as she waved the waiter over for another bottle, such was the rapidity with which they were all drinking, still she laughed. But it was the empty laughter of a coward, Bill thought, the laughter of a woman who didn't have the courage to stand by her convictions, to challenge someone equal to her. Bill feared his own acquiescence, not just tonight but every single day, meant it applied to him too.

"Only joking, Mrs Laws," said Adam. Bill feared what was coming next, where this was headed, and took another big swig of champagne. "I wouldn't want to corrupt your lovely son."

"No," she said sternly, wiping her mouth with a dry crusted tissue like the one Bill knew she always kept up her sleeve. It was as though she was wiping away any trace of a smile. "No, you wouldn't want to do that, would you?"

"Menus, guys," said the waiter, appearing above Bill, a welcome intrusion on Dolores' growing intensity, like a circling great white sensing blood.

118

Bill leafed through the menu, handed to him by the ever-smiling, eager-to-please waiter who alternately enthralled and repulsed him. But even as he read the words off the page they formed a nonsensical, jumbled mass, another barrier to be overcome before he could be rid of this gutting experience, be rid of her.

"Oh, Bill, they've got your favourite, sausages and mash," piped Dolores, reaching over and touching his hand, almost motherly, but he knew she was just covering for her earlier outburst, momentarily dulled by drink.

Now it was Sarah's turn to glower at him. She had mercifully kept her counsel throughout, but he knew that look. The look of righteous indignation, honed at her boarding school debating circle that left him with no choice. "Actually, I'm a veggie," he said, almost inaudibly, but sure he saw the approaching waiter suppress a giggle behind a slender hand.

"A what?" hissed Dolores.

"A vegetarian," shot back Sarah smugly, tugging affectionately at Bill's arm and he was grateful, so grateful that someone else was absorbing his mother's wicked stare, her fury at the world.

"I know what a vegetarian is, thank you," she said. "I just can't believe what *he* is."

"What he is?" said Sarah at her argumentative best, questioning Bill's pariah status for eating greens, as if for Dolores it defined his whole being. "He doesn't eat meat because it's murder."

"What?" screeched Dolores, shaking with anger.

Bill could imagine the vitriol that would explode out of her mouth, vomit like, if she knew everything: the dalliance with Helen and worse, far worse, the sin which had taken him to the dark place he now inhabited, his attraction to men. He felt the weight of the crucifix heavier than ever in the charged silence. Even Adam was quiet for once and the waiter had disappeared to the refuge of the kitchen, politely giving them more time to order or so he'd said. He was probably just repulsed by the whole ugly scene, Bill thought ashamedly.

"He doesn't like to eat meat," Sarah said finally, slow and deliberate as if talking to a very young child.

Bill was cheering inside. He knew from experience that most bigots only got away with it because their views were left unchallenged. They simply battered the weak into submission with the bluntness of their prejudices. Dolores had beaten him and his father down but not confident, middle-class, politically correct Sarah. It was like seeing two extremes, the cool waif at his side and the mound of glowering human flesh opposite him.

"Oh, doesn't he," Dolores said, signalling the waiter who'd just reappeared.

"Ready to order now?"

"Yes, I think so," she said, looking around the table, all of a sudden maternal, concerned but still unwavering. "Bangers and mash for birthday boy and me."

"Sure."

Bill turned away from the waiter's pitying stare at the sound of Sarah scraping back her chair. It felt like he was being attacked from all sides.

"I'm sorry Bill, I can't do this," she said, getting to her feet.

And as he looked up at her he only saw pity for him in her eyes. He felt pathetic, worthless, like Dolores always made him feel, wanted him to feel.

"I can't see you suffer like this and if you're not prepared to walk out of here, I am," Sarah continued, turning from the table, shooting Dolores one last hateful look as she headed to the exit.

"Well, she's a right little madam, isn't she?" said Dolores, laughing loudly, hollowly, as the restaurant door slammed shut and there were just three of them. No one joined in her laughter.

"She's fine," said Bill evenly, looking Adam in the eye pleadingly, hoping he'd order a dish, that he wouldn't leave him all alone *with her*.

"Vegetarian lasagne," said Adam finally, grinning the broadest of grins at his friend.

"Madam's not coming back?" quizzed the waiter, arching an ironic eyebrow at Bill.

"No, Madam isn't," spat Dolores.

"Right you are," he replied, fussily clearing away her place, the half-finished flute of champagne with an imprint of Sarah's lipstick on the rim the only forlorn remnant.

"All that champagne's gone right through me," said Dolores,

thrusting her chair back, her bulky figure throwing a shadow across the table as she awkwardly rose. "Got to pee."

"Nightmare," said Bill, breathing out and shaking his head at her schoolgirl crudity once he was sure she was out of earshot. He hoped Adam wouldn't see the tears springing to his eyes. He knew that, like Dolores, his friend preyed on any weakness.

"Hey, are you all right?" Adam said tenderly, reaching a hand over the table but quickly recoiling as though he'd made some kind of mistake, an admission.

"No, I'm not fucking all right. What do you think?" hissed Bill, knowing at that moment he didn't just hate the fawning queer sat opposite him and the grotesque Dolores, he hated everyone because he despised himself, his weaknesses.

"We can't choose our family," Adam replied softly.

"I suppose not," he said, looking at the table top, his aggression having drained out of him to leave a horrible kind of resignation in its place as, being so attuned in her footfalls, he heard her returning to the table. The fear never went away.

"Hey, you don't have to stop gabbing on my account," she said, tapping Bill not so lightly on the head and easing her considerable frame into a chair obviously designed for the skeletal arse of a Soho model or a bubble-butted out of work actor. "Unless you were talking about me of course."

"Not everything's about you, Dolores," he said exasperatedly, swigging back another glass of champagne, fortifying himself because he knew she'd pick up on his snide tone. She didn't really need an excuse.

"Well, I've had quite enough of your lip today," she wheezed, batting at the sweat running down her flushed face, visibly affected by the exertion of getting to the toilet and back. "I don't know what they're teaching you at that university of yours but I better see some results sooner rather than later."

"I'm doing all right," he lied.

"Yeah, Mike Smale, our English Literature tutor, says Bill's got a particular bent for it," chirped Adam, sniggering into his champagne glass.

"All right?" she shrieked, ignoring Adam, fixated on her son, wobbling in her chair indignantly. "All right? For that amount of money you should be getting straight As. How about you, sonny?"

"I'm doing great," Adam replied, avoiding Dolores' eye, knowing his grades were hardly any better than Bill's and not wanting to prolong the conversation.

Bill was grateful when the waiter finally brought their food. It signalled the ordeal wouldn't last too much longer. Dolores bowed her head as if to say grace. He did too but winced at the busy scraping of cutlery from Adam's plate.

"Don't you say grace in your family?" Dolores said, head shooting up from the table, glaring at Adam.

"No, Mrs Laws, I'm a non-believer," he said with a provocative smirk. "I don't think they'd have me."

"Shush now, the church is for everyone," she said magnanimously, like she'd decreed it.

Yeah, for those who want to live a life in denial, noses buried in a centuries-old piece of irrelevance for guidance, Bill thought savagely, keeping quiet.

"That's what's wrong with the youth of today," she mumbled without any great conviction, as if Adam was beyond saving, beyond clichés. It wasn't long before her latest diatribe paled into the sad clatter of cutlery on bone china.

"Everything all right for you folks?" said the waiter, hovering busily over the table again, staring intently at Dolores as if to provoke her.

Bill feared an outburst but knew it would only come when the waiter was safely out of earshot.

"Fine," said Adam, nodding, sending the waiter sashaying on his way.

"If one of my kids turned out like that, I'd disown them," said Dolores, spitting the words out hatefully, sausage gravy dribbling down her ample chins. There was a grand air of finality about her statement, like she'd said her piece, like the whole evening had been leading up to it.

"Turned out like what?" said Adam, voice high and whiny, as if he really didn't know.

Bill wished the faggot would shut up. He was only encouraging her.

"You know," she said, angrily flinging her knife and fork to the plate with a crash.

"No, I don't know," he replied. "Why don't you tell me?"

"Queer," she said through twisted lips, like she was tainted even for just uttering the word.

"And how do you know your son or someone around this table is not?"

"I'm not," shouted Bill, his face flushed red. He just wanted to grab Adam by his ridiculously fashionable shirt and crush the air out of his slender neck.

"And how about those of us that are?" said Adam so loudly that other diners turned around to stare, the waiter once a blur in the distance moving closer as if sensing trouble. "Should we all burn in hell?"

"None of my business," Dolores said, trembling, avoiding Adam's accusatory stare as she rifled through her handbag.

Bill had never seen her looking so lost but then he'd never seen her so challenged. All these years she'd just gotten away with it.

"Why did you say what you did?" continued Adam, not letting go, asking her to justify the unjustifiable.

"I'll leave you two boys to dessert," she huffed, addressing the ceiling as she threw a wad of cash onto the table that Bill knew he wasn't in a position to turn down. Then, without another word or even the cold peck on the cheek he was so accustomed to, Dolores, his mother, pushed back her designer chair and made her cumbersome way out into the night, away from the bright lights of Soho and back to the shadowy corner of her prejudices, the same ones she'd saddled her son with.

"Why didn't you warn me?" said Adam, panting with rage.

"Why don't you stop being so gay?" shot back Bill, tears stinging his eyes, unable to stop the hate spilling from his lips, more scared and confused than ever.

"No wonder you can't be yourself with a mother like that."

"What's that meant to fucking mean?" he shouted, unable to even regulate the tone of his voice. The waiter was back from escorting Dolores from the premises and was standing nervously at the head of the table, the waiter who he'd wanted to fuck but now would like to beat till unrecognisable.

"Until you stand up to her you're always going to be pathetic. Is this how you expect your friends to be treated?" said Adam, rising agitatedly to his feet, flinging a glassful of champagne over his friend.

Feeling the liquid coat his hair, seep across his shirt, sensing the eyes of the whole restaurant on him, humiliation complete because he couldn't stand up for himself, couldn't even admit what he really wanted *to himself*, he swung a heavy arm at Adam. There was a sickening crack as Bill's fist ploughed into his friend's face propelling him backwards into another table, diners diving for cover, blood splattering white cloth.

Bill ran right through the raised voices and panic and straight out of the door like he was running from his feelings. His eyes were clouded by tears as he jogged erratically up Dean Street not knowing where he was going, colliding awkwardly with those confidently heading for a destination. He couldn't shake the image of Adam from his mind, hysterical as he clutched his bloodied nose. A friend betrayed, but worst of all, Bill knew he'd betrayed himself.

CHAPTER TEN

The neurotic din died down to a hum as though people were embarrassed they had enjoyed the violence so much. Maybe they wanted more, Adam thought, as the waiter, mercifully silent for once, took him gently by the arm. He guided Adam back to the table, handed him a large napkin to staunch his wound and quickly cleared away the debris and the blood-stained tablecloth, leaving the wad of cash Dolores had left behind.

"Stiff drink?" he asked, emphasis on the stiff and affecting a wink like that of a grotesque caricature on a saucy seaside postcard.

"Just water," snapped Adam, turning away from the hungry desire in his eyes, wondering why everyone had to be selfish, so opportunistic, though it agitated him because he knew he was guiltier than most.

He sat staring into space, trying to understand how things had got so ugly. The waiter came and went again, silently placing down a glass of iced water. Moving to take a sip he noticed two paracetamol arranged neatly next to the glass. He smiled to himself as he swallowed them down but his moment of reassurance was pricked by the unwelcome throb of pain as the adrenaline stopped surging through his body. He put his hand up, felt the heavy swelling, the half a golf ball protruding from his once slender cheek. At least his nose had stopped oozing blood.

The ringing of his mobile phone was a brief respite from self-pity but he cursed loudly when he saw it was Sarah and started to feel even sorrier for himself. Obviously she was going to ask where Bill was. For all he knew he could be on his way to Helen's but he wasn't about to cover for him, he thought, reluctantly accepting the call.

"Hello," she said coolly, the hell they'd all been through over the course of the evening failing to instil even a smidgen of camaraderie, indicating just how divided they were. "Where's

Billy Boy?"

"Well, after he punched me out in the middle of *The Evening Standard* 'Place to be Seen 1997'," Adam said, almost recoiling from the icy coldness emanating down the line, "he did a runner. So in answer to your question, I really have no idea."

But all his dramatic purpose was lost by the silence coming from the other end. She'd already hung up. "Bitch," he said aloud, smiling back at yet another bemused stare from a woman at an adjacent table, no doubt itching to tell her friends how much the "Place to be Seen" had gone down. Intimidated, she finally turned away. Adam winced with pain as his cheek throbbed harder.

"I'll have that stiff drink now please, er, make it a double whisky," he said to the waiter who was still hovering nearby.

The only reason he hadn't been thrown out was the fact they'd racked up such a healthy bill, he thought, scooping up the sheaf of crumpled notes in the middle of the table with as much haste as Dolores had discarded them.

He felt another stabbing pain in his cheek, took a large swig of the whisky the waiter had obediently dispatched and steeled himself for the moment he had been dreading. He rushed to the bathroom to scrutinise the wound. As he looked at the ugly red swelling on his cheek, his nostrils caked in dricd blood, he felt as ashamed and humiliated as he guessed Bill must have. He splashed his face with the icy cold water, impatiently waving away the irrelevant flunky standing behind him with a towel, the liquid providing only fleeting relief from the fluctuation between ache and excruciating pain. Even as the tears of hurt and frustration flowed with the running tap water, he knew he couldn't cleanse himself from his want, his desire for Bill.

Adam was jolted out of his sorrow by the phone ringing irritatingly in his pocket again. He pulled it out and through the blur of tears saw it was Bill. Anger rose within him as quickly as his sadness had, but he felt there was still no room to hate him. Letting the phone ring and ring, he knew tomorrow or the next day he'd still pull out that dog-eared photo of Billy Boy from his wallet and study it longingly, feeling the same desperate want he'd suffered the first time he set eyes on him in an English Literature tutorial.

Bill elbowed past Soho's al fresco drinkers, delaying their trip back to suburbia for *just one more pint,* he thought disparagingly. The sweating, suited army spilled out of the pubs, blocking the pavement, so deep that they even littered the road, often hurling abuse at drivers for having the temerity to use the thoroughfare. Their banter, their forced laughter lingered infuriatingly behind him on the balmy evening air as he increased his pace.

Blundering his way onto Old Compton Street it was as though he didn't know where he was going, but unfortunately for him, he knew exactly. The after-work Dean Street crowd – blokes winding each other up about girls and football or barking into mobile phones trying to justify their time in the pub by dictating that last bit of irrelevance to a harassed secretary or letting wives know they were going to be late for dinner *again* – gave way to clones of a different kind. For Bill they were a far more intimidating kind, devoid of suits, most sporting the summery uniform of jeans and singlet. As he made his way aggressively along, unlike those just a few hundred yards back, these outdoor drinkers didn't regard him as a potential fist fight, a bundle after the rigours of another 10-hour day. No, he sensed their eye contact but he didn't dare look back. He knew he was being eyed for another reason.

He was shamefully drunk but knew it was no excuse. He moved through the street-side crowd with their tempting vapour of perfume and staggered into the gloomy confines of a pub. A bulky black bouncer nodded to him at the entrance and he subconsciously filed away an image of this immense character with a jagged scar that ran from lip to ear.

The pub had a huge rainbow flag outside and he'd walked past enough times to know just how far he'd fallen. He looked at the pinpoints of light that vaguely picked out men standing in clusters. Most seemed alone and no one was really engaged in conversation. The need for chatter, the ebullience of outside, was replaced by the flatness of a thumping disco soundtrack. Sweat pulsed messily down his forehead in response to the drunken smiles and desperate winks aimed his way. He didn't reciprocate. He couldn't. It took all his effort just to approach the bar and attempt buying a drink. He hoped he wouldn't stumble under the weight of collective scrutiny. It felt like being on some kind of perverse catwalk. Bill tried to kid himself he was there just to get pissed, to *drown his sorrows*. It was the nearest pub, he thought through the haze of alcohol. His conscience bugged him again, *well it had been the closest, hadn't it?*

"You all right there, love?" screeched the barman above the thump of the music, high sing-song voice piercing the urgency of his thoughts.

"Beer please, pint," Bill said flatly, staring blankly at the row of optics behind the barman, anything but respond to his smile. He had to be disciplined, he reasoned, fumbling about in his pocket for his cigarettes.

"What beer?" said the barman, pouting, hands on hips. As Bill looked at him fully for the first time, there was the faint flicker of an amused smile on the boy's lips. "We've got Carling, Kronenburg, Stella ..."

"Lager," snapped Bill, cutting him off and slapping a tenner down on the counter.

"First time is it?" he snapped right back, effortlessly pulling the pint and then handing him the overflowing glass along with his change before turning nonchalantly to serve another customer, like he'd already lost interest in the new kid in town.

Bill looked across the bar and through the window at the people chattering happily outside. He thought about the time his friends had told him they'd hung around a pub on Old Compton Street at closing time and followed two ageing queens, dragging them down a side alley and beating them until they were unrecognisable. He caught some boy looking at him and stared back into the bottom of his glass like he was ashamed to be thinking about what his friends had done *being in a place like this.* Back then he'd nodded along vigorously as they'd recounted their sick tale, letting out an appropriately filthy laugh at the climax as if to underline how detached he was from the faggots. He was anything but laughing now. He dared to look up again and caught the barman's eye. A stool had become free at the bar and the boy gestured to it. This was all the encouragement he needed to make his way over and sit down. He'd felt so uncomfortable standing, so conspicuous, he'd been edging closer and closer to the exit.

Bill took another gulp of his pint, but as he put it down on the chrome counter he was disturbed to see he'd almost emptied it. The barman caught his eye again and then regarded the nearly empty glass, comically raising an eyebrow. He couldn't help but laugh but was afraid the boy might think they were more than just a barman and a punter. He buried himself in a magazine that had been tossed on the bar by some long-departed customer. Like coming into the place itself, it took him a while to focus on what was in front of him, but as he impatiently flicked through the magazine he realised it was page after glossy page of men. The pictures showed a variety of openings and appendages, finally causing him to sling the rag back down as though his fingers had been burnt.

It was then, as he regretfully drained the last dregs of his pint, that he felt the enormity of what he'd done just by being in the pub. The excited chatter barely audible above the incessant disco only made him more edgy, as did the growing insistence of the stares, but he didn't dare confront one of the faggots for fear of pummelling a face with the empty beer glass he was still wielding agitatedly in his hand. Anger was rising in him along with nausea brought on by the night's excesses, but instead of running for the exit, as he knew he should have, he ran for the toilet.

Bursting through the door of the cubicle, he knelt down on the piss-soaked floor and vomited loudly into the far from pristine toilet bowl.

"Are you all right in there?" came a concerned voice from the other side of the cubicle door.

It was concern he knew he would never have got in a straight pub but he answered by vomiting again, even more violently this time, an attempt to get everything out of his system. He finally rose to his feet, swaying, his head swimming with thoughts of Dolores, Helen, Sarah, Adam, all muddled together with the repetitive beat of the music outside, incessant and relentless like his needs, his desires. Needs and desires that he couldn't stop, couldn't change.

He was sniffing hard as he finally exited the cubicle, vaguely aware that the front of his jeans were soaked through by the contents of the toilet floor, his acid-green shirt encrusted with particles of the expensive dinner Dolores had paid for. Probably only to salve her conscience for all the years of suffering, he thought bitterly, but he was still suffering.

"You got any more coke, mate?" said a guy, grabbing his shoulder, invading his personal space.

"What?" Bill replied, aggressive, confused, finally catching the eye of the attractive boy standing before him just inches away. He could smell the temptation of his perfume even over the disgustingly pungent smell of the toilet and his own vomit.

"You were sniffing," said the boy, stepping back as if on guard, as if reacting to Bill's aggression, his dishevelled state, unsure of himself. "You were sniffing hard in the toilet, you got some cocaine left?"

"Fuck off," he said, feeling that anger, that hatred, rise again, but it was only panic at the unstoppable surge of attraction he'd just felt. The boy ran out of the toilet, ran away, leaving him as lonely as he'd ever been.

"Just fuck off," he repeated but to himself as he looked in the mirror and began cleaning up.

He splashed the cool water over his face and scrubbed desperately at his stained shirt with a tissue. His mobile rang and he tried to ignore it. Finally pulling it out of his pocket, he saw it was Sarah, his pregnant, devoted, "lap dog of a girlfriend" as Adam dubbed her. He let it ring and ring as he re-entered the bar, knowing her infuriating persistence would be swallowed up by the music. He sought out his stool, determined to order another drink, determined to forget.

"All right, love?" asked the barman, studying him closely as Bill sat back down.

"I'm fine," he lied, his monotone contrasting sharply with the barman's sing-song, knowing he could see something was wrong, something was askew, his appearance clashing horribly with the contrived perfection of the other customers. "One more pint."

"*Please?*" the barman said, like he was addressing a five year old.

"Please," Bill replied obediently, flinching nervously as the colour rose to his cheeks. Everything in his life had suddenly become so unpredictable, he felt off balance.

He tried to calm himself by the fact that the pub had emptied out a lot. The after-work crowd had moved on and he could almost convince himself he was in a "normal" bar. As he tentatively sipped another pint, Bill began to take solace in Adam's one moment of candour about being gay. Well, it was the only time he'd been prepared to listen to his friend. He'd talked about his first visit to a gay pub, how liberated it had made him feel, how he'd wished he'd done it sooner. Bill was relieved not to feel that about where he was now. He clung to that admission as though it proved something, the difference between them and chuckled into his beer glass, relaxing for the first time, lighting a cigarette with almost steady hands. But then he noticed the boy from the toilet, waiting at the bar, standing at his shoulder, looking even better than on that first, snatched, desperate glance and it happened again. An overwhelming desire coursed painfully through him, frightening in its intensity.

"Bottle of Budweiser, please," Bill heard him shout across to the barman in the same appealingly self-conscious voice that he'd used when asking for the cocaine.

He feared the boy would turn from the bar and catch him looking, but was sickened by the fact that he was willing it to happen. When their eyes did inevitably meet Bill wasn't able to turn away and hide like he'd been doing for far too long. He stared right back.

"I'm sorry about before, I shouldn't have assumed anything, I always do. Want a drink? Whisky chaser?"

To Bill he made it sound all so easy, all so inviting, all so plausible, as Dolores would have said. "Yes," he replied, looking at the boy's face side-on as he ordered his whisky. He hardly seemed old enough to be in a pub, let alone drinking. Then he realised, with a creeping horror that the fine features, the blond hair, the easy, charming manner all reminded him of Adam.

"There you go," he said, their hands brushing as he passed Bill his drink.

"Thanks," he said, barely able to look his new acquaintance in the eye, making a ridiculous attempt to appear manly by swigging the whisky down in one. As he banged the glass on the bar, far from being impressed, his blond friend seemed to be regarding him with what he guessed was pity.

"You all right?"

"I'm not normally like this," he slurred, instinctively shooting a hand out as if to hold the guy, to stop him moving away, but ending up slapping the bar top instead.

"Well, I've actually got friends to see here," he said, edging backwards, but Bill looked hard at the one drink in his hand and sensed that the bottle he was holding was his friend.

"Sorry about before, I've had a hard day," he said pleadingly, trying to appear sincere and not desperate, hoping through the haze of alcohol that the sentence had come out in the right order, knowing that there wasn't any magic combination of words that could recover the situation, make him sound more plausible.

"Want to talk about it?" said the boy finally, using the practised, slightly jaded air of a counsellor who'd heard it all before, but placing his beer gently down on the bar between them like he meant to stay, like he was actually interested in talking.

"Yeah," replied Bill, exhaling after a prolonged drag of his cigarette, hoping it would sober him up, stop him viewing the room from what felt like a manic carousel.

"Go on then," he encouraged softly.

"Look, I had a fight with my best friend tonight," Bill said, and as he did so he couldn't help his eyes filling with tears, threatening to overflow down his flushed cheeks. He felt the weight of the boy's questioning stare, he knew that look, it was Smale's.

"Your boyfriend?" he queried, barely suppressing a smirk.

"I'm not fucking gay, all right?" he shouted, paranoid, irrational, wheeling around, eyes blazing, blinking away the tears.

An intense rage raced through his body, his hands, like an electric charge and Bill was soon gripping the boy's neck. He felt him trying to wrestle away under the strength of his grasp like a panicked animal and he looked down at the cigarette he'd ditched, smouldering away on the floor, looked away rather than at his face, anything but his face. He knew he was going to kill him, rid himself of desire, the fucking disgusting temptation, as he squeezed tighter and tighter. The boy's breath rasped in Bill's ears, but just as suddenly he felt an immensely powerful force grip his own back and send him reeling. As he cannoned against the bar he involuntarily let go of the boy, catching the aghast look of the barman and another montage of eyes staring back at him through the blur as he toppled over. Pain crackled through him, the hurt obliterating his will to fight.

Bill offered no resistance as he was roughly dragged to his feet. Warily opening his eyes he came face to face with the lip-to-ear pink scar on that unyielding black face he'd taken in at the pub's entrance. The bouncer's body odour pervaded his nostrils, the roughness of the cheap leather jacket chafed against his throbbing face. Panicking, humiliated, he began struggling again but it was as though the bouncer was carrying a bag of feathers. He was dragged swiftly across the floor, in front of excited, self-satisfied smiles barely concealed behind pint glasses and pushed roughly to the exit. Then he was outside, so grateful for the freshness of the air, panting as he breathed it in in great gulps.

"I'll kill you next time," said the bouncer menacingly into his ear, finally letting go and giving him a push in the back that sent him stumbling up the street.

Bill didn't look back. He felt pain all over his body, but it didn't compare to the turmoil in his head as he stood on the corner of Dean Street, trembling, not knowing who he could turn to, where he could run next.

CHAPTER ELEVEN

"What the fuck is this?" said Adam, eyeing the large bouquet of flowers on the dining-room table that appeared to be already wilting behind their ugly cellophane wrapping.

"Look at the card," Bill replied, smiling up at him from his plate of toast as though last night had never happened, while Sarah looked on mutely, her mouth forming one of those disapproving pouts.

He knew he really shouldn't have but he ripped the card off the front of the bouquet in a crackle of cellophane and as he did so gently turned his face so the bruised side was facing the two housemates. *"Sorry, sorry and sorry, love Bill,"* it read. The words coupled with the childish scrawl on the tacky rose bordered card meant he was fighting back tears, but he was determined not to show any kind of emotion in front of the couple, anything that could be seen as a weakness.

"Happy now," barked Sarah, glaring at him as though she'd put Bill up to it but he knew she hadn't.

"I shouldn't have hit you, mate, I know that," he said, contrite, even caring, in contrast to his girlfriend's coldness. "Come 'ere."

Adam looked at Sarah and it was as though she was willing him not to move, but with legs leaden from a mix of nerves and excitement he made his way across the room, as instructed, to Bill. He'd never felt so comforted yet so conflicted, sinking into his friend's outstretched arms; into the embrace of the one who'd hit him, the one who'd called him a "faggot". Suddenly none of it mattered, as he breathed in the musky aroma he loved, spiced with the decadent odour of cigarettes, last night's beer and the hint of washing powder and cheap deodorant.

"I'm sorry, too," said Adam as he finally, guiltily, untangled himself from Bill and stood back facing his friend, if friend wasn't too moderate a word for the intensity of his feelings.

"For God's sake, it's like two lovers making up," shouted

Sarah, words dripping with contrived outrage and clashing horribly with Adam's hangover. She stood up and began collecting up the empty plates with an aggressive clatter.

"Adam, sit down," said Bill, ignoring his girlfriend's mood and nodding at the seat opposite his. "I want to talk."

"I'm going shopping," she said, like it was some kind of threat, struggling to be the centre of attention even as she exited the room, but no one was really listening to her, no one was interested.

Despite Bill's invitation to talk, Adam was still uncertain and remained standing, unsure whether he actually wanted to listen to what his friend had to say. Their discussions so often ended in a fight, or some homophobic jibe, like he'd become obsessed with denouncing homosexuality.

"Come on, sit down. I don't bite," he said, voice tinged with impatience, breakfast left largely untouched. "I've got the hangover from hell, by the way."

"Only for a few minutes, then, I've got lectures this morning," he lied as he sat down, feeling weak for bowing yet again to Bill's demands, but then Bill was his biggest weakness.

"That's never stopped you before," Bill said, laughing, bringing a hand to his temple like he was in considerable pain.

"No, I suppose not," he said resignedly, sliding the unwanted bouquet away from him.

"I really am sorry."

"Look, Bill, I know, but you really shouldn't have hit me," he said shakily.

"You threw a glass of champagne over me in a crowded restaurant, remember?"

"Yeah," said Adam, finally conceding that Bill did have some mitigating circumstances in his favour but putting a hand up to his bruised cheek as if to make a point.

"Look, I'm totally sorry about last night and if I could go back and change it I would. I'm really sorry about Dolores, too," he said, looking down at the table, like he was ashamed.

"I shouldn't have said anything, she's your mother. More than anyone, I should know that we can't choose our parents. We're not to blame," Adam said, reaching a hand halfway across the table to comfort his friend, then recoiling, not wanting to provoke

140

another outburst. "I'm tired of all this fighting, I used to think this was a dream house, that you and Sarah were the dream couple, but I can't take much more."

"Adam, come on, we can work it out, believe me," he said softly as they locked eyes.

"Then why are you so fucking hateful all the time?" he blurted out, finally sensing he had some leverage, some currency with his friend. Bill was hardly ever a captive audience. He'd always shied away from any conversation other than the superficial, and after meeting Dolores Adam could see why.

"What?" Bill said, looking genuinely surprised but Adam knew he knew his behaviour was unacceptable, irrational even.

"I asked why are you so damn hateful?"

"You saw Dolores, that's what I had to put up with for 20 years of my life before I got a sniff of freedom. She's a hateful bitch, so it's lucky I take after my dad," he said, laughing bitterly, face flushed.

"Don't think you have the monopoly on abusive parents," said Adam, sighing wearily. "And what's this about freedom? You didn't look very free last night."

"Your parents are as bad as Dolores?"

"Look, I'm just saying, don't think you're the only one who's been hard done by," said Adam, determined not to elaborate, not wanting to lay bare his own trauma. "And don't use it as an excuse, Bill, you've got to start looking after number one, you've got to be comfortable with yourself, not who Dolores wants you to be. Did she ever hit you?"

"You know when I was a kid," he said hesitantly, almost breathless with emotion. "I ... I was in the bath with my best mate, Jamie, from down the road. You know we were little nippers and we were fiddling with each other's dicks in the bath, like you do, just kids ..."

"Go on," said Adam encouragingly as his friend trailed off.

"Well," he said stridently, like Adam's little prompt had given him the strength he needed to go on with his confession, "the bitch Dolores, my mum, she burst in like she was always doing, broke the lock clean off the bathroom door and she saw us, two kids playing, just curious. She stood there, hands on hips, and waited as Jamie dried off and put his clothes back on, then she shooed him down the stairs. I remember just standing in the bathroom dripping wet, shivering, with a tiny towel around me, hearing the front door slam as she threw the little boy out, then listening to her every footfall on the stairs as she came back, fear creeping all over me like the coldness of that autumn day. You know how big she is and she loomed horribly in the doorway with a belt in her hand. She used to keep it hanging in the hallway as a warning, one of my departed dad's leather belts, and before even opening her mouth she swung it at me, brought it whipping down on my back again and again. After it was over, I was just a puddle of blood and tears. Dolores said she'd kill me if she ever saw me do something like that again ... she gave me no reason to disbelieve her."

"I'm so sorry," Adam said, watching his friend bury his head in his hands, not knowing what he was meant to say, sensing there was nothing that could possibly comfort him.

"Sorry to tell you all that but I want you to understand why I'm weird sometimes," said Bill tearfully, finally looking up from the table. "I'm ... I'm not gay or anything but I want you to understand why I freak out."

"Yes, I'll bear it in mind," said Adam, letting out another sigh at the familiar rejoinder Bill always offered. "But are you sure there's nothing you want to tell me?"

"I better go and see if Sarah's all right," he said, tone hardening again, totally ignoring the question as he got to his feet.

Adam rose too, moved to grab his friend, to offer some kind of comfort, but Bill shrugged him off and elbowed him out of the way as he left the room. He slumped back into his chair and looked sadly at the colourfully cheap flowers, such a pitiful consolation for what he really wanted.

As he climbed the steep stairs, every one of which seemed to take a toll on his already fatigued body and mind, he listened intently as sounds of conflict echoed through the old house once again, like a fierce wind ripping through the eaves. He heard Sarah's raised, whiny voice almost at breaking point and couldn't help letting a smile form on his lips. Adam stood outside their bedroom door just as he had a few days ago, eager for any sign of the unravelling of their relationship, a relationship he was so desperate to end.

"It's like he's more important to you than me," she screeched and it was then Adam knew she would hurt, that she'd suffer as much as he had these last few months. "What the fuck are the flowers about? When. Have. You. Ever. Bought. *Me*. Flowers?"

"Sarah, come on, calm down," Bill said in his lethargic monotone.

To Adam it was as though Bill was at a total loss of how to handle his hysterical girlfriend, or maybe his resigned approach was the first sign that he no longer cared. How he hoped so.

"I'm carrying your baby," she shouted, voice cracking, choked with tears. "Unless you start taking an interest I'll make sure you never see me again and you'll never get to see your child, *your* child, Bill."

"I told you, after this year we can live on our own. I promise. Madam can go and live with his faggy mates. They're better interior designers than us anyway," Bill said.

The horrible sound of her attendant, fawning laughter filled Adam's ears and he bit so hard into his lip that he tasted blood seeping into his mouth. The raised voices had dissolved into an incoherent mumble as he continued to stand forlornly outside their door and pictured them making up, Sarah, no doubt stupidly pawing at her lying bastard of a boyfriend.

Adam opened the door, his own bedroom door. Angry as he was, he couldn't confront them for fear he'd simply shrivel in the face of their newly united front, even though he knew it was a pathetic fallacy. Instead he slammed his door shut, just to let them know, let Bill know, that he'd heard every duplicitous word.

He lit a cigarette but strangely couldn't get the cheap bouquet of flowers out of his mind. It seemed such a worthless gesture but Sarah had actually been right, boys didn't usually send each other flowers, not unless there was a death involved. Adam studied himself in the mirror, the wound on his cheek bruised and yellowing and he shook his head as he picked up the phone, dialling the only person he knew could make sense out of the mess he was in, though he also knew Smale was partly responsible.

He was confirming tonight's meeting but the professor's office phone (he didn't have a mobile, said they were the "devil's spawn") rang and rang and he pictured him having thrown a seat cushion over it to dull the shrill ring as he gave another young student the benefit of his particular brand of personal tuition. Corrupting another young mind, thought Adam, devouring silken flesh with the reptilian-like tongue and the soft, podgy hands he knew only too well.

Just 10 minutes later his phone rang and he saw from caller ID it was the professor. It gave him a little start that they seemed so much on the same wavelength.

"Hello, dear boy," Smale said cheerily, sounding the most strident he'd been since the fight. "Did you call? Sorry, I couldn't get to the phone, otherwise engaged."

"How did you know it was me?" Adam replied, noting the mischievous chuckle in the professor's voice, the one he knew usually bubbled up during sex.

"Adam, dear, you're one of a select few that has my office number and even less of that select few call me like you do."

"How about the person you've just been with?" he snapped, surprised at the jealousy in his voice.

"Now, now," said Smale, chuckling again. "Let's cut to the business at hand."

"So you did have someone with you?" he said, knowing the professor's laughter always concealed a multitude of sins.

"Adam, whoever I was entertaining in my office is really no business of yours," he said in the practised professorial tone that often revealed a discrepancy but brooked no argument. "Now about tonight, it's cause for a little celebration. Dinner at eight thirty, okay? Don't be late."

"Well, I hope you enjoyed entertaining in your office," Adam said sniffily. "What celebration?"

"All will be revealed tonight," he replied, chuckle reverberating down the line and then silence, leaving Adam to contemplate the inexorable shifting of power back into the professor's greedy hands.

He could hear Blur's *Parklife,* the summery sound of Britpop so at odds with his feelings, vibrating through the bedroom wall so he knew everything was obviously all right in paradise. It only served to give him the added incentive to make that next telephone call.

"Helen," he said, breathing out, relieved as she finally picked up.

"Hello, you, what's wrong?"

"Nothing," he said as he knew their type of friendship forbade any negativity. She was a fag hag after all and he was meant to be the funny gay friend. "Well, just about everything is wrong actually but I don't want to go there."

"No?" she said. "I'm fine, by the way, thanks for asking."

"Sorry," he replied, realising he wasn't sorry because being selfish was what he was all about, even the call was to serve his own ends. "Can I come over?"

"Babe, I've got company today."

"Bill?" he said questioningly, noting the sheepishness in her voice.

"Look, Adam, I'm sorry but Bill and me are really none of your business."

"No, I guess not," he said but he couldn't help but picture the two of them together, writhing around on that awful floral-print sofa.

"But he did just tell me he loves me," she said, like it was some kind of triumph.

"What?" he yelped.

"He said he loves me and I love him."

"But ... but what about your so-called boyfriend back home in Cambridge, the one you said you hoped to get back together with, work through your problems, eventually marry?" Adam said, desperate, hating the thought of Bill and Helen more than he hated Bill and Sarah but knowing it was hopeless because she'd already excommunicated her former lover.

"And yes, I am coming to Barcelona, we can talk there," she said, ignoring his question.

"Helen?"

"No more lectures, I'm a big girl now, all right?" she said, rudely cutting him off.

"You off out?" said Adam with an accusatory glare as he caught Bill on the stairs.

"No ... I mean, yeah," he replied, giggling nervously, his heart beating a little faster, wishing his friend didn't make him feel like he did. The hatred gnawing away underneath, but he hoped Adam hadn't heard the argument, the nasty little joke about "faggy mates" and "interior designers". He hadn't even meant it but he was so desperate to put Sarah off the scent he'd have said anything, stopped at nothing.

"See you later," Adam called down the stairs behind him.

"Yeah," he said flatly, opening the front door, irritated that his friend was always present in the big shadowy house like the insatiable desires that lurked in his mind.

It was raining hard out and he cursed the British summer as his flimsy leather jacket offered little protection. He'd told Sarah he was off to the library and now wondered why he'd told her a lie that would be so easy to check up on. Bill feared he was close to the answer when he realised that being found out would bring him face to face with his choices, force him to confront things. Breaking into a light jog towards the Tube station on his way to Helen's, he knew he was spinning the web of deceit even tighter, so tight it was threatening all who were caught up in it. After the last time he'd been with her, he'd resolved to at least be honest with himself, but he was retreating from that vow with each forward step he was taking.

He was vaguely aware it was Wednesday as he pushed his way past the afternoon shoppers, a mix of immaculately coiffured Hampstead mothers, women who obviously had far too much time on their hands, and American tourists wide-eyed and marvelling at the quaintness of it all. Still jogging, he absently bumped into someone who'd been a blur as he raced along. Stopped in his tracks, stepping back, he took in a sight that caused his muscles to painfully contract, fight-or-flight. A shameful flush rose to his cheeks, faced with the moisturised-to-within-an-inch-of-his-life gay man whose pooch was as perfectly maintained as his ridiculous waxed moustache. The dog owner who had just regained his balance and composure after being sent stumbling, stood arms folded, awaiting an apology. The animal yapped impatiently, saliva spilling from gnarled teeth. Bill wanted to say something, lash out, maybe follow him up to the heath and pull apart his moustache waxed hair by waxed hair.

"Sorry, mate," he said instead and jogged away, but he caught sight of the sickening twinkle of affection in the man's eyes, like he'd seen, no, like he'd felt in Soho that evening in the pub on Old Compton Street. "Queer Street" they called it. But he shrugged it off, tried to forget it, struggled to concentrate on Helen as he descended in the lift to the grubby Northern Line platform.

He had contemplated buying Helen chocolates or flowers, the default setting of the dishonest charmer, but as he made the now familiar walk to the halls of residence he realised it would have made him look as cheap as he felt. So he was empty-handed, heading towards the building at a trot and looking up to her floor through the incessant rain. He thought he could discern her slim outline behind the curtains like she was waiting, like she really couldn't wait. His stomach knotted in that all too familiar pain.

"All right?" she called breezily from the open front door, only confirming that she had been watching from the window, sunny smile at odds with his gloomy mood.

"Fine now I've seen you," he lied, somehow managing a smile, stomach pain enough to make him wince as they embraced.

"Ugh," she said, grimacing as she pushed him away. "You're all wet."

"It's this bloody summer weather," he said, shaking his head like a dog's, droplets of water flying from lank black hair.

"Let's get you dried off," she said, leading him into her room with that motherly kind of fussiness he was always suspicious of, couldn't quite trust. He noticed a half-smoked joint in the ashtray and the room smelled of pot, like she'd only just put it out. "Helen?"

"Look, that's been there since your last visit," she said, noticing him looking at the joint, pre-empting his uncharacteristic concern.

"Don't lie to me," he said, picking it up and examining it like a crime-scene detective, worried about the aggression in his voice, but fearing he might actually care about someone.

"I'm trying to cut down," she relented, a flush tainting her swarthy cheeks, mouth slightly askew.

"It's your life."

"Thanks a lot, I'll remember that," she said, angrily flinging the towel that she'd just fetched from the bathroom at him, nicking the corner of his eye.

"What the fuck?" he shouted. Helen cowered as he strode towards her, but despite his anger he didn't want to spill blood, a woman's blood. Instead he punched the cheap sofa.

"I ... I thought you were going to hit me," she stammered, staring at him, tears rolling down her cheeks.

"Don't be silly," he said, forcing a thin smile but still keeping his distance, not convinced he wouldn't hit her, not trusting himself to get too close.

"I'll make tea," she said, sniffing back the tears.

Bill stayed silent, flexing his broad shoulders in the confines of the tight leather jacket, finally sitting down as she went to the kitchen.

"Tea," she said, announcing her arrival back in the room, the room that seemed as grey and depressing as the day outside, as this afternoon's encounter.

"Thanks," he said but not looking her in the eye as he took the proffered cup.

"Where does she think you are this afternoon?" Helen asked. It was like she was looking for a fight, sitting uncharacteristically in the armchair opposite rather than on the sofa with him. "All dressed up aren't we? Sarah must have said something."

"I don't want to fucking talk about her," he shouted, thrashing about agitatedly but still seated.

"Look, I want you Bill and I'm coming to Spain to get you," she declared, eyes blazing into him. "What do you want?"

"I don't know," he replied in a pathetic mumble, feeling totally cowed by the incisiveness of her question. As he listened to the rain tapping on the window in the ensuing silence, although he was totally conflicted about what he wanted, he knew it definitely wasn't Helen *or* Sarah.

Adam knocked lightly on her bedroom door, his attention drawn to the *Meat is Murder* poster tacked up like some kind of warning of what was to be expected beyond. His knocking went unanswered but he could hear the whistling of a radio turned down low. The door was slightly ajar, so he gave it a light shove. Sarah was face up on the bed, staring up at the ceiling. She barely moved at the intrusion.

"Sarah," he said gently coaxing, ready to prime her for information, to stir things up a little more.

"What?" she whined, finally sitting up, looking in his general direction, her face impassive, her smile just part of the usual mask of civility, Adam thought.

"You all right?"

"Like you care," she snapped, turning away from him and looking towards the window, illuminated by the amber street lamp outside.

"I heard raised voices earlier, I just thought ..."

"That's your trouble, you think too much," she said cutting him off, still fixated on the window.

"Is everything okay?" he persisted. He knew she was right and didn't really care, but there was a time he cared very much and that made the whole bitter tang of their severed alliance even harder to swallow. What was left of their relationship, he mused, was like the plight of a handsome teenager who'd been horribly deformed in a car crash and there was nothing to do except turn the life-support machine off. He persisted. "What happened?"

"What do you mean, what happened?" Sarah asked, looking at him now for the first time. He noticed her eyes were red from crying. "*To us?*"

"Yes, to us," he spat, unable to hide the aggression in his voice, as though she was somehow to blame for everything that had gone wrong. "We used to be so close."

"People drift apart," she said, like she was explaining away something insignificant, not what had once been an all-consuming friendship.

"But why? We used to do everything together," he said almost pleadingly, like he wished they could revert to how they once were, cooking together in the kitchen, sinking a bottle of wine together, dancing together at a gay club, picking out the cutest guys together.

"I'm sorry for being a crap fag hag but I've got other priorities now," she said coldly, a statement of intent that things could never be the same.

"Yeah," he replied flatly, knowing she was right, knowing that she knew what had changed their relationship forever, that it was the arrival of Bill, but it still didn't make him feel better about what he'd lost because he'd gained nothing, only bitterness.

"And if you want to know where Billy Boy is, I can't help you. He said he was going to the library but that was hours ago," Sarah said, lips twisted into a snarl, like she didn't think what they'd had was even worth reflecting on, like she didn't want to talk any more.

"I'm concerned about you and the baby. You've been through such a lot," he protested but he was secretly warmed by the fact that Sarah was questioning what Bill was up to and he wasn't about to disabuse her of those suspicions.

"You don't think he's seeing someone, do you?" she said, eyeing Adam closely, a renewed interest in their conversation, looking vulnerable for once, fragile even. "It could be that Helen. What do you think? You know her."

"They do sometimes study together but there's nothing going on. At least I don't think so," he said, cruelly teasing out an element of doubt as he finally sat on the bed and put an arm around her shoulders, fantasising that he could just as easily strangle her. "Look, Helen's one of the top students and Bill's got a lot of catching up to do, it's good he's got a study partner."

"Yeah, I suppose," said Sarah unconvinced, wrestling free from his arm as she stood up and walked over to her PC.

"I think everything's going to be fine."

"Look, I've got to be getting on with this assessed essay, speak to you later," she said impatiently, not even bothering to turn away from her computer screen.

He gave Sarah a single-digit salute as he left the room, but didn't notice that his rude gesture was reflected in the monitor screen for her to witness, a metaphorical full-stop denoting the end of their friendship and hinting at a darker future.

Adam stopped off for a Chinese on the short drive up to Highgate. It was customary for him to buy a takeaway for his meals with Smale. The professor could barely boil an egg, such was the sad extent of his bachelordom, and while his housekeeper made a go at cooking it was cuisine straight out of the Second World War, corned beef being her staple. She was a huge fan of Salad Cream, too.

Placing his order, he chuckled at how he'd introduced Smale to the delights of Chinese food, but he still couldn't shake off an overwhelming sadness. Adam didn't want to drive up to the professor's big old house where the mostly unused rooms carried an odour somewhere between cheap furniture polish and decay. Even the fragrant delights of the Chinese kitchen were beginning to make him feel nauseous. There was a time when a thrill buzzed through him at the thought of seeing Smale, the thrill that someone of such intellect, such standing, wanted to see him, spend time with him, but now he knew it was all about *fucking* him. Take that out of the equation, he thought, and there wouldn't be an English Literature professor hanging on his every word, telling him how bright he was, laughing at his jokes.

He drove past the heath on his way up the hill to Highgate and from the car it appeared strangely alluring, bathed as it was in the dull glow of the street lamps. He imagined, in spite of the wet weather, what was going on beneath sappy trees, behind lush bushes. Adam slowed as if to stop, but the clock on the dash indicated it was already eight thirty and Smale was a stickler for time. He cursed under his breath as he reapplied his foot to the accelerator and the old sports car lurched forward. The whiff of Chinese, which he really didn't feel like eating, made him feel sick again and he wound down the window fiercely, grateful for the coolness of the evening air. He knew he'd partake in the professor's usual strategy of plying him with red wine as it was now the only way he could get through their meetings. Smale was something of an expert when it came to wine, though to Adam an aromatic bouquet was small compensation for being leered at or far worse for an entire evening.

"My dear boy," bellowed Smale effusively, flinging open the

front door before he'd even got halfway down the path. He pecked Adam on the cheek, breath already tainted by wine. "Come in, come in."

As the professor turned to lead the way, he noticed the head wound sustained in their fight was already covered by the resplendent mane of grey hair, as if nothing had ever happened, and he knew Smale wanted to keep it that way. Gallantly grabbing the boxes of takeaway from him, he fussily waved Adam into the usual armchair. Adam noticed the empty bottle of red wine on the coffee table next to a fully drained glass. He watched Smale also eyeing it somewhat shamefacedly, probably wishing he'd not started quite so early.

"I'll get plates," the professor said, scooping up the empty bottle as he went, as if out of sight it didn't really matter.

It was the same principle he applied to affairs with students, Adam thought, looking edgily around the living room, noticing not much had changed. A Beethoven CD was playing as was customary, but then he noticed the gaping space on the mantelpiece where the professor had kept one of his school portrait photos. He'd given it to him as a birthday present and he couldn't help but feel jarred.

"Peking duck, my favourite," he said as he re-entered with the plates of food on trays, licking his lips hungrily but staring lasciviously at Adam.

After pouring two more glasses of wine, Adam sat down and glanced at Smale. He took in the yellow silk shirt, top two buttons cheekily undone, face unpleasantly flushed with wine but it was the still lucid eyes that locked coldly with his which made him shudder. It was like they were grappling with him, with his feelings.

"Expecting someone?" asked Adam, smiling.

"What?"

"You're all dressed up," he said through a mouthful of chow mein.

"I always dress up when I'm entertaining, love, you know that. Particularly when it's a celebration."

"Oh, yeah, do tell."

"You'll have to wait till after dinner," Smale said, smiling indulgently and tapping a finger against his protruding red nose.

The professor humming along to classical music as he greedily swallowed down the food was almost enough to make an already mildly nauseous Adam completely sick. But instead of barking at him to stop, he desperately tried to initiate conversation. "So who have you been entertaining in your office?"

"We're jealous, are we?" yelped Smale, engaging in his normal trait of leaping on any perceived insecurity. "It really is a green-eyed monster."

"No," protested Adam, the unwelcome sound of the professor's mocking laughter in his ears. "Just curious."

"Well, you know what they say about curiosity," said Smale, pushing his plate of food away, preparing to unleash yet another homily but deftly refilling Adam's glass of wine, along with his own instead.

"Anyway, how's that boy of yours?" the professor continued, changing the subject, sat on his haunches expectantly as though he derived pleasure vicariously through Adam's life. "Any, what do they call it now? Shagging?"

"What?" he replied, laughing at Smale's loose grasp of the latest slang, which he often picked up from his students and liked to deliver deadpan into a conversation. He was on form, disarming with jokes and wine but Adam always feared the punchline.

"No, there's been no *shagging*, far from it. We met his mother, who is a dreadful homophobe and then we ended up having a fist fight ... well, I threw a glass of champagne over him and he slapped me."

"Slapped as in punched, I hope you mean. Yes, I had noticed the bruise on your cheek but I was too polite to ask, for once. I know how you like rough sex," he said, chuckling again.

"Well, he sent me flowers the next day by way of an apology."

"Flowers?" said Smale, panting with disbelief. "Dear boy, straight men don't even send flowers to their wives or girlfriends except maybe on Valentine's Day or to atone for some mortal sin, but they certainly don't send them to male friends."

"That's what I thought."

"Well, I shall look forward with interest to my next meeting with Mr Laws, but I meant to speak to you about that."

"About what?"

"There's been a bloodless coup at the faculty. Dowdy's resigned with immediate effect and I'm now dean of the school," he said, smiling and raising a glass that Adam felt obliged to clink.

"No rival bids for the post?"

"My colleagues all think it's a poisoned chalice, a lot more responsibility for not much more money, but what about the prestige?" he said, lovingly stroking his hair.

"Well done then," Adam said grudgingly, concerned that promotion would add to the professor's already burgeoning armoury of manipulation.

"Not so good for you, though," said Smale, fixing him with the steely eyed stare that always signalled trouble.

"How do you mean?" he replied, barely concealing the growing hint of panic in his voice, the professor looking on, ingratiating and intimidating all at once.

"I mean, I'm going to have to end our little meetings, with immediate effect."

"What?" Adam said, voice rising, aware that a split could mean the end of his university career. He'd relied on the professor's liberal marking and realised he couldn't really do without him, at least till he passed the first year. "What about the emailed love notes? I have contacts at the university newspaper."

"Adam, dear, I'm dean of the school now and at the end of the day it's your word against mine and my word simply carries more weight," he said evenly as he effortlessly refilled the wine glasses, like he'd never been calmer. "However, I am willing to negotiate. I play fair after all."

"Yeah, right," Adam mumbled, feeling he'd been beaten again, slurping back his wine and wondering, seriously contemplating, whether he should just walk out on the professor now, walk out of university for good. But then Bill came to mind and he realised with a terrifying clarity how much he had to lose. "Negotiate?"

"I knew you'd come round," said Smale, reaching from his armchair (he always made sure they were in touching distance be it in his office or at his home) and placing a hand on Adam's knee as he took another glug from his glass. "You've got something against me, the pesky emails, I've got something

154

against you, the grades, but I'm afraid I've trumped you with my promotion, that's a royal flush."

"Huh?" said Adam, horribly certain of where the poker analogy was leading.

"Now you've got to bring something else to the table," said Smale, rising drunkenly to his feet, his hands already ruffling Adam's blond hair, moving fast across his torso, hot breath all over him in the suffocating room.

"Okay," he stuttered as the professor climbed off of him, sick that he was about to acquiesce again.

"Lead the way," commanded Smale, eyes drilling into Adam's skull.

And he did lead the way, like the very first time the professor had made that particular order, even though he'd had no idea where the bedroom was back then. Now Adam knew only too well. He could almost taste it. He stumbled up the stairs, head thick with wine, feeling the effort of every reluctant step, riveted to the sound of the heavy footfalls behind him like he was being marched to his fate by an executioner. As they finally entered the darkened room, Smale bounced athletically across the floor and wrenched the curtains shut with a sad finality before snapping the light on.

He felt hungry eyes all over him, consuming him as he undressed in the terrible silence. Smale wrestled him onto the bed but Adam ended up on top. His powerful swimmer's arms rested just inches from the professor's throat. He looked disgustedly at the sunken chest and the sprinkling of brittle grey hairs that betrayed his age, realising how easy it would be to kill. Adam bit down heavily on his lip, through his rage, falling into the familiar embrace of the old man for what he vowed would be the very last time.

CHAPTER TWELVE

They started the day with a champagne breakfast, Adam's idea. As he brought in a plate of smoked salmon and eggs, which he really didn't feel like eating, to the dining room, to face them, the three of them, he was so on edge he wasn't sure how he'd react if anyone said the wrong thing. It was all smiles as he sat down at the table, Sarah brandished the deceit she'd grown up with. It must have taken years of practice to be that good, thought Adam, but he knew she was only compounding things, lighting the fuse for the coming apocalyptic explosion.

"Here he is," she said, glowing smile fixed in place as she pointed out the obvious. "Today's chef and all round good egg."

"Hello, babe," piped up Helen, wedged awkwardly between Sarah and Bill at the table, taking too big a swig of her champagne. "You *are* a great cook."

"Thanks," he said, putting down his plate and angrily snapping off the radio from which the *Today* programme had been droning.

"Hey!" shouted Sarah, mask slipping as she glared at Adam. "I was listening to that."

"We do have guests," he retorted, looking over at Helen, but she was too involved in Bill to notice the commotion. Bill in turn was leafing noisily through *The Mirror* – his breakfast ritual.

"Never mind," Sarah said, muttering something under her breath, finding refuge in *The Daily Mail*.

"Why do you like the *Mail*?" asked Helen boldly. In this new Blairite era it seemed akin to asking someone why they still voted Tory or why they preferred sex with children.

"Oh, no particular reason," she said, keeping her head firmly buried in the paper, like it provided the legitimacy for her very existence, and justified her world view.

"Just wondering because it is a little bit right wing," replied Helen.

"Just a teensy-weensy bit," chimed in Adam, enjoying the

159

opportunity to wind Sarah up, knowing she would find it difficult to keep an even temper despite the trip being in the name of reconciliation.

"It's about as right wing as New Labour," grunted Bill, finally looking up from his newspaper and catching Helen's eye.

"Why are you all ganging up on me?" Sarah said as she angrily flung the paper onto the table where it landed messily in her plate of unfinished food. "It's just a fucking newspaper."

"Sarah, come on, we're students, we're only having a reasoned debate, or as reasoned as you can with a *Mail* reader," Adam said facetiously, knowing it would only inflame her more.

"Well, you don't have to debate about me," she said, huffily pushing her breakfast away. "I'm not hungry now."

"I spent ages slaving over a hot stove for you," he said, hands to his chest, mock aggrieved.

"Anyway, what paper do *you* read?" Sarah asked, ignoring Adam, addressing Helen as though it was an accusation.

"*The Guardian*, of course," she replied smugly, like she'd won the argument, her tone questioning how Sarah could possibly compete.

"She's an intellectual," offered Bill, laughing, not wasting an opportunity to touch her as he patted Helen's hand, which only earned another glare from Sarah. "Why do you think I'm always copying her essays?"

"Bill, we're not even on the same course," protested Helen, causing Sarah to drop her paper to the table again, eyes blazing back at all three of them.

"No, though you do share the sociology module," Adam said, but only after he'd let a deadly silence resonate with Sarah, the silence where he knew she was contemplating the lie he'd spun about them all doing the same course, contemplating the fact that Bill and Helen definitely weren't classmates but probably were sex partners. He smiled to himself.

"I don't mind helping him with sociology, it's meaningless anyway," lied Helen, attempting to atone for her earlier slip of the tongue. Adam wondered whether she'd actually intended to alert Sarah to the fact she was being deceived.

"Yeah, she's great," said Bill with a beaming smile but Sarah simply stared dubiously from one to the other. Adam was delighted because insecure was exactly the way he wanted her to feel.

"Yes, she always comes top of the sociology class," he said, protesting the legitimacy of Sarah and Bill's relationship far too strongly.

"Right," said Sarah, taking a large gulp of her champagne and then hurriedly scooping up the empty plates, "we'd better get going."

Adam helped his two housemates to the kitchen, dispatched some things into the sink and then made as if to leave but hovered instead just outside the doorway, waiting for the fallout from the conversational incendiaries he and Helen had planted at the table.

"I thought you were doing the same course, that's why you were so friendly," said Sarah, her voice was low because she had guests, but with barely contained fury.

"We are doing different courses but we share a sociology module, we're in the same class for sociology," Bill said a little too pleadingly. Adam waited for the coming outburst.

"This is your last fucking chance," Sarah said, anger replaced by a weary resolve. "The baby will go first, Bill, *your* baby, and then I will go."

"What are you saying?"

"Let go of my fucking arm. Ouch! You're hurting me, I'll shout out."

"Listen good, anything happens to that baby and I will hurt you," Bill said flatly, voice devoid of emotion, firm with the hint of a promise. "Got it?"

Sarah didn't reply. Adam heard the sound of dishes being crashed angrily into the sink and then heavy footsteps, but it was too late, Bill was standing in the doorway, eyeing him.

"What the fuck are you doing there?"

"Nothing," Adam said, shrugging uselessly, unable to offer any defence.

"I catch you listening in like that again and you'll get more than a bruised cheek," Bill hissed as he brought his large hands menacingly around Adam's throat.

"Remember what I know," he whispered, almost inaudible with fear.

"Was that a threat?" spat Bill, grabbing Adam angrily around the collar, two buttons springing from his shirt as he was backed up against the wall. Bill pounded his head painfully into the plaster. "Don't do anything silly."

"No," he squeaked as Bill finally let him go and strode back to the dining room, to Helen. Adam followed but at a distance.

"Are you all right?" said Helen as Adam returned. "You look a little flushed. And what's happened to that shirt? It's nearly open to your navel."

"Cheap shit shirt, the buttons fell off," he said, still managing an accusatory glare at Bill, trying to laugh it off but knowing there were some things that couldn't be put to rest with a joke. At least the miracles of foundation had enabled him to cover up the fading bruise on his cheek.

"Don't worry about Madam, he'll be fine," said Bill, laughing cruelly, staring at Helen. "Are *you* all right?"

"I'm fine," she said, smiling. "Though I like to think I'm a little bit more classy than *The Daily Mail*."

"Oh, don't worry about that, of course you are. You're far too classy for us," Bill said indulgently. Adam felt his stomach contract, the pain of jealousy taking over his life.

"Come on," said Sarah, clapping her hands above her head as she re-entered the dining room like she was bringing to heel a disobedient dog, doing what she did best, acting like nothing had happened, like everything was right with the world. "Let's go guys and girls. We've got to get to the airport. The taxi will be here in five minutes so if any of you need to use the loo, I suggest you go now."

"Little Miss Organised," said Bill, ruffling his girlfriend's hair. Adam marvelled at the hollowness of his friend's gesture, his unending capacity to delude, but knew they were one and the same on that score.

"I've got to powder my nose," said Helen.

"Turn right and it's the first door on your left," said Sarah, smiling thinly.

"Good call," said Bill, sniggering. "I don't want to hold the party up, you know what me and my bladder are like, I better use the one upstairs."

"Speaking of organised, Adam, I meant to give you these,"

said Sarah once the other two had left the room, flinging a bunch of keys onto the dining table "You know what Bill and I are like for losing things, this is a spare set for the house in Barcelona, to be kept with you at all times in case I misplace mine. We don't want to end up sleeping rough."

"Cheers," he said, picking them up, noticing the one labelled "*front door*". He put them in his pocket, felt the comforting weight of them there and couldn't help but think they might somehow come in handy.

Adam was impressed as they entered the old Spanish villa, rented from one of Sarah's distant relatives, sunlight dancing in the tiled hall through classically louvered windows. She guided them up the broad, shadowy wooden staircase to their respective bedrooms, all close to one another. He threw his holdall on what was a rock-hard bed and rattled open the shutters. He surveyed the old street below and the house opposite, just a few feet away. He felt he could almost reach out and touch it. The intricate but sturdy architecture, so unlike the drably uniform boxes most people called home in England, he thought. His view of the busy street, his appreciation of the young boys whizzing about on scooters, of wrinkled old ladies weighed down with shopping, was cut short as the heavy wooden door of the bedroom swung open. He spun around hoping it would be Bill but it was Sarah standing there, smile in place. She wanted something, he guessed.

"Hi," she said. "Lovely, isn't it?"

"Yes," he said, looking at her questioningly, one eyebrow raised ever so slightly, unused to social calls from the matriarch. He heard voices coming through the wall and hoped Sarah would hear it too, Helen and Bill. He knew for sure they wouldn't be discussing sociology.

"Look, I still haven't bought Billy Boy a birthday present, I'd like to give it to him tonight and you're great at shopping," she said hesitantly, like it was an effort to be civil, to actually ask him a favour. "Would you help me find something this afternoon? It'd be good if you could help me buy dinner too. You cooked a mean breakfast this morning, by the way."

"Love to," he said, "but what about them?"

"Them?"

"Helen 'n' Bill," he replied, like they were an item.

"That's okay. Helen said she wanted to do some sightseeing. Bill will probably have a nap, a siesta, knowing Bill."

"Okay," he said, laughing to himself, amazed she could be so gullible as to leave the two of them alone in the elegance of the villa, on a sultry Mediterranean afternoon that promised dappled sunlight and hard beds. He half suspected she wanted to test them and knew that Bill failed most tests.

"Be ready in ten," she said.

He nodded as Sarah closed the door gently behind her and a smile spread over his face at the plan that was flowering in his brain, causing even him to wince at his own deviousness. He mindfully patted the set of keys in his pocket.

"Bill said he might pop out. There's a Starbucks or something down the road," she said, a thin smile on her lips.

"Starbucks?" he said, throwing his hands skyward. "Doesn't Spain own a third of the world's coffee plantations or something and he has to go to an American chain."

"This is not Spain, it's Catalonia," she said flatly, humourless as ever. She had had a sense of humour before she'd met Bill which made it even more galling. His lies had seemingly drained her of the capability to find anything funny.

"Whatever," he said as they made their way to the front door. "What's Helen up to?"

"She said she might take a siesta but we'll wake them up when we get back anyway. I've left them the keys, in case they do decide to explore, but they should be back before us."

"Thoughtful of you, particularly if they want to get a latte," he said, patting the bunch of keys in his own pocket that she seemed to have forgotten about. "Or maybe they can help each other with that long overdue sociology assignment."

"Adam," Sarah replied, glaring at him and cuffing him around the temple. He laughed under his breath.

Heading up the sun-drenched street amid the historic buildings bowed with age, each undoubtedly with their own tale to tell, Adam pictured Bill gently peeling off Helen's thin cotton clothes, their young, writhing bodies artfully reflecting the late afternoon sunlight beneath shuttered windows, and felt the stabbing pain of jealousy again.

"Oh, I'm in agony," he croaked pathetically, putting a hand dramatically to his forehead in the brightly lit supermarket. "You know I get migraines, it must be the heat."

"For God's sake, Adam," she said exasperatedly, picking up a dusty bottle of wine from the shelf and putting it into the shopping basket. "Maybe if you hadn't had all that champagne and then the gin and tonics on the plane ..."

"Oh, don't," he grumbled as he put a hand to his temple again. "How else was I to get through a flight on a *budget* airline?"

"Look, do you want to go back?" she said, refusing to laugh at his joke, anger all over her face.

"Well ..."

"Look, I will take you back and then I can get on with the shopping, maybe I should have come alone in the first place."

"Oh, don't worry about me, sick in a foreign country, I can find my own way," he said stroppily.

"Don't be so silly," she snapped, finally showing some concern as he reluctantly let her take his hand. "Let's get you home."

"Thanks," he said, looking away from her as a smile illuminated his face, thinking of what they were headed back to, what they'd be walking into unannounced on their surprisingly early return from the aborted shopping trip.

Sweat ran messily down their foreheads as Sarah, like some permanently incensed school matron, marched him back through the winding streets to the house. As they reached the front door, she was about to ring the bell when Adam snatched her hand away.

"What?" she asked agitatedly.

"Let them sleep," he said, bringing the bunch of keys from his pocket and holding them aloft triumphantly like a magician. He saw what he took to be a mixture of surprise and fear in her eyes, fear at what they'd find inside.

He slid the front-door key quietly into the lock and as Sarah entered the hallway it was her turn to hold up a demonstrative hand.

"Shush," she whispered as she tiptoed ahead to the foot of the stairs, clinging tight to the bottle of wine she'd bought in preparation for the evening's celebrations, before the shopping trip had been brought to a premature close.

He quickly clicked the front door shut and followed. She was in such a hurry she was now halfway up the stairs. It was only when he caught up with her and they were near the top that he realised why Sarah's head was cocked quizzically to one side. There were hushed voices floating from the end of the corridor. Sarah perceptibly slowed down as if she really didn't want to know, like she was about to turn back, but Adam beckoned her on as carefree laughter suddenly bubbled up from the slightly open bedroom door on the far left.

As Helen emerged from the room into the shadowy hallway, skinny frame vulnerable in bra and knickers, it was too late for all of them. "Oh fuck," she said on seeing Sarah and Adam, dropping the clothes that had been in a bundle in her arms, burying her head in her hands.

Sarah raised the bottle of wine above her head, launching it with such ferocity that it seemed to crackle through the air before it smashed explosively against the wall just inches above Helen's head. Red wine was sent splattering all over her and the whitewashed walls. Glass splintered violently across the wooden floor. Bill looked on from the bedroom doorway, indefensible in only a pair of briefs, Calvin Klein, Adam noted. Helen stood as if rooted to the spot not daring to look up.

"Get the fuck out of this house," shouted Sarah, wild eyed as she grabbed Helen roughly around the neck, pushing her back against the wall, unconcerned about the shards of glass around the girl's shoeless feet.

Bill remained in the doorway, impotent, pathetic, like he had been that night with Dolores. Adam moved to pull the two women apart. Helen had allowed herself to be thrashed around like a rag doll until his intervention. She obviously didn't have the heart to defend herself, such was the weight of her guilt, shagging Sarah's so-called fiancé in a house owned by her family, in *her* bed.

"Fucking whore," croaked Sarah, her larynx seemingly shredded by the emotion of the afternoon as she watched Adam lead Helen away to her bedroom.

Tears were spilling down her cheeks but Adam was unable to say anything to make her feel better. He helped as she hurriedly packed her things. Usually placid and organised, Helen was stuffing clothes into her suitcase as fast as she could. There was a shamed silence save for her sobs and the slamming of Bill and Sarah's door that seemed to reverberate for some time throughout the house. The quiet was soon punctuated again by Bill and Sarah's raised voices coming from the room next door, frightening in their intensity, thundering through the ancient brick, like the whole house was quaking with emotion. It was then that Adam feared the power of what he'd unleashed, the nightmare he'd created in his flawed quest to satisfy his own desires.

He sent Helen inconsolable out into the street to get a taxi. She was still sobbing, stooped under the weight of her suitcase. Ten minutes later, Adam managed to flag down a passing cab. They hadn't spoken a word by the time she slid silently into the back seat, her face an ashen grey. He watched as the vehicle roared off without her offering so much as a backward glance. Walking back inside the house he was confronted by a tearful Bill and Sarah, arm in arm. He stomped wearily back up the stairs and was sickened to realise he was no nearer his goal. They were a threesome again.

What before had been a pleasantly shaded room, now seemed dark and depressing, coloured by the mood of what had gone before, Bill and Sarah's voices rumbling ominously through the wall. He'd promised his mum he'd "do a bit of culture" so he fished out a tourist map from his bag. Antoni Gaudi's Sagrada Familia seemed a great choice for the lazy tourist. He didn't really feel like broadening his horizons but he was desperate to get away from his two housemates.

He toured the ground level of the huge unfinished cathedral

with its weird sculptures sprouting like so many afterthoughts, and thought sadly that it would be the same for him and Bill. Despite all he'd tried to create, all the foundations he'd laid in terms of a relationship together, he was only going to end up with something vast, soulless, never to be completed.

Determined, he climbed one of the spiralling staircases in one of the oddly rocket-shaped spires. Gothic images loomed out of the darkness at him as though he was in the warped mind of the structure's very creator. Finally as the staircase petered out into crumbly stone and he couldn't climb any further, he poked his head out of a window, a vent really, like an arrowslit, and looked down at the other tourists, milling around like so many ants far below. Now he knew exactly what he was going to do. He had known since he'd seen them arm in arm back at the house. He drew out the dog-eared picture from that familiarly worn place in his wallet, but for once he didn't look at it. He ripped it into tiny pieces until he couldn't rip any more, then opening the palm of his hand, he watched as the strips of colour paper floated down on the breeze like confetti. He turned away before they'd disappeared completely out of view, knowing it would be longer before the image in the photograph left his mind, if ever.

Descending the steep stairs, having to concentrate on almost every step, the ring of the telephone made him jump in the gloom. He was still full of hope that it would be Bill telling him it was over between him and Sarah but was disappointed to see it was Helen, another casualty of his jealous cravings.

"Hi."

"Hello," she said a little breathlessly, like she'd only just managed to compose herself, like she'd just stopped crying. "I'm sorry."

"You don't have to apologise to me."

"Then who should I fucking apologise to?" she barked, sniffling again. "He came on to me almost immediately the front door had slammed."

"Helen, hey, I didn't mean it like that," he said softly. "You've got absolutely nothing to apologise for. Everyone knows it apart from that bitch, Sarah."

"It looks so bad, though," she protested, sounding on the verge of tears again.

"Look, their relationship is the rockiest one I know. Bill's absolutely desperate for a way out but I think he'll be the last one to actually realise it. Maybe with the baby on the way and everything he decided enough was enough and wanted to get caught."

"Baby on the way? What fucking baby?"

"Oh, Helen, sorry, I only found out myself recently," he said, knowing if he'd told her in the first place, she never would have come to Spain.

"*Recently*? Why the fuck didn't you tell me? Too late now but it would have changed everything and I wouldn't have wasted my time on that lying bastard," she shouted, tears replaced by an angry resolve. "He was just fucking using me. And I can't believe you let me down as well, it's almost like you were willing this to happen."

"I'm so sorry Helen but none of this is anyone's fault. You certainly can't blame yourself. I care deeply about all three of you. Of course I didn't want this to happen," said Adam, feeling guiltier than ever, feeling every word he uttered must have sounded like the huge lie it actually was. "We can meet up."

"It's okay, I've checked into a hotel. Knowing what I know, Adam, I really don't feel like meeting you just now but if I do get lonely I'll call you," she said. "We'll meet for dinner in London and try to forget about all this. Bye, babe."

"Bye."

He was at the airport alone, knowing they'd all be there. All four of them were booked home on the same flight. He'd hardly seen Bill and Sarah in the big house over the weekend since he'd sent Helen off in her taxi. Bill had come into his room once, solemn, contrite and totally insincere when he informed Adam that he and his girlfriend had a "lot to talk about" and that the best thing Adam could do was "make himself scarce". That was that, he was discarded for the remainder of the trip, surplus to requirements, second as usual to the lovely Sarah, who he cursed as he wandered aimlessly around the streets and dined uncomfortably alone, awkward in his solitude.

He'd caught glimpses of the pair of them in the house, sometimes smiling, at other times in tears. The most pervasive aspect was the noise of their voices, alternately raised and angry, then dropping to low, soothing murmurs. On the final night there had been scented candles to precede the lovemaking. The fucking had been so loud that he'd had to leave the house for what seemed like endless loops around the block.

Now in the airport lounge, he laughed bitterly at the thought of them, all thinking the same thing, all desperately trying to avoid one another. He saw Sarah emerge from the ladies' toilet, but on seeing him she looked the other way, caught Bill's hand and shepherded him off in the opposite direction. As he watched the pair disappear behind the safety of a mountain of duty free cigarette boxes, he had never hated anyone more.

CHAPTER THIRTEEN

Adam had looked out of the aircraft's window as the plane landed two days ago to see leaden grey skies and driving rain. Now sitting in his bedroom in Hampstead it was as though that short burst of glorious sunshine, the promise of summer on that first afternoon in Barcelona, had been wiped out for good. When they'd arrived in Spain, he'd been so overcome by optimism that he had fantasised they'd all get on. Then of course, his own selfishness ensured it could never happen. Yes, Helen and Bill had acted out their own desires, but he had planned the outcome, he'd given a mighty push to the first domino in that tragic chain.

Earlier he'd bumped into Bill downstairs, surprised to see him up so early. It was the first time they'd had a chance to chat since Spain but he only muttered something about having an appointment (Adam guessed he was seeing Smale) and complained about being woken up by the "fucking Pet Shop Boys". It was true, Adam had purposely played the duo's latest album over and over because he knew how much Bill and Sarah hated them. Bill derided any band from outside of Manchester, but particularly those limp-wristed purveyors of synthesized pop with a penchant for irony. But he had dubbed Blur honorary Mancunians, presumably because it would have been so uncool to hate the coolest band in the civilised world.

Adam had shut himself away since Barcelona. It had only been a couple of days, but he saw how easily it could become a habit as he sank deeper into depression. He hadn't been near the university. He hadn't answered his phone, even to his mum who'd sent him numerous text messages fearing that he'd crash landed somewhere in continental Europe. And Helen, poor Helen, had called five or six times but he hadn't picked up.

In the last 48 hours, he had only ventured as far as the toilet or the kitchen and then back to his room. He had even resorted to stealing a large portion of Sarah's vegetarian pasta bake, normally almost a hanging offence. She must have known he'd taken it, but hadn't dared challenge him about it, nor about the fug of cigarette smoke that had been wafting under his door in the supposedly "no-smoking" household. Relations were so strained.

He'd given up even pretending to be the obedient houseguest, given up adhering to the "house rules" she'd so proudly explained that sunny early autumn day, the ecstatic day that he'd moved in, so excited by the possibilities of his new life and his new friend. It had been a warm day but there had been a chill behind the warmth and he'd wondered even then, whether they were really friends, whether it would all go wrong like things had a habit of doing. And it did, when a few weeks later, Bill, who he was stunned to recognise as the guy he'd obsessed over in his English Literature class but who he'd never spoken to, answered the ad they had placed for a housemate on the university noticeboard. He remembered how they had both competed for his attention, both flirted with him at the "interview" on the sofa in the living room while he had smouldered with a morose kind of sex appeal. Adam now regretted where that playful afternoon had led the three of them. He couldn't shake the divisions it had ingrained from his mind.

He snuck out of his room intending to plunder some more of the food the lovers always bought together on their weekly shopping trips to Tesco. He knew it was horribly domesticated and laughed at them cruelly for it, but he also knew it was part of the certainty he craved, part of what every lonely person wanted, desired.

Adam was at the top of the stairs preparing to make the steep climb downwards when he heard the sound of sobs coming from Bill and Sarah's room. He was going to ignore it, literally laugh it off, but it sounded so pitiful that some sliver of humanity pricked at him. He pushed the door open. Sarah was sat at her desk, back to him, shoulders shaking as she cried. He looked closer and saw she was hunched over, writing something on a single sheet of paper with countless others screwed up and littering the floor like she was trying to compose a difficult letter. Now he was intrigued.

Instinctively, as if sensing his hate, his far from honourable intentions, she swung around to face him, her cheeks flushed and her eyes red with tears.

"What do you want?" she said aggressively, sniffing back her tears, an accusatory glance that he attributed to her humiliation in Spain. It was the first time they'd spoken since.

"Don't blame me for Barcelona," he said as evenly as he could, feeling the hate and anger coursing through him again as he involuntarily clenched and unclenched his fists.

"Well, I do. I blame you and I blame my fucking boyfriend and I blame that bitch Helen," she spat. "You know, I just can't get over it, the sick feeling in my stomach that seems like it's eating me alive from the inside out. It's just not going away. I've been betrayed by three friends in my family's own house. I've got to make a fresh start."

"Sarah, I know it's hard but you'll get over it. You're over dramatizing," he said, cringing at the hollowness of his own words.

"*I'll get over it. I'm over dramatizing*," she said into his face, breath fetid, as if tainted by everything that had happened. Rising from her seat she grabbed him by the collar. "You should feel how I feel, then you'd know how fucking wrong you are."

"I'm sorry," he said, but he wasn't. He wasn't even close.

"Adam, do me a favour."

"What?" he replied, eyes boring into her, despising her, knowing what was coming next.

"Piss off," she said, turning back to her writing.

But he stood his ground and peeking over her shoulder saw a letter addressed in her trademark flowery handwriting "*Dear Bill*". The other words that stood out in his brief delighted skim of the first couple of paragraphs were "*I'm leaving you*".

"If you're not going to fuck off, then I am," she shouted as though sensing him behind her as she signed her name to the letter and threw down her pen.

She got up and brushed past him, glancing back nervously from the door to the piece of paper on the desk like it was a bomb primed to go off. Adam followed her as she moved onto the landing, hounding her, right up close as she approached the top of the stairwell.

"The letter! The letter! You're leaving him, aren't you?" he said, insistent, childlike, maddening. "What about the baby?

175

What about the baby?"

"Listen," she screamed, spittle flying from her lips as she grabbed him, shoving him hard against the wall, his head thumping painfully against the Artex, "you're just an evil little faggot that's been trying to get into my boyfriend's pants since day one. I never want to see you, any of you, again."

"You know he's still shagging Helen, don't you?" he lied, the calmness of his tone intended to rile her more.

"Fuck you, faggot!" she barked, projecting a frothy stream of spit into his face.

Her words reverberated in his ears, but all he heard, all he needed to hear as he batted her arms away like she wasn't even there, was "faggot". Stung by the hated playground taunt, her spit dribbling disgustingly down his cheek, Adam with his swimmer's bulk edged her skinny frame to the top stair. Then, as the accumulation of months and months of jealous hate consumed him, he summoned all the strength coiled for so long in his muscled arms and pushed her.

He watched her slight body tumble with gaining momentum down the steep stairs. There was a sickening yelp as she somersaulted hopelessly from one to the next, blood splattering the white walls, barely visible in the stairwell's gloom. Finally she hit the hall floor with an obscene thump and then for what seemed like several minutes writhed and twitched grotesquely. Only in the eerie, inevitable stillness that followed, did Adam, transfixed at the top of the stairs, realise what he had done.

CHAPTER FOURTEEN

Bill was knocking on Smale's door, rapping hard, stunned he'd reached this point but not having anyone else to turn to. The previous evening he had lurked outside the Lesbian, Gay, Bisexual and Transgender Society's office, but decided a group with such a confused name was unlikely to be able to help him unpick his own confusion. Then when the chairman of the LGBTS had poked his head out of the office to leer at him, revealing a studded tongue, he'd blundered away in embarrassment.

As he rapped again on the professor's door, desperately now, he knew finally that he needed to be honest about his feelings, not only for his own peace of mind but for those around him. He also knew that he didn't want to become some statement, some gross caricature like some of the casualties he'd seen around campus.

"Hello," said Smale, breaking Bill's train of thought as he emerged in the doorway, squinting dubiously over half-moon glasses. "What brings you here unannounced, Mr Laws? I thought you were in sunny Barcelona."

"No, we got back a couple of days ago, I need to talk."

"That's all very well but I'm a busy man and you don't have an appointment. I don't know whether I told you, but I'm now dean of the school so these meetings will have to end anyway. But I can always make exceptions," said Smale, thoughtfully tapping his chin with a long forefinger as though enjoying yet another student in his thrall. "Let me see ..."

"Er, don't worry," Bill said, interrupting the professor and turning to go, "some other time."

But as he began walking along the corridor, he felt a firm hand on his shoulder, mouth breathing into his ear, almost touching it. "No, I can see you now, if you'd like."

He didn't reply but let Smale turn him around and guide him

into the office where he flopped into the armchair, listening as the key turned in the lock. The professor sat opposite, eyes all over him as usual, like he was looking for a weakness, an opportunity to pounce.

"Cigarette, Mr Laws?" he said, waving a packet under his nose, resembling a pushy detective sergeant in a police interview room. "You look like you need one."

"Yeah," was all Bill could muster as he nervously took the proffered cigarette and watched the professor light it with a flourish. Previously he'd hated Smale's clipped tones, outlandish mannerisms, dandy clothes. Now he knew it was futile, realising he only hated the professor because he hated himself.

"Problem?" asked Smale, exhaling a stream of smoke at the ceiling, fixing his subject with an icy stare, but his question went unanswered in a silence as chilly as his gaze. "Look, Mr Laws, Bill, as I said, I'm a busy man. If you come to my office you're expected to contribute at least something, to reciprocate. If I tell you something, you tell me something, deal?"

"Deal," he replied in a mumble, though the deluge of feelings welling up inside was threatening to spill out and engulf both of them. He felt himself trembling.

"I'll start," said Smale, smiling thinly. "Adam came round to dinner recently, nasty bruise on his cheek. He said you did it and then bought him flowers. How sweet."

Bill felt himself blushing as the professor stared even harder but still he couldn't find the right words, the right combination that would articulate his feelings, so he remained silent.

"You feel so strongly about him that you send him *flowers*?" the professor continued, pressing, probing like that busy detective sergeant, growing obviously impatient as he aggressively stubbed out another cigarette.

Bill stared at the ceiling as he prepared to speak, gripping the cigarette tight in his hand. "I like men and women but, it, er, doesn't make me a queer," he said, spewing the words out, unnerved by the panicked tone in his own voice.

"You realise there might be another queer in this room incredibly offended by your remark," said Smale, but Bill saw the professor was smiling and they laughed away some of the tension. "Mr Laws, it really does take all sorts, I've always said sexuality isn't a fixed thing. It's society that is obsessed about putting labels on everything."

"But what can I do?" Bill said pleadingly, laughter having died in his throat, chest filling with emotion.

Smale slung a box of Kleenex at him, rested a hand on his leg, fingers a little too close to his inner thigh. "It's a cliché I know, but do whatever feels right. Some people when they come out ..."

"I'm not coming out," snapped Bill, the professor instantly pulling his hand away. "I said I like men and women and maybe not in that order."

"All right, some people when they finally get close to accepting who they are want to shout it from the highest rooftops but you've no need to. You don't need to indulge in any flag waving," said Smale as he lowered his voice conspiratorially. "But you need to be comfortable, be honest and be yourself, for your own sake and that of your friends. And, dear boy, indulge some of those desires and see where it leads. You're a young lad ... all this brow beating ... just enjoy yourself."

"Thanks, but ..."

"No, there are no buts, Mr Laws," Smale said, rudely cutting him off as though bored with the conversation. "There's one thing I'd like to know though, how do you feel about Adam?"

"I love him," said Bill, stalling for time under the professor's unflinching stare.

"Yes, I know all that," he replied, thrashing his hands about. "But, now we've got everything out in the open, how do you really feel?"

"He's attractive, I can see that."

"For Christ's sake, Mr Laws, this really is like getting blood out of a stone," bellowed Smale. "Don't tell me half a story."

"Okay, I ... I fancy him, I can imagine us lying in bed together."

"You can imagine *fucking* him?" said Smale in barely a whisper, like he was that detective finally on the verge of eliciting a confession to murder through his gentle coaxing.

"Yes, okay, yes. What more do you want me to say?" shouted Bill, up on his feet now, bringing up a fist as if to strike the professor but letting his arm drop back down and striding to the door. He knew the door was locked of course, but that didn't stop him wrestling aggressively with the handle.

"One more question and then I'll let you go," said Smale, calm as ever in spite of Bill's aggression, holding the key tantalisingly up to his face. "Why don't you just tell Adam everything?"

"I can't right now. I don't want to make my life more complicated than it is. I'll wait till I'm stronger," Bill stammered, unconvinced, moving anxiously from foot to foot. "Now let me out of here."

"Don't worry, this won't go any further," said the professor, self-satisfied grin etched on his features, nudged up as close as he could to Bill in the doorway, finally turning the key in the lock.

The professor patted him on the back as he hurried through the exit but Bill's relief at being in the corridor was obliterated by the realisation that what he'd revealed in the office meant the world, his world, had changed forever. Far from being liberated, Bill only felt fear at the decisions he was going to have to make. His mind drifted back to a priest who had taught him in First Communion classes years ago that in bad times he just had to think of one person or thing to be grateful for and it would lead to another and another. Then as now he was a total blank.

Smale sat back down and surveyed his now empty office, nothing left of Bill save the linger of his cigarette smoke and a strangely musky allure that caused the professor to lick his lips as he picked up the phone to call Adam. But halfway through dialling he stopped, dropping the phone back in its cradle. He baulked at letting him get everything he ever wanted. His jealousy of the boy's youth, his beauty, rose hatefully to the surface.

No, he thought, chuckling to himself, he would tell Adam about Bill only once he had slipped just out of reach. As long as Bill didn't confess, and somehow Smale knew he wouldn't, didn't have the guts. Catholics loved confessions, but it was mainly to authority figures not to 20-year-old boys, he'd found. No, Bill couldn't possibly tell all to Adam, thought Smale, Bill was the football-loving "straight" guy, a Manchester City fan for goodness sake, he wouldn't just turn round to his friend one day and admit he liked boys' bits. Adam would want to dress him in high fashion and take him on Saturday afternoon shopping trips, dragging him from the radio where he'd no doubt made a habit of listening to *Sports Report*, mused the professor laughing uproariously.

As Bill hovered with intent outside the Student Union bar, part of him wanted to get drunk, then go home, sink into Sarah's arms and tell her it was all a big mistake, that what he'd just admitted in Smale's office was just an aberration, that he knew they'd be together forever with the baby, in a cottage with roses around the door. But for once he walked past the entrance of the bar, instead of seeking solace in its murky interior, knowing he was finally going to have to say something, the truth. He headed resolutely to the Underground wondering what reaction awaited him at home, realising that even though he loved her, he now had other priorities and was no longer sure he could stand the intensity of them living together.

CHAPTER FIFTEEN

Adam moved down the stairs, slowly at first, then running, stumbling as he approached Sarah, panting, out of breath. Her body was so still after those final spasms. A head wound was leaking onto the immaculately polished parquet, spreading like ink on a blotter and blood ran crimson from her mouth, pooling thickly in a dimple on her pallid chin. Adam knelt down to study her more closely, her eyes were open but unflinching, her face swollen and bruised like an outsized fruit that had fallen from a tree, left to putrefy on a damp summer lawn.

He searched for a pulse, his first-aid training coming back to him, but he had not acted nearly quickly enough. He couldn't find the slightest beat. His eyes flicked back to her skinny, twisted body and he imagined the foetus suffocating inside, giving one last kick. But he didn't even attempt resuscitation, couldn't imagine breathing life into someone he hated so much. He wasn't that much of a hypocrite. Instead the need to be practical overtook his rising panic and disbelief. He rifled through her pockets and located her mobile phone. Rather than dialling 999 he switched it off and slipped it into his own pocket. Then he ran back up the stairs, frantic, two steps at a time, jumping like a hurdler. Entering the bathroom he grabbed some towels, one still damp from Sarah's morning shower.

When he got back downstairs he gently lifted her head, flinching at the blood on his hands, propping her up with a white fluffy bath towel that soon turned crimson. He used one of the other towels to soak up the blood on the floor, his fingers stained red, sweat dripping from his brow with the effort of scrubbing. He was wrapping a third towel around the back of her skull, trying to staunch the blood from the gaping wound but dropped her with a sickening thump as his phone rang. Dragging it out of his pocket he saw it was Bill. The ring tone pulsed in his ears together with his own heartbeat, but he let it ring and ring, fearful of how close his friend was to Hampstead, not really wanting to know. As it finally rang off he grabbed Sarah aggressively, by the hair this time, and successfully wrapped the wound in the towel, tying a knot at the two ends with great dexterity like it was simply a job to be done. Adam could now see the horizon ahead, plot a way forward, wary of anyone upsetting his plans. Wary but ready.

He assumed that Bill had just arrived at the Tube station and calculated that he had 20 minutes at the most. He pictured him strolling back, mouth in shape for his lunch and ran, actually sprinted, the few feet to the cellar door. He opened it and the gloom from below was so deep and impenetrable it threatened to envelope the whole house. He shuddered. The smell of the cool, damp air wafted over him as he scrabbled around in the darkness for the light switch, hand grazing the rough concrete of the wall before he finally located the old pull cord. There was a brief flicker, a pop, then total darkness again.

"Shit," he said on his way to the kitchen, where he knew Sarah kept light bulbs, when he heard a noise at the front door.

He ran back out into the hallway, carving knife in hand from a kitchen draw, ready for anything, just in time to see letters tumbling onto the mat and to hear the postman's cheerful whistle vibrating through the thin glass of the front door like everything was normal on this obscenely abnormal day. A neurotic giggle bubbled up inside him. Even if it had been Bill, he thought, he could always have pretended it was an accident. He clung to that, but he wondered what his friend would have made of the clean-up operation, the attempt to conceal. He went back to the kitchen, letters in one hand, knife in the other, knowing the answer.

He threw the knife back into the drawer and flung the letters on the counter. Noticing blood on the manila envelopes, he angrily scooped them up and buried them deep into the contents of the swing-top bin. He then located a fresh light bulb, held it aloft in triumph and wondered why he was finding it all so easy, wondered whether this was what he'd really wanted all along as he screwed in the bulb, lighting his way forward, illuminating his grisly task.

Returning to Sarah's body, he slipped her trainers off and began to drag her towards the open cellar door. He'd only got halfway down the hall when he began to boil with anger again at how such a skinny, insignificant person in life could be so heavy and cumbersome in death. Sweat running from his brow and into his eyes, his whole being straining with the effort, he flung both her legs to the floor, bony feet bouncing horribly, and took a rest. He stripped off his T-shirt, which was drenched in perspiration, caught a glimpse of his relentlessly pumped torso in the hallway mirror and saw wild eyes staring back, killer's eyes. He looked down at his hands as he prepared to lift her again, and saw they were stained with Sarah's blood. He knew he could wash it away but like Shakespeare's Macbeth, Adam feared the stain of this bloody morning would never really leave him. He knew it wasn't just a case of removing the physical evidence.

Panicked again, glancing at his watch he saw it had been about 10 minutes since Bill called, but he tried to blank it from his mind, he had work to do. He swiped up her feet again and with one great effort finally dragged her to the cellar door. He dropped her again, breathing heavily, hands on hips, but didn't look down at her body, at her face, he couldn't. Instead he scanned the floor for signs of blood, anything that could give him away. He was relieved to see that even though there was a patch where she'd fallen it almost exactly matched the deep burgundy of the stained parquet. He could hide it by slightly moving the Oriental rug in the hallway, but the old house was so gloomy anyway, it could retain limitless secrets within its shadows.

He looked at his watch again with what was becoming paranoid regularity. Fearing he didn't have long, he picked up her legs and dragged her feet first. The phone rang in his pocket, its loud insistence making him jump, but he wasn't about to stop now. He edged her to the top of the cellar stairs that tapered off into darkness below.

Pulling her down step by step, Sarah's body gained momentum the further they descended. The speed of the movement finally caught Adam off balance and sent them both tumbling into the blackness at the bottom of the stairs. He cursed as he fell heavily onto the filthy concrete floor, her body landing partially on top of him, causing him to kick one of her legs savagely away with a disgusting crack. It took a minute for his eyes to focus but then he noticed bits of furniture in the darkness, family heirlooms of those long since dead, he guessed, his heart pounding, wondering what spirits he was stirring up.

He dragged the body with a terrible scraping sound across the crude floor, as far into the darkness as he could until he reached an old closet. Dropping her, Adam wheeled quickly around, anxious to get out of the gloomy cellar and saw what he was looking for, a dust sheet. He whipped it off an old sofa, sending a cloud of thick particles spiralling through the air, making his eyes water, clogging his throat with decay. As the air cleared he threw it, like a shroud, over what had once been his friend. Then he ran, as though he was running for his life, up the cellar stairs, face to face with her trainers in the hallway. He slung them back down into the basement along with the bloodied towels and slammed the door, only then realising how violently he was shaking. He hugged himself in an effort to stop, to calm himself.

He dragged the Oriental rug across the stain where Sarah's lifeblood had leaked away and was transfixed by Bill's silhouette framed ominously in the glazed front door. The key sliding into the lock had all the inevitability of the cocking of a gun. But instead of waiting to face his friend, he scooped up his T-shirt and ran upstairs, passing Sarah's dried blood on the skirting that he hadn't had time to wipe away, wondering how he would explain that away to her boyfriend. He locked himself in the bathroom and listened intently to Bill pacing around downstairs, his whole being wracked by fear at how close he was to the body, how close he was to the truth, willing him not to notice how everything was amiss, praying the shadowy stairwell would conceal the gruesome evidence until he'd had time to delete all traces of her.

"Sarah," he heard Bill shout as he washed the blood off of his hands, watched the evidence drain away down the plug hole, frantically scrubbed at his fingers, his eyes blurred with tears.

"Sarah, babe, I'm home. I'm sorry," Bill shouted again, his closing footfalls audible on the stairs.

Adam emerged from the bathroom to face Bill at the top of the stairs. He couldn't help feeling that he and Bill were closer in some way, drawn together by the morning's terrible events. He wished he could tell him she'd gone, gone and was not coming back, ever.

"Where is she?" he said, panting, a tub of Ben & Jerry's ice cream in one hand, spoon in the other.

"I ... er ..." stammered Adam, wondering if Bill could read the guilt in his eyes, see that his hands were raw with scrubbing. "I don't know how to tell you."

"For fuck's sake, tell me what?"

"She's gone," he said evenly, fighting a chaos of emotion inside, sweat springing to his forehead as he thought of Sarah's body lying in the dark, dusty cellar already beginning to decompose.

"Gone?" said Bill, voice rising with indignation. "Gone where?"

Grabbing Bill's arm, his sturdy arm, Adam pulled him towards the bedroom, what used to be *their* room, Sarah and Bill's.

"Look," he said, pointing to the desk and the letter, which was where everything had unravelled just an hour ago.

Bill picked it up gently and put it down again, as if it were so precious, so fragile it might disintegrate at his touch. He looked at the letter intently as it lay on the desk but it was as though he wasn't really seeing it, the powerfully blunt words having no impact, no sign of recognition on his face.

"You read it," he said to Adam, picking up the letter again and handing it to him.

"What?"

"Just read the fucking thing out loud," Bill shouted, sitting down at the desk where Sarah had penned it minutes ago, kicking angrily at the other balls of paper on the floor, scattering them as he buried his head in his hands and prepared to listen.

The flimsy sheet of paper shook in Adam's hands. The words written in her immaculately looping script were blemished with smudges which he guessed were the result of her tears.

"*Dear Bill*," he read, taking a deep breath, wiping the sweat from his brow. "*I'd like to start off this letter by saying sorry but I'm actually the one who's got the least to be sorry for. I just can't get over what happened in Barcelona, I cannot rid myself of the sickening pain of having been betrayed by three of, what I thought, were my best friends in my family's own home.*" He looked up to see Bill's reaction, taking a minute to compose himself.

"Just fucking read it," barked Bill as he took his hands from his face, eyes burning into Adam.

"*I'm leaving you. I'm going to take myself and your baby away for a while, probably for good. Bill, I need to think and I don't know when I'll be back, if ever. Don't bother trying to contact me because you won't be able to find me. You can stay in this house till the end of term and then that's it. Dad's thinking of putting it on the market and I don't want to see you or Adam here again. Anyway, my gut feeling is that it's over between us. Sarah.*"

He cleared his throat to indicate he'd reached the end, surprised at himself for having got through the emotive jumble of words, amazed at his capacity to conceal.

Bill just stared up at him, disbelieving, face drained of his usual colour. Adam put a hand on his friend's shoulder and even though he'd never felt more fraudulent, left it there, holding himself back from hugging Bill, stopping himself from grazing his cheek with a kiss, fighting the urge he'd been fighting all these months.

"I've fucked everything up," said Bill, voice cracking, swatting Adam's hand from his shoulder like it was an irritating, unwanted fly. "Leave me alone for a while, will you?"

"Okay," Adam replied meekly, sloping off from the room, moving slyly with the calculated movements of the killer he'd become.

"Look, babe, please come home, I'll do anything, anything," he heard Bill leaving a desperate message on Sarah's phone, the phone he had in his own pocket. The voice trailed away as he entered the confines of his bedroom, looking frantically around like a fugitive making sure his refuge hadn't been infiltrated.

Adam listened as Supergrass' *Alright* drifted up the stairs from the radio that was still on in the kitchen. It had been playing all morning but he hadn't really noticed. Now the sunny, familiar tune jolted him back to the carefree time when they had sat around, Sarah, Bill and him, the threesome, in the back garden on the sunny late autumn day that Bill had moved in. He recalled how they'd collapsed into fits of giggles to a soundtrack of Britpop and how they'd all been so hungry, so stoned, they had emptied virtually the whole contents of the fridge into one baguette. He felt sick that such a moment could never be recaptured, so sick to his stomach that the pain was eating him from the inside out as Sarah had so memorably said, in her almost last words, words that now seared themselves into his brain.

Bill slammed the phone into the desk with a crash after leaving his message on Sarah's mobile. He hoped that hearing his distraught voice would encourage her back, or at least encourage her to call him, give him some kind of window where he could attempt to persuade her she was being rash. In some ways though he knew she was absolutely right, her gut feeling that it was over between them showed a frighteningly keen instinct, he thought.

He closed the door, drowning out the unwelcome sounds from the rest of the house, sounds of normality like the Britpop coming from the radio, which he used to love but now found almost physically painful to listen to because it reminded him of what he was missing, that nothing was normal. The rain beating against the window was hardly a comfort either. He stood up and looked around the room, their room, like he was taking it in for the very first time. Even the indented mattress on the unmade bed reminded him of her, set him thinking. He picked up the letter again to see if it could possibly offer any more clues as to what had happened that morning. Sarah had obviously left in such a hurry she hadn't even had time to do the things she seemed pre-programmed to do, like fold the sheets. It was her pet peeve and she always complained when Bill failed to do it if she got up first.

He moved to her closet looking for more evidence that she'd gone but as he roughly pulled open the door, instead of being short of clothes it was so full, garments threatened to spill out onto the floor. As he ran his fingers through some of the items, the swirl of garish colour almost made him dizzy and the smell, the maddening smell, the scent of her, made him tearful and angry all at once. He grabbed one of her favourite dresses, an outfit he'd bought for her. He brought it to his nose and buried his tears in the soft fabric. She'd worn it to the Christmas ball. He remembered her throwing up in the bushes from drinking too much sparkling wine, and he'd embarrassed himself for nearly punching one of the waiters for flirting with him. Similarly panicked thoughts bombarded him now, like dazzling headlights coming straight at him some filthy night on a treacherous country lane. He clung to the dress, cradled it like he was cradling her, like he had to hold onto something. He crumpled to the bed still gripping the dress, wondering if he was ever going to see her again, wondering if he was to blame.

Bill was scared, so scared of what to do next as he lay on the bed, tears streaming down his face. He was inconsolable, impotent. Scared of where it might lead if he got up. The simple fact of putting one foot in front of the other, terrifying because he feared it could lead to another night like the one in Soho. There was an inescapable and nagging temptation now that he was free. This was the scariest prospect of all in losing Sarah.

As a youngster he always seemed to be looking for a way out of some horrible situation. Then, as now, it was like he was scrabbling around in the dark for a light switch he could never find. He dialled Dolores' number, not because he thought it could help, but because he thought she might be able to derail him from the path he was on with a few hateful words. Deep down though, Bill knew it would take a lot more than words.

"Are you still living with that faggot and the silly vegetarian girl I'm guessing is your girlfriend?" she said, disgust oozing through the handset as she delivered her opening line to the son she hadn't spoken to in days.

"Dolores!" he said admonishing her but really just stalling, not wanting to answer her question, wondering why he'd bothered searching for the answer here.

"Answer me," she barked.

"Look, Sarah's left me," he said, trying to keep the rising emotion out of his voice, knowing how she hated any sign of what she called weakness. "I don't know what to do."

"Do? Do?" shouted Dolores down the line, forcing him to hold the phone away from his ear. "Maybe she thinks you're being a faggot with your faggot friend."

"What?" he said, her cruel, humiliating laughter making his ears burn, bringing him back to his childhood, making him feel little and insignificant like she always did.

"Maybe she knows the truth," she said slowly, as if she

194

wanted to give her words time to resonate. "Remember when you were a wee kid and I caught you in the bath with your best friend? Remember the disgusting things you were doing? I've always thought you were a filthy faggot."

He drew the phone away from his ear again, imagined her standing there, rolls of fat wobbling in time to her demeaning laughter. Bill could still hear her words babbling from the earpiece but he couldn't listen to her abuse any more. He knew as he cut her off that he was cutting her off for good. She'd given him an answer even though it wasn't the easy way out he'd been looking for, but then, it never was.

On his way out, Adam had left the radio playing in the kitchen because he didn't want to pass by the cellar door. He had already decided where he was going to dump Sarah, not that he thought of her as Sarah any more. It was just an inanimate object, he insisted, pathetically trying to reassure himself. He walked down the garden path to the MG, barely noticing the half inch of surface water left by the torrential rain. He was sizing up the dimensions of the small snub-nosed sports car, asking himself whether it would fit, whether the body would fit.

A nosey neighbour eyed him from a front-room window like he was mad, as he walked around to the back of the car, oblivious to the drenching rain, and unlocked the boot. He surveyed it for space, picturing Sarah, *the body*, he corrected himself, crumpled in the cellar under a dust sheet. He wrestled frantically with the retractable rear seat, until he finally managed to dislodge it, creating sufficient space for what he gauged to be a bulky load, a body.

He backed out of the boot space and slammed down the hatch. Running a hand through his drenched hair, he now realised how wet he was. Teeth chattering and his hands shaking with cold, he unlocked the driver's side door and jumped in. The car started at the third try and he was assailed by Blur's *Parklife*. It had been in the cassette player when he'd last driven, when everything had been different, he thought, snapping off the stereo and wishing there was a way to reverse things. It was an effort to pull away from the house that held so much horror, but he reluctantly did so. He switched the heater on full, but the blast of air felt chilled against his sodden clothes. He gripped the steering wheel tighter to prevent himself shaking so much.

At the top of the street he didn't know which way to turn. He didn't even really know why he was in the car, but when the impatient driver of a white van behind him hooted at his indecision he turned left making a snap choice to visit Helen. He was going to confess, he thought. Well, he was going to confess something.

Adam didn't often turn up unannounced because he knew Helen didn't like surprises. Her life, like her appearance was very ordered, almost calculated. As he knocked on her door, he was at least reassured that Bill would not be wrapped around her elegantly skinny shoulders. He wondered how much he should tell her, how much he *could* tell her.

"Hi," she said, opening the door after a significant pause.

"Hi," he replied, guessing she had taken a while to decide whether to let him in or not. They hadn't seen each other since the Spanish embarrassment.

"How are you, babe?" she cooed, pecking him on the cheek, pale, unreadable, a little fragile, a little too affected, her hair in a sexy bob and a cigarette arched in her hand like a fashion accessory.

"Fine," he lied as she led him inside, the glare of daytime TV making the small space look grimmer than usual. "Can we turn this thing off?"

"Off?" she said, looking at him quizzically like it was a weird command, like he might actually have something important to tell her.

Adam realised that they'd never really sat down and talked to each other without the intrusion of television or some other distraction. It was like they always put obstacles in the way, never really *talked*, he thought sadly.

"You can leave it on if you like," he replied resignedly as she flopped down on the sofa next to him. There was nowhere else to look other than at the pouting TV couple opposite, filling up their airtime before yet another commercial for haemorrhoid cream,

Adam thought savagely.

"You want to tell me something?" she said, her tone softening, the so in vogue, often harsh mock London accent melting away to reveal something more real.

As he looked into her eyes, wondering how often over the last few months they'd actually made eye contact, he opened his mouth to speak, closed it, then opened it again, the theme tune of the daytime chat show obscene and absurd in the background. "I have got something to tell you," he said.

"You're gay?" she said, laughing nervously, bringing a fresh cigarette to her lips. "I already knew that."

"No, look Helen," he said, trying hard to sound sincere, never having enjoyed playing the queen in her fag-hag routine, despising it really, tired of being just a joker, a joke to her. "I've done something very silly."

"Silly?" she said, patting his knee, half smiling, turning back to the TV as if she really didn't want to know if it was something too dramatic, too heavy. It caused him to hesitate, to back away from a full damning confession.

"It was me I was talking about when I mentioned the student and the lech. I had an affair with Smale, my tutor," he said, and while having confessed something, such was the weight of his guilt, he wished he'd told her what he set out to tell her. His eyes filled with tears and he began to tremble.

"Smale?" she repeated, like she couldn't quite comprehend it. "You mean that dapper old thing that hangs around the arts faculty? The one who wears the cravats?"

"He doesn't wear cravats," he insisted, forcing a laugh but knowing the professor did have a penchant for the colourful silk monstrosities.

"He's not so bad," she said, sounding far from convinced, "but I don't understand this gay thing for older men."

"What gay thing for older men?" he said piqued, unclamping his teeth from his lower lip. "It's just something that happened, a fling. It's over now."

"Adam, babe, I'm not judging you, I'm just surprised that's all."

"Yeah, well I'm full of surprises, just you watch," he said cryptically, wishing he hadn't as the humour he'd intended seemed to die in his throat, his words taking on a sinister edge.

"What did you talk about?" she said, eyes full of wonderment, like she was actually interested.

"He's a very intelligent, charming ..." he began but trailed off as though it really didn't matter, like nothing could possibly matter.

"I'll make us some tea," she said, sidling out of the room.

Helen was reverting to the old British default of dealing with an awkward situation by not dealing with it, except to the extent of saving her own embarrassment, Adam thought sadly. He felt hollow, soulless. Even his overwhelming desire to have Bill, for so long his raison d'être, seemed to have waned, but he was still intent on taking people down with him, making them suffer like he had. Sarah wouldn't be the last.

"Helen?" he asked as she came back in the room, her eyes focused on the TV as she handed him the cup of tea.

"What?" she said, still avoiding the insistence of his gaze.

"I want you to do something for me before the end of term," he said. "I know it's going to cause a bit of a scandal but I want you to publish my story, mine and Smale's."

"You know it may jeopardise your own university career," she said, business-like, unconcerned, like she was inwardly licking her lips at the possibility of such a scoop, "and I'd need evidence."

"I don't intend to be around next year."

"What?" she said, scrutinising him, finally turning her attention away from the television.

"I mean, I don't want to continue at this university," he added hurriedly. "Too many bad memories."

"I understand," she said with a tangible lack of concern for her supposed friend, "but the end of term is very close, so I'll need your story pretty soon."

"You'll have it, I have emails documenting our liaison," he said, but even this moment of triumph had a hollow, tainted ring. "I want Smale's ordered little world to fall apart, and see how he looks."

"Want to go out this afternoon, watch a film or something?" Helen said airily as though drawing a line under all the unpleasantness, ignoring the rage in Adam's voice.

"Nah," he said, getting up, patting her on the shoulder, aware that he'd probably never see her again and troubled by how unconcerned he actually was. "I better get going, got some last-minute revision to do before the exams start."

"I know the feeling," she said, forcing out a giggle. "How about Bill?"

"Oh, he's fine," Adam said curtly, moving swiftly towards the front door.

"And *Sarah*?" he heard her say from behind him.

"Fine, too," he lied as he opened the door, the air in the corridor refreshingly cool on his face. He made for the stairs without looking back. He couldn't look back.

"And then I pushed her down the stairs," he tapped into the computer, aware of Bill moving around in the next room, listening for any sign of him coming closer. He had to confess somewhere, even if it was just to an electronic diary. *"I just couldn't take it any more, her any more, but I didn't mean for her to die. God how I wish she hadn't died, anything but that. It was an accident, only an accident ..."*

CHAPTER SIXTEEN

Adam had been awake most of the night, listening as the wind ripped ferociously through the eaves of the old house, creaking and groaning menacingly in the early hours. On the one occasion he drifted off he saw himself at the top of the stairs with Sarah again, but this time instead of pushing her he turned and walked away. The dream was cut short and he woke with such a start that he nearly fell out of bed. He then sat clinging to the covers, his body slippery with perspiration.

Dawn approached, bringing brittle daylight to end his long night and illuminate the horror of what had gone on only a few hours before. He couldn't get the image of Sarah and the cellar out of his mind. It was occupying a permanent space there, a grainy horror film on a loop. He listened intently for any sign of Bill moving around. The previous evening, Bill had mentioned through his tears, that his first exams were that morning. Apart from that, they had barely spoken. Adam couldn't bear his friend's speculations about how long it would be before she came "crawling back". Not only was he nauseated by Bill's seemingly endless sorrow that had such an obscene edge of self-pity to it, he was also sickened by the thought that having the place to himself while his housemate had exams would leave him no choice but to remove Sarah, *the body*, and complete his terrible deed.

He was jolted by the alarm clock ringing in the adjacent bedroom. Looking at his own clock he saw it was 8am. He knew it would be a while before Bill actually left the house. He would have to get through the laborious rituals of showering and shaving first. Normally he found the remnants of Bill's shaving foam and whiskers in the sink so manly, but now he just wanted him out of the way as quickly as possible so he could get down to his task in the basement.

As the front door finally slammed about an hour later, Adam simultaneously opened his own bedroom door, anxious to complete what he'd started. The smell of fried breakfast that hit him at the top of the stairwell reacted horribly with his raw, nervous stomach. When he entered the kitchen and saw a packet of bacon open on the counter he couldn't help laughing, amazed at how quickly Bill had ditched Sarah's vegetarian manifesto. He'd always suspected that his friend strayed occasionally. He was so good at putting up a front, Adam thought, taking a swig from a carton of orange juice. It was Sarah's own "100 per cent freshly squeezed juice" that she had forbidden him to have. He laughed before swigging down the remainder of it and slinging it into the overflowing bin, the bin she had always emptied.

He calculated his next move and recalled his mother burning her lover's notes over the sink when he was a teenager, recalled the flames reflecting in her determined, unswerving gaze. Now that same ruthlessness coursed through him. He knew exactly where he was headed as he opened the front door, undaunted by the overgrown driveway, littered with weeds and the discarded innards of the house from its recent refurbishment. Sarah's dad was in a dispute with the builders and they'd left behind a lot of debris just to spite him. Surveying the old, dusty ceramic bathroom fittings and chintzy furnishings, once enthusiastically picked out in catalogues by those long forgotten, Adam rolled up his sleeves. He was preparing to clear a path so he could edge the car right up to the front of the house and conceal it behind the overgrown bushes, away from prying eyes and off the radar of Neighbourhood Watch. Yesterday he'd noticed a house a few doors down was being refitted and there was a skip outside so he figured to slip the builders a few quid if necessary to dump the driveway rubbish, dump unwanted memories.

He strode through the surface water on the drive, thankful the rain had now stopped, and dragged a sodden armchair behind him towards the street. The rusted wrought-iron gate squealed when he opened it as if in protest at finally being called into action again. He pulled the rotting piece of furniture purposefully to the skip, desperate to get what was set to be a long morning over with. He used all his strength to haul the chair into the void, the garish yellow container swallowing it with a metallic echo.

Next came the cast-iron bathtub, heavy rust coming off in

flakes as he grabbed uncertainly at its sides. Looking at the once white interior now blackened with decay he imagined another bathtub and Dolores towering over Bill and his little friend, rolls of fat quivering with rage. Anxious to wrest the image from his mind he dragged the tub to the skip with renewed vigour.

Returning breathlessly to the driveway he swiped at an old ceramic sink but a sharp, searing pain electrified the nerve endings in his hand and caused him to drop it. He stood transfixed by the one-inch cut that leaked blood and throbbed with his pulse. Lightheaded, he knelt down and looked at the sink more closely. He saw where the side was cracked, it had splintered into a razor-sharp edge now spotted with his own blood. He got up and again felt dizzy, swayed from side to side, but he was determined to finish the job. He pulled a handkerchief from his pocket and wrapped it around the wound, tying it in a knot. As he watched the white cloth turn red, all he could see was Sarah's misshapen head leaking out onto the parquet flooring.

He picked up the sink, more gingerly this time, the pain in his hand growing, his head swirling, but relief swept through him as he finally sent the offending bathroom fitting tumbling against the side of the skip. Adam was glad there were no builders around to impede his progress but he had been aware of several pairs of curtains flapping up and down the street. The pathetic casualties of suburbia, he thought bitterly, desperate for something to happen to break up the banality that retail therapy, daytime TV, sleeping pills and alcoholism couldn't quite mask. He'd watched *Crimewatch* enough times to know that some nosey old bastard who always put two and two together and made five could actually hit the jackpot for once and be his undoing. Neighbours getting their names in the paper or, manna from heaven, on the TV, would revel in justifying their sad little lives, Adam guessed, laughing to himself and scooping up another armful of rusty bathroom fittings.

As the piping weighed down his hands Sarah's story came back to him. She'd told him how her great aunt had slit her wrists in the very bathroom he was disposing of. It had never bothered him before since her presence had been erased by aerodynamic tiling and pastel shades, but as he held the detritus of years in his hands he couldn't help thinking of the woman's blood spurting over the clunky white surfaces. He flung the rubbish angrily into the skip in a bid to rid his mind of the sepia-tinged image of the great aunt that Sarah had shown him in a photograph one sunny afternoon before death had become so tangible.

Turning away from the skip she was almost in his face, Adam's earnest neighbour, a bag of shopping in each hand, wearing an overcoat so old it had taken on an uncertain colour, an insignificant dog making a significant yapping sound at her feet.

"What are you up to?" she said, her voice alien to him as they'd only ever really communicated before by banging on the adjoining wall. She'd rap when he played his music too loud and he'd bang right back.

"Clearing the driveway," he said evenly, palm outstretched, not wanting to get into an argument, draw unnecessary attention to himself.

"About time. You can do the garden while you're at it, it's become an eyesore. If my Albert was here he'd give you all what for," she snapped, betraying all the bitterness of her husband's premature death, the death that left her totally alone, her head bowed solemnly as if in memory.

He edged right up to her, nudged the dog away with a booted foot, eyes fixed on her pale features, brightened only by a shock of lipstick, the sole concession to femininity in her sexless appearance.

"Go fuck yourself," he said, spittle flying, digging a forefinger aggressively into her ribs to emphasise each word as she rose out of her trance to meet his gaze.

"I beg your pardon?" she said but backing away, looking genuinely frightened, dog going barking mad, two bags of shopping suddenly appearing very heavy in her hands.

"You heard me," he spat, striding back into the driveway to complete his task, knowing she wouldn't dare come near him again after seeing the anger in his eyes.

He dragged the huge empty TV packing case, which they'd left in the lounge since it had been delivered last winter, across the floor. They had been meaning to throw the unwieldy mass of cardboard out for a long time, but with typical student practicality it had doubled as a table. That morning however Adam had an idea when he recalled Bill's trick of hiding himself in it then jumping out to scare them. The idea made him shudder now as he drew the box level with the cellar door. The box that had the capacity to hide a human body. The word "*fragile*" on its side caught his eye and made him shudder, shudder at the thought of returning to the darkness of the cellar.

He entered, snapped on the light that illuminated only the top half of the stairs and followed the echoey concrete steps down into the gloom. He felt panic wash over him as he scrabbled around at the bottom of the stairs, the uneven flooring almost sending him off balance again. He could hear his own breathing loud in his ears and felt his heart beating hard as he finally located the dust sheet with its familiar lumpy shape underneath. Adam whipped the cover off and with tentative fingers felt that the flesh was noticeably cooler than before, cold even. Attempting to move the body it felt stiff, the rag-doll suppleness of the previous day replaced with heaviness, and a sickly sweet smell that already suggested decay. Flies swarmed menacingly into his face like the very harbingers of hell. He swatted the insects aggressively away but they seemed so enamoured with their putrefying host they kept coming back for more.

He tried pulling her, it, through the darkness towards the light from the stairs, but the sound of the body scraping along the floor disturbed him. Instead, with great effort, he scooped her up in his arms. Although for a moment the hellishness of the situation made him falter, such was the power of the adrenaline pumping through his muscles, such was the desire to get the job done, the weight became manageable. He slung her over his shoulder like a heroic fireman, but one who had come to bury not save, he thought grimly, grateful she'd been almost anorexic as he shuffled one foot in front of the other and they climbed the stairs together.

Reaching the top and the full light of day it was like she was putting on one final performance. She slumped grotesquely back from his shoulder and into his arms, glassy eyes looking ghoulishly straight at him and a face that was an off-white otherworldly colour he'd never seen before and would never forget. He breathed out as the box came into focus, tension easing slightly as he hovered over it. He lowered her inside, still face to face, his lips momentarily grazing her cheek like he was kissing her, like he used to when they were friends, he thought, not understanding how it had finally come to this as he let her go. He closed the flaps of the box and stood back up. It looked just like a packed up Japanese television again, but Adam knew it was only a piece of thick brown card hiding the horror within. The weight of deception was so incredibly light.

He dashed to the kitchen, bacon still on the counter in what seemed like a final affront to Sarah, and quickly located the Sellotape and scissors, bought for a more innocent purpose last Christmas, the pleasure of wrapping presents for his housemates. *Now he was wrapping one of them up.*

Returning to the hall, Adam frantically secured the top of the box with strip after strip of tape to guard against it springing open and letting the abomination out. Feeling the weight of the phone, *her* phone, in his left-hand pocket he remembered another crucial detail that had to be attended to, another item that needed careful disposal.

He kicked away the rug that covered up her bloodstains, a width of carpet to conceal his guilt, and dragged the box to the front door and out into the garden. Next to the car it looked bigger than the old MG but he knew he'd be able to wedge it in somehow, anxious to get the body away from the house and forget that any of it had ever happened. When his phone rang and he saw it was Bill, Adam realised that even if he got away with it he would never be able to forget or erase the guilt, and that would be a kind of punishment in itself.

Ignoring the still ringing phone he unlocked the hatchback and, undeterred by its dimensions because he had no choice, he hauled the box over the tailgate and partially inside. The top of it was slightly blocked by the roof so he hammered the cardboard down with his fist until he hit something solid. Wedged up against the tailgate the box was caved in but still sealed and he was finally able to slide it over the retracted seats and fully into the car. Adam looked at his injured hand. It was bleeding again and an appropriate red smear now blotted the box's sagging lid. He tried to shut the boot, slammed it down but felt it hit something gristly, something human.

"Shit," he shouted and was about to slam the hatchback down again when he turned his attention instead to a neighbour who had momentarily stopped at the end of the driveway. Adam's glare caused him to move on without a word, without looking back, like he'd never been there.

"Fucking Neighbourhood Watch," he muttered aggressively under his breath, thinking how these nosey neighbours hadn't prevented their house being burgled during the Christmas break. Not that there'd been a lot to steal, the TV had obviously been too big to take.

He ran back through the house and rifled through the kitchen draws knowing exactly what he was looking for but unsure where to find it. Throwing things onto the floor in his haste Adam suddenly remembered where it might be. He unbolted the kitchen door and went out into the back garden, through the knee-high grass to the shed. There on the dusty worktop was the garden twine Sarah had used to tie up her crop of beans that were now sprouting wildly at the end of the garden but which would soon rot and die with inattention, never to make it to the dinner table like she'd planned.

He looked at the debris on the kitchen floor, skipped over it and hurried back to the car. Winding the twine around the boot handle he drew the hatchback down over the slightly protruding box and tied the ends neatly under the rear bumper like he was tying a bow on a gift. He stepped back, briefly admiring his handiwork before jumping in the front seat. Uncomfortable with the box behind him he slid his seat forward a notch but the package was still all he could see in his rear-view mirror. He lit a cigarette with a trembling hand and turned the ignition key. Unusually the engine fired first time and he blew out a thick cloud of smoke with relief.

Coming to a halt at the junction at the end of the street he glanced down at the key ring hanging out of the ignition. A rusty key stood out, the one to the pokey old family beach chalet on the South Coast. His mum had forgotten about it since he'd grown up and she'd discovered Mediterranean holidays. He'd stolen the key a few years ago while he enjoyed, if that was the right word, an affair with someone he'd met in a Brighton toilet. The beach hut had become a sordid bolt-hole for the married man and desperate schoolboy. It was this dark, desolate cabin where Sarah was going to be dumped, he thought as another downpour commenced and he switched on the windscreen wipers, summer nowhere to be seen.

Shoreham-By-Sea, announced the sign and just the name brought back memories of his childhood, of harsh pebbles, egg sandwiches and chilling waters, the kind of austere form of "entertainment" forced on the family by his father. Passing through the little town with its dusty junk shops, greasy fish 'n' chip bars and grim pubs it looked even more inconsequential than he'd remembered, even sadder. Since his sex in the beach chalet with the man whose name he didn't want to remember, it had taken on a more sinister edge – *Sodom-By-Sea*. He'd been made to kneel obediently on the hut's floor, scraping his knees to pleasure the man who refused to take off his wedding ring, as though it offered him some kind of pathetic legitimacy, atonement for his sins, when in fact, for a husband and father it only compounded them. Adam tried to forget as he pulled into the seafront car park, passing the boarded-up kiosk where a colourfully dressed man had often plied him with too much ice cream and a wink, and he realised how hard it was to forget.

It was raining hard again. Thick blobs pelted the windscreen. Unsurprisingly the car park was empty. Even on sunny days, very few people ventured to the seaside town *they forgot to close down*, Adam thought, recalling the Morrissey song, and only then to walk their restless dogs. He listened as the tyres crunched over the pebbles, pebbles he'd run across twinkle-toed as a kid. It all seemed like so long ago, like it belonged to another lifetime, a better time. He drove up as close to the chalet as he could, no chance of missing it as it was the one right at the end of the beach, the one that had been neglected. Others stood proudly in summery pastel shades but Sarah's resting place was a sad study in grey that sickeningly complemented the miserable sky and the pea-green sea frothing angrily in the distance.

His hot, rapid breath was steaming up the windscreen. Reluctantly he flung the car door open with some difficulty against the wind. Drops of rain hit him fiercely in the face like small projectiles as he got out. Running around to the back of the MG he ripped at the twine that he'd knotted so well in Hampstead, his shirt soaked through by the time he managed to pull it free. Adam lifted the box then dropped it again, realising he'd need all his strength if he was to make it the 50 or so metres to the front of the chalet.

He edged the box out, rain thumping on his back, drenching his hair, but he didn't really feel anything except numb. He turned slowly and headed to the hut with the box. Rain drummed against the cardboard soaking it in seconds. It was as though it was melting in his hands, crumbling. By the time he reached the porch a discoloured hand was lolling grotesquely out of one side of the disintegrating package and he threw the load down in disgust. Listening to the rain hammer on the porch roof he recalled his mum reaching into a garish orange picnic hamper, wondering what she was going to draw out next, a time when all he had to worry about was the variety of sandwich he was going to munch his way through. But he didn't let his memories dominate him for long. He knew he was near to completing his gruesome task. He pulled out the rusting key and plunged it into the padlock, which clicked open after a short, impatient struggle.

Adam peered inside through the semi-darkness, flinching at how the debauchery of the past had caught up with him. Used condoms and their wrappers littered the floor and mattress, which he'd finally brought along to protect against splinters. Empty beer bottles and a liberal sprinkling of cigarette butts almost filled the rest of the musty and airless space. He couldn't help but recall how horribly sordid it had all been as he grabbed for the box. The cardboard came away in clumps as he clawed at it, through it, and there she lay in the grey light, looking up at him through milky eyes. He scooped her up aggressively and using all his remaining strength, threw her into the hut, listening as she fell to the floor with a sickening thump, as useless as the used condoms and empty beer bottles that now surrounded her. He fiddled frantically with the padlock again, puffing out his cheeks when the key at last clicked into place. From the edge of the porch he took out her phone and hurled it almost triumphantly through the air. It was swallowed up by the waves, another piece of evidence now a secret of the sea.

The storm was passing over the horizon as he ran back to the MG. Gulls swooped down low making him cower, their screeches ringing unsettlingly in his ears like a reminder of the pain he'd inflicted, the pain he was in.

As he knocked on Smale's door he couldn't help thinking of the last time they'd met and the unpleasantness in the bedroom. This time however, Adam wanted to surprise him, catch him off guard, but he still feared stumbling across his likeness, some new boy in the professor's thrall sitting in a state of semi-undress in the office armchair like he'd done himself not so long ago. He was about to leave, when Smale appeared. His mane of hair seemed to have lost its lustre, his eyes were bleary.

"What are *you* doing here?" he boomed.

"I've come to say goodbye," said Adam, almost overpowered by the high scent of whisky on the professor's breath, revealing that he'd taken to drinking earlier and earlier, like he'd finally given up.

"Goodbye?" questioned Smale indignantly, concern flickering all too briefly in his eyes.

"I mean we won't be meeting again like this, so I just want to say goodbye to an era," added Adam quickly, hoping to conceal his panic, his intention to run away.

"Oh, but you make it sound like you're disappearing for good," he said, perceptive as ever, with a world-weary sigh like he didn't have the energy to challenge the impulsiveness of youth any more.

"No, really, I just want to, you know, draw a line under things," Adam replied, wondering whether the professor's melancholy indicated another student having slipped through his greedy hands.

"In that case you better come in," he said, sliding a hand easily around the small of Adam's back, a move he'd been performing for years, like a well-practised smash in tennis.

As Smale sat down opposite him for what he guessed would be the very last time he felt lost, the rhythm of his life completely upset. Looking into the professor's resolute stare, like he was looking at some impenetrable granite rock face, Adam knew the

212

certainty he had brought with his books and his cultured asides, even his sleaziness, would be gone forever when he walked out of the office. He couldn't really count on Helen since she'd been lost to him since Spain, Sarah even before that, which only left Bill, yes Billy Boy.

"And how's our Mr Laws?" said the professor uncannily, like he was reading his young companion's mind, lighting another B&H, settling back into his chair, seeming to take strength from Adam's uncertainty and suddenly looking more composed than ever despite his obviously growing penchant for whisky.

"Bill's all right," he said. "But it's er ... oh, it's nothing, just forget it."

"No, no, do go on, Adam, I'm all ears, dear boy. It's what *exactly*?" goaded Smale, leaning in just that little bit closer.

"It's Sarah," he replied, pausing for fear of babbling out the words, of letting a rush of guilt overwhelm them both. He knew how with just a conspiratorial wink the professor had unpicked him before, all those months ago during his first one-to-one tutorial. "She's disappeared."

"Disappeared?" Smale said, voice rising sceptically like he was questioning a poor excuse for a late assignment.

"We had a fight and she left," he blurted out, knowing how much of an admission that would have been if he'd been sitting across from a police officer. He scrabbled nervously around in his pocket for a cigarette but Smale was alert enough to already be waving one under Adam's nose, like a metaphorical carrot. With a trembling hand Adam grabbed it. Despite his nicotine habit Smale normally dissuaded guests from smoking, unless he wanted something of course.

"A fight? She left? It must have been a pretty serious fight."

"I guess, yeah," said Adam, unable to offer anything other than a lazy obtuseness that made him sound even more as though he had something to hide, not having the energy to fight.

"Hmm," said Smale, thoughtfully blowing out a large stream of smoke. "Then may I suppose there was some kind of aggression on your part. A struggle? An accident? You're a strong, passionate boy and I know how these things can escalate."

Adam was stunned but let the silence implicate him, listening to the clock on the wall tick ominously on and on, like he had on his very first visit alone to the office when he'd sat there impotently as Smale undressed him. Their eyes finally met but Adam could only look away from the professor's questioning gaze.

"By the way, I'm thinking of going to Hong Kong and taking Bill with me. So you won't be seeing me around for much longer anyway," he said, breaking the awful hush at last. "I think I'd better go, professor, we've caused each other enough trouble."

"I think you better had, Adam," Smale said.

For once Smale remained in his chair not bothering to accompany his student to the door, not letting his hot breath rest on the boy's ear, Adam felt untouchable now, tainted in some way. Entering the corridor, he walked slowly off, waiting for the concerned patter of the professor's footsteps behind him like there had always been after they'd quarrelled, but not this time. This time he knew he was alone.

CHAPTER SEVENTEEN

He was waiting at his bedroom window when they arrived, as he'd known they would. It was a typically dull morning and the police squad car looked particularly garish with its fluorescent stripes and white finish. As Adam looked closer, blinking away another hangover, he could just make out two figures moving darkly around inside, waiting, like they were taking in the whole scene, trying to suss everything out. He imagined himself facing them at the police station, staring across at them, being sized up as his arms rested on a cheap Formica table, the cigarette they'd given him dwindling away in an ashtray as precarious as his freedom.

He watched as at last they got out of the car, identical buzz cuts, the kind of men he saw in straight pubs and averted his eyes from to avoid trouble. They should have been obscured by the hedge but they were both big and burly. The caps they'd just put on poked menacingly over the foliage. He watched with a rapt kind of fascination as they made their way down the garden path, one black, one white, presumably for variety, walking single file, being too big to stand abreast on it.

As if to emphasise their authority, instead of ringing the bell like any normal visitor, there came a heavy knock on the door that reverberated throughout the house. He waited, almost paralysed, but the rapping came again and again, more urgent, like they weren't going to go away until they got what they wanted. Adam finally ran down the stairs and saw them silhouetted against the glass of the front door, blocking out the light. He edged it open. The white man was right on the doorstep as though poised to come in even if uninvited, his rotund face disturbingly featureless save for ruddy cheeks and a blonde moustache that had barely graduated from bum fluff.

"Police," he said from a little slit of a mouth, pink tongue poking out from behind discoloured teeth as he unnecessarily and officiously held up a warrant card. "I'm Sergeant Price and this is Police Constable Symons. Are you the occupier here?"

"Occupier?" he said confused, intimidated by the formality of the two towering men in blue uniforms on his step.

"Are you a tenant?" said the constable, leaving aside his colleague's gruffness, exhibiting the slight hint of a Welsh accent, a hint of humility.

"Er, yes," Adam replied, glad to have been finally able to answer a question, though he was concentrating so hard he'd even had to think about that.

"We've come about a Ms Sarah Darwood," said the sergeant, dispensing with any attempt at pleasantries, hopping agitatedly on the step from one large booted foot to another. "Can we discuss this inside?"

"Yes, yes," he replied, terribly eager as he led the pair into the house, their bulk filling the hallway, hats almost touching the ceiling.

He waved them into the living room with a bandaged hand he immediately wished he'd concealed. The sergeant paused outside for a moment, looking left then right, before nodding like he was satisfied everything was in order. Adam, still in a state of denial about the seriousness of events and in a desperate bid to appear plausible, was left fretting about the officer's body odour, a horribly stale aroma that was likely to linger.

They stood and hovered awkwardly in the middle of the lounge, the sergeant picking things up and putting them gently down again like everything was a vital clue, while the constable stood still with his hands clasped in front of him, staring ahead with the odd reverence of an undertaker.

"Sit down, please," said Adam, waving them to the sofa, wishing the pair would stop casting such a shadow over him, his life.

"No, we're all right standing," the sergeant said hurriedly, answering for both of them as though anxious to get on with proceedings. "By the way, how did you injure your hand?"

"Oh, this," said Adam, nervously waving the bandage under the sergeant's nose, but composed enough to deceive, realising most of his teenage years had been about deception, hiding who he really was, which he guessed was why he filled the role of killer so easily. "I did it when I was clearing the driveway. You know, I've been so hyper since she, I mean Sarah, went missing that I decided I had to do something. There was a lot of debris left over from the house's refurbishment ..."

"I see," said the sergeant cutting him off, an edge to his voice now, like the rambling answer had been more than enough. The constable however was scribbling something down in a notebook. "Now, about Ms Darwood. Sarah. The parents have recently filed a missing person's report as she's been gone for a number of days now."

"Yeah," he said morosely, the verbal equivalent of shrugging his shoulders, unsure whether he was being asked a question or not, angered and frightened by the intrusion but desperate not to show it. He sat down on the sofa and looked up at the pair of them peering down at him.

"We understand her boyfriend, a Mr William Laws, lives here, along with an Adam Wright. Which one are you?" said the constable, briefly taking over questioning like they were some well-oiled machine but all the while looking down at his notebook, his prompt.

"Adam," he replied, wishing they'd just go, unnerved by the sergeant's stare and his growing sense of impatience which, Adam thought, either meant that he had him down as prime suspect or that he wanted to get away for the sizable lunch he obviously indulged in a little too frequently.

"And where is Mr Laws today?" said the sergeant.

"He has exams."

"I see," said the sergeant as his colleague made another scribbled note. "We've seen from her parents that she left a letter but in the light of not having heard from her for a few days we'd like to know some background. Runaways happen all the time, of course, but what made a supposedly happy student just disappear? We'd like to maybe ask a few more specific questions, take a little look around."

In the ensuing silence the constable looked up from his notebook, indicating they were awaiting an acknowledgement of some kind.

"Go ahead, sure," said Adam edgily, rattled by all the procedure, aware he was sounding stroppy and uninterested, the survival instinct beating so strongly within him.

"Is her going off like this out of character?" said the sergeant, exhaling loudly, a film of sweat on his forehead as though it was all such an effort.

"No, not really," Adam replied flatly, eyes wandering to the silver buttons on the officer's jacket as he tried to see his own reflection, see how guilty he looked.

"Explain," said the constable, obviously eager to fill more pages.

"Well, her and Bill, William, they fought pretty often. Like cat and dog you could say," he said almost triumphantly, like he'd found the right combination to a complicated lock and was near freedom. A faint grin appeared on his lips as though he was absolved of all blame.

"Once a day? Once a week? Once a month?" said the sergeant, seemingly unable to get the dripping scepticism out of his voice. "How often exactly?"

"Well it would go along fine for a while and then things would just blow up."

"Blow up?" questioned the constable, an eyebrow raised.

"Yeah, you know they'd have a blazing row over something silly," said Adam, sighing, tired of them parroting answers back to him like it was a game of psychological tennis, wishing the sergeant would leave and take his smell with him.

"Was it ever violent?" said the officer, removing his cap to scratch his head and sending flakes of dandruff onto his jacket that he then brushed almost obliviously to the floor.

"No," Adam said conclusively. The police constable looked up from his notebook thoughtfully as though preparing to take over questioning. The not so thin blue line were standing side by side now like a comedy duo but without the laughs.

"She was pregnant, wasn't she?" he said right on cue, biting the end of his pen as though trying to suppress a smirk, like he'd finally stumbled on something, when obviously it was written down in front of him.

"Yes," he replied, throwing his hands up in the air, sick of being spoon-fed questions they obviously knew the answers to.

"William's the father?" asked the sergeant, taking over again, looking dubious as he ran a hand through the sparseness of his moustache, an action so clichéd he could have been a TV detective.

"As far as I know," Adam said, biting into his lip, anger and fear rising as he took another glance at the silver buttons.

"Why, did she sleep around?" shot back the sergeant, nose wrinkled with distaste as though he'd got to the dirty nub of the whole sordid affair.

"No. Look, would you like a drink either of you? Tea? Coffee?" he said, trying to break the monotony of the questioning, the awful wilful rhythm, wanting to go into the kitchen, throw cold water over his face and cleanse himself of the taint of their suspicious gaze.

"No, you're all right," said the sergeant, authoritatively answering for both men, offering the slightest hint of a smile. "And what was your relationship with her, with Sarah, Mr, Mr er ..."

"It's Adam Wright," he said, enjoying the policeman's embarrassment at having forgotten his name, calmed by how easily the professional act had unravelled to reveal bumbling incompetence. "We were friends, Sarah and I, the best of friends."

"She told you *everything*?" said the constable, pen at the ready.

"She told me she was leaving that day, I tried to talk her out of it but she insisted. She just brushed me off," he said, feeling lightheaded with the weight of his lies, willing them to leave, easing further back on the sofa in an effort to relax but all he could see were two big heads looming over him, unrelenting.

"Are you okay? Mr er ..."

"Mr Wright," said the constable, impatience in his voice as he came to his superior's rescue.

"I'm fine, it's just been an upsetting few days. We were all very close, the three of us."

"A happy threesome," said the sergeant, looking across at his colleague, tapping a finger against his chin. "But in the letter she wrote when she was leaving, Sarah talked about being betrayed by three of her best friends."

"Bill had a fling, she found out, that's it really," he said, shocked at how matter of fact he sounded implicating his own friends, but prepared for what he took to be an attempt to catch him out. "She thought I'd betrayed her, I guess, because I was not only a friend of Bill's but also best friends with the person he had an affair with, we all went to Spain together."

"I see. And who was the other woman? *If it was a woman.* You never know these days," said the sergeant with a judgmental sneer aimed directly at Adam.

"Helen Tidy, she studies at the university too, sociology."

"Okay, we can get her details from Mr Laws," he said as though he was thinking aloud. "When is he due back?"

"He has exams all day today, as I said," Adam replied. "Try tomorrow morning, I'll let him know."

"Mind if we have a quick look around? Then we'll be out of your way, Mr Wright," said the sergeant, smiling at last, presumably relieved that he'd finally got to grips with Adam's name.

He led them back out into the hallway, away from the cellar and towards the stairs, though they both stood briefly looking up the steep flight, big boots just half an inch of fabric away from Sarah's blood, from the truth. Adam only breathed out when they finally followed him to the bedroom.

"This is their room, Sarah and Bill's," he said, throwing open the door.

"Hmm," said the sergeant, giving the neat room a cursory glance like it told him almost all he needed to know, the constable peering over his shoulder like an over-eager child looking around a new home.

He was just about to turn on his heels when with a sudden burst of inspiration, Sergeant Price strode across the room in three quick steps and pulled open the built-in wardrobe doors with a flourish, like a magician showcasing his latest trick, to reveal the clothes so densely packed, they were about to spill onto the floor.

"She didn't take anything with her?" the policeman said, running a hand through the fabric of a dress as if it could possibly offer up a clue. "Now that seems a bit odd."

"She may have done," said Adam, trembling very slightly. "You know what girls are like, they have so many clothes."

"Well, it certainly looks like she left in a hurry," said the

222

sergeant, gently closing the closet doors and fixing Adam with another glare. "Were you here the day of her disappearance?"

"You were here since you said you tried to stop her, *right*?" reiterated the constable, making up for the sergeant's forgetfulness yet again with a worrying kind of efficiency, adding to the chorus of doubt in Adam's head. The policeman's bright, inquisitive eyes like those of a curious cat.

"Yes, constable, I was here, as we've already established. We'd made up since Barcelona but she was still upset. I heard her crying that day and saw her writing the letter and tried to talk her out of leaving. But I didn't realise she intended to leave right away," he said breathily, exhausted by the effort of answering questions, unsure whether the sergeant was totally incompetent or if it was all a ruse just to try and trip him up. "I went out to the shop and she was gone by the time I got back. I'd only been gone about half an hour."

"Did you have another disagreement that day?" said the sergeant, eyes boring into Adam.

"No, we did not, sergeant," he said firmly, finding strength from somewhere.

"We'll be back to see Mr Laws tomorrow," said the officer and it sounded more of a warning than an appointment.

They both moved out of the bedroom and Adam watched as the two bulky figures made their way awkwardly down the stairs to let themselves out. From the window he observed them walking down the garden path and shuddered as the constable made a point of looking back at the house as if he hadn't yet seen enough to satisfy his curiosity, not nearly enough.

CHAPTER EIGHTEEN

"What the fuck did you tell them about Helen for?" shouted Bill bursting into Adam's bedroom, the familiar smell of Issey Miyake hitting his nostrils, agitating him further, as did the life-sized poster of Damon Albarn grinning down cheekily from the wall. "It was you, wasn't it?"

"They're the police, what do you expect me to do?" Adam replied, turning sharply around from his computer screen, looking preoccupied, like he was doing something he shouldn't have been. "They were asking loads of questions, Tweedledum and Tweedledee, or whatever their bloody names were."

"Symons and Price," Bill said aggressively, not in the mood for his friend's attempt at jocularity.

"What?"

"Their names, Symons and Price," he growled, keeping his distance, fearing he'd lash out again as Adam turned back to his computer and switched it off with the sigh of someone who had been rudely interrupted.

"Oh, yeah, Symons, the big black guy," said Adam, running a bandaged hand through his hair then bringing it down to his side so rapidly it was like he'd developed a nervous tic.

"What's with the bandage?" Bill said flatly, trying hard to dismiss his friend's attempt to draw him in to his sordid appreciation of big black men, his mind drifting back to the bouncer from the gay pub in Soho. It was Bill who was twitching nervously now.

"This?" he asked, holding his bandaged hand aloft, playing for time, looking out of the window as if to search for an answer. "I did it cleaning up the driveway."

"Cleaning up the driveway?" Bill replied, bemused, knowing it was usually an effort for Adam to screw the lid back on the toothpaste. He moved across to the window that seemed so fascinating to his friend and ripped the curtains fully open to look down at the newly pristine drive.

"Yes, Sarah's dad came over and gave me a few quid to clean the place up. I guess he's thinking of putting the house on the market or something," he said, panicked into saying the first thing that sounded plausible, still staring out the window, past Bill, not wanting to catch his eye as he threw another few ounces of metaphorical earth on Sarah's grave, burying her under the weight of his lies. "I also chucked away some other rubbish like the TV box in the living room, Mr Darwood said the place was a mess."

"His daughter's run off and he's thinking about the fucking driveway, spring cleaning?" he said questioningly, pulling Adam roughly around to face him, their eyes locking, but instead of an answer he saw tears and uncertainty that mirrored his own grief and confusion.

"He's a mess like the rest of us, Bill."

"Yeah, I guess, but why did you have to bring Helen into this? She's got fuck all to do with anything," he shouted, anger rising again, threatening to spiral violently out of control.

"Brought into what? It's just questions, it's a missing person's inquiry not a murder hunt," Adam said airily, regaining his composure, sitting down again and fiddling disinterestedly with things on his desk.

"What the fuck," said Bill, covering the short distance between them and grabbing Adam roughly about the neck, pulling him around to face him again, desperate for him to take something seriously, for once. "This is my girlfriend we're talking about, *your* friend, and she's been missing for more than a week. You don't even seem to care."

"I care, Bill, of course I do," he said softly, their eyes meeting again, prompting Bill to let go of Adam's neck and sidle bashfully away, embarrassed by his outburst. "But you've read the letter. I'm sorry but I don't think she'll be back for a while."

"But what if something's happened?" Bill said, throwing his hands up in the air, frightened of reaching out but needing something, *someone.* "Why hasn't she called her parents?"

"Look, this isn't Hollywood, it's Hampstead. We're not characters in some slasher movie. The reality is people do run away. Even the police seem convinced that's what's happened."

"I don't know," he said, looking uselessly down at the carpet as if it could actually offer an answer.

"Bill," said Adam, standing again, putting a hand on his friend's shoulder, so close the smell of his perfume made Bill feel lightheaded but for once he didn't push him away, "no matter how hard it is, you've got to move on, forget her."

"Forget her?" he screamed, eyes blazing, fists raised, overcome by anger again, but Adam stood firm.

"I don't mean forget as in delete but try and imagine a life without her. There is a chance she might never come back you know."

"The police asked so many questions, so many," he said, feeling the anger dissolve into a sapping tiredness as he slumped onto the edge of his friend's bed. "It's as though they think I did something to her."

"Bill, they're just being thorough. You saw the letter, she's run away. What she went through in Barcelona, you know, that was a big blow," Adam said, positioning himself on the bed next to Bill.

"Did she say anything to you before she left? Anything? *Think*, even the slightest detail might help."

"Like what?" Adam shot back, soothing tone morphing into indignation, like he was defending himself from being accused of something, like he was trying to distance himself from that day, but his eyes remained an unnerving blank. "I talked to her but her mind seemed to be made up. There was nothing I could say."

"What I don't understand is why she didn't pack any clothes," he said, still eyeing Adam as if he could tell him why.

"Search me," he replied, shrugging his shoulders, standing up like he wanted to disrupt the conversation, alter its course.

"Don't you care?" said Bill, looking up accusingly.

"Bill, I care, but we've been over this a thousand fucking times," he said, voice rising to that horrible pitch that Bill so often wanted to squeeze right out of him, but instead he sat rooted to the bed for fear of what he might do. "You've really got to move on or you'll go mad."

"I know," he said quietly, realising Adam was actually making some sense in a period of his life that was making no sense at all.

"Look. Now the exams are over I'm thinking of going away

for a while, Hong Kong."

"Hong Kong?"

"My old man promised to give me some money in the summer, if I behave myself, you know, like a bribe. I'm meant to be working at Mars but I'm so over handing out Bacardi Breezers with a smile on my face," said Adam, laughing, his laughter strained, at odds with the mood.

"Money to get you out of his hair more like," Bill snorted, daring to imagine the pair of them sat knee to knee on a long-haul flight, terrified yet thrilled by the possibility of intimacy now that Sarah, part of his conscience, wasn't around to disapprove.

"He doesn't have any bloody hair," Adam said with perfect comic timing and they both laughed. "This is his way of never having to see me, the best solution for him and me. I'm sure I'd have enough money to help you out, you know, if you want to join me."

"I don't know," said Bill, uncomfortable at the large smile that had formed on Adam's lips. "I'll have to think about it for a while. I'm not sure about the situation here, the police. And why Hong Kong?"

"Fuck the police," Adam spat. "We're not under arrest. Think about it seriously. And as for why Hong Kong, it's just a place I've always really wanted to go to, especially after getting into Wong Kar-wai. His films make it look so edgy, so real. Plus it's in the news right now what with the handover and everything."

Bill had already turned away and was heading to the door, not sure what he was going to do in the next few minutes, let alone the hours and days that stretched ahead, and the awful yet tempting possibilities his newly independent status seemed to be offering up. The thought of Hong Kong began to preoccupy him almost as much as Sarah's disappearance.

Bill fingered the card in his pocket, Sergeant Price's business card, thinking it odd that even policemen had business cards now. The officer had asked him to call if he thought of anything else "relevant to the inquiry" or, of course, if he heard from Sarah. But days had gone by slow and grey and he still hadn't, still couldn't think of anything that would be of relevance to the piggy-faced sergeant, still had no idea where she might be. A sickening sense had crept up on him and become an inescapable anguish that he had to wrestle with every hour, the feeling that he would never see her again. Her last words to Adam, maybe *her last words,* seemed to haunt him. She "hurt from the inside out". That's how he was afflicted too.

Staring out of the window as he imagined her doing before she'd left so suddenly, staring out into another miserably long midsummer's day, he watched as an immaculate red sports car drew up outside the house. The Alfa Romeo Spider looked so stylish. Its aura of late 1960's cool contrasted with the neighbours' boxy Japanese saloons and its maverick appearance clashed with the certainty of today's blandness. But knowing who was inside made Bill as anxious as the policemen's visit had. He peered into the car and saw Smale behind the wheel. He feared letting him out of his sight, didn't want him to be obscured by the hedge before he'd got a good look at him and been able to gauge his motives. But the professor didn't appear to be in a hurry, he sat staring at the house as though attempting to decipher something too.

He finally clambered out of the car, waving a hand vainly through his grey mane of hair. Bill contemplated not opening the door to the professor, not letting him into the house, back into his life, but he heard music coming from Adam's bedroom and realised he was home too. Adam was sure to answer the door to Smale as he'd no doubt done before. It was horribly clear to Bill that the professor was no stranger to the house as he marched confidently up the garden path. *Bittersweet Symphony* reverberated through the wall, the song of this dreary summer, sounding absurdly resonant, but the impatient buzz of the doorbell cut rudely through it making him jump in anticipation of what was coming.

Typical Smale, he thought angrily as he reached the bottom of the staircase. Even through the frosted glass of the front door Bill could discern the professor's face twisted in irritation.

"Who's that?" cried Adam from up above him, nosey, intrusive as ever. Bill knew the professor could be there to see either of them *or both* but was too preoccupied to answer his friend.

"Well, hello Mr Laws, very nice of you to get out of bed," Smale said testily.

"I wasn't in bed," Bill replied, running a hand quickly through his straggly hair, feeling watched, as though scrutinised for any kind of flaw. He feared the professor knew exactly where he was faulty.

"Very unfortunate about Ms Darwood," Smale said casually, offering his usual understatement. "Was a lovely girl by all accounts."

"Still is," said Bill, glowering, outraged the professor had spoken about her like she was gone, dead.

"I didn't mean ..."

"That's okay," he said more evenly, slightly embarrassed by his outburst and waving away the professor's apology. He kept Adam's cautious optimism in the back of his mind. *People did run away, didn't they*? he thought, trying to convince himself.

"Who is it?" said his friend, more urgent now and so close he could feel hot breath on his neck.

Bill turned around and Adam was almost leaning on his shoulder in the doorway, panting as though desperate not to miss anything.

"Oh, it's you," he said as he rudely nudged Bill aside and came face to face with Smale. "What do you want?"

"Actually, I came to see Mr Laws. Why do you always insist the whole world revolves around you?"

Bill looked at Smale and then back at Adam as they gouged at each other with their eyes. He felt like a spectator at a contest he hadn't been invited to. He motioned to go back inside but his friend beat him to it, disappearing into the shadowy hallway like some wounded animal.

"Are you going to invite me in or am I going to stand outside in this blessed drizzle all day?" said the professor bullishly as though the exchange of almost murderous hate with Adam had never happened though it still seemed to blight the air around them.

"Yes, I'm sorry, er, sir, come in," Bill replied, finally motioning the professor inside. He felt unsure of himself, even more intimidated by the man outside the familiar four walls of his office, though the mix of perfume and cigarette smoke that he was now wafting around were uncomfortably familiar. And, yes, the high, sweet smell of alcohol was familiar too.

He showed his guest into the front room as he had the two police officers. It was semi-dark in the late June greyness. The TV was illuminating the farthest corner, illuminating Adam who was sat in moody silence in an armchair.

"Bloody weather," said Smale, sinking back into the sofa uninvited, making himself thoroughly at home as he pointed to the screen, the rain cascading off some spectator's umbrella on Wimbledon's Centre Court.

"Yeah," said Bill sadly. Even though he enjoyed tennis, all-round sportsman that he was, he had never really understood the two-week ritual in SW19 that the country seemed to cling to as though it offered some kind of comfort, like the royal family or Sunday roasts, the certainty that nothing would change. He grimaced as the cameras zoomed in on perennially depressed Henman fans, painted faces as garish as flesh wounds against the leaden skies.

"Do you think he can do it this year?" asked Smale to be met only by resounding silence. "No, neither do I."

"Can I get you a drink?" asked Bill, wanting to hurry Smale into revealing the point of his visit, feeling uncomfortable on a sofa that was mostly taken up by the professor's awkward frame. He placed an ashtray in front of him even though the fact someone was smoking in the house seemed an affront to the memory that Sarah had become.

Smale waved the offer airily away, blowing another stream of cigarette smoke at the ceiling. "I'd like to invite you to lunch, Mr Laws," he said magnanimously, like it was some longed for treat. "As you probably know I'm dean now, which means I won't have time for the minutiae of university life any more, for instance our weekly chats."

"Er, yeah," he replied, embarrassed at Smale revealing the existence of their meetings in front of Adam, but then he was beginning to suspect his friend already knew and had known all along. The professor terming him minutiae made him feel even more insignificant, compounding the inferiority complex Dolores had already drummed into him over the years.

"I take it that grunt means you'd love to come to lunch with me?" he said, chuckling at his own witticism and running another hand through his luxuriant grey hair.

"Yes," Bill replied, reddening, worried about how he'd get through lunch under Smale's scrutiny, concerned by the prospect of wandering hands in the compact sports car and edging a little further away from him on the sofa. But the professor's eyes continued to pore all over him like he was a racy piece of art on a gallery wall.

"I want to come," piped up Adam pleadingly from the corner, sounding like a sulky child.

There was an air of desperation there, thought Bill, like his friend was jealous of the idea of the two of them being at lunch alone together or worried he'd miss something. He realised this was exactly what Smale wanted Adam to feel.

"To keep an eye on us, Adam? Oh, I suppose it's all right," said the professor mock aggrieved. "But you'll have to squeeze into the back seat of the car. You've been acquainted with that before of course."

Bill laughed nervously as the grotesque image of Smale moving breathily over Adam's taut body in the cramped convertible came to mind, but his friend's hateful glare caused the laughter to die in his throat.

"Come on then children," commanded Smale as Bill meekly followed the professor to the front door with Adam right behind.

The drizzle had stopped and walking down the garden path as the sun peeked through the clouds, Bill imagined the sturdy-legged ballboys whipping the covers off to reveal the lush green of Wimbledon. A far more pleasant scene, he thought, than he was to face this lunchtime.

"The police have been over," said Adam flatly from the back seat.

Though the space was so confined that Bill felt he was talking directly into his ear and wanted to turn around and punch him, shut him up. He didn't want to talk about Sarah. He didn't want *anyone else* to talk about Sarah. He wanted to bury those feelings with the other horrors in his furthest recesses but he knew even they weren't distant enough.

"Ah, our very own boys in blue are on the case," Smale said with an inappropriate chuckle. He didn't so much as drive the vintage sports car as caress it, thought Bill, cigarette in one hand, classical music on the stereo, like he was a budding Inspector Morse. "They give you the third degree? The Spanish inquisition?"

"And why should they do that?" snapped Adam, the intensity of his voice grating again.

"Why?" parroted back Smale, driving noticeably more aggressively. "Oh, I don't know. You do happen to be the last person to have seen dear Sarah, that's all."

Dear Sarah, thought Bill. The professor hadn't even known her, had probably only ever set his greedy eyes on her from his office window. It was like he was deliberately trying to rile Adam, pin something on him, pierce through that horribly innocent sheen he'd perfected that made him irresistible to lecturers and elderly women.

"Well they should concentrate on catching real criminals for real crimes," said Adam indignantly, voice filling the whole car. "This is nothing more than a runaway."

"*Nothing more*," Bill yelled, wheeling furiously around, but Adam's aura of righteous indignation remained fixed and he wanted to choke it out of him. "My girlfriend's disappeared and that's all it amounts to, nothing?"

"Now, now boys," said Smale, voice rising an exasperated octave.

Bill guessed from the way the professor's mouth was perversely turned up at the edges that he was enjoying their squabble, but his interjection did have an effect and an uneasy silence descended, raised voices replaced by classical music and the purring of that vintage engine.

"Welcome to The Willy," said the professor, leading them into the pub at the end of Hampstead High Street.

Smale's hand seemed glued to Bill's shoulder, but it was hardly comforting.

The King William IV looked like any other pub, but he knew it was a gay pub, remembered how many times he'd walked past when he should have been walking home. That heady mix of temptation and self-loathing came back to him and it was an effort to put one foot in front of the other. Bill felt the sweat spring to his forehead. He swayed with the mixture of stale cigarettes and beer in his nostrils, concerned the pub's patrons would sense his fear like perceptive dogs and move in for the kill. Then as his eyes adjusted to the gloom, a fruit machine winking in the corner being the brightest, liveliest feature about the place, the array of middle-aged and elderly men caused his fear to morph into aching disappointment. It didn't have the buzz or danger of *that pub* in the West End, something he now knew he had to taste again.

All he felt were the eyes of the desperate, in varying degrees of decay, on his young flesh as Smale, obviously concerned by the competition, sat them down at a table closest to the wide-screen TV and furthest from the lecherous stares. The television, in contrast to earlier was now showing a Wimbledon bathed in sunshine. The coverage, artful shots of balletic play and the "pop, pop" sound of the ball, embodied the very rhythm of summer. Watching it Bill longed to be out of the pub, away from prying eyes, away from Smale, sat on Centre Court with other lazy sunbathers and nothing else to think about than watching a ball going back and forth.

"I like Sampras myself," said Smale inanely. "Pistol Pete they call him."

It was possibly an attempt to break the silence or to "connect" (one of the professor's favourite buzzwords) with his students, Bill thought derisively, feeling uncomfortable at the unrelenting gaze of the dinosaurs standing at the bar, thinking how in a straight pub they'd be glassed. He imagined their tight, wrinkled flesh coming easily off the bone, but guessed their constipated expressions wouldn't change.

"Lunch is on me, guys," Smale prompted again, above a splash of applause from Centre Court and a "good shot" from the commentator. "Let's get a drink and then we can think about food," he continued fussily, grabbing two menus from the adjoining table.

Bill looked over at Adam, who'd been unusually quiet apart from the outburst in the car, but he appeared to be engrossed in the tennis, even though he professed a hatred for sport of any kind. It was like Adam also wished he wasn't there, Bill thought, like the lure of the sunshine streaming down outside the dingy pub was too inviting. He dared to imagine the two of them immersing themselves in it, like they were plunging naked into a hot bath together.

"Mr Laws, would you accompany me to the bar, please?" said Smale in his commanding tone.

Bill looked across at Adam again. His expression had changed with the professor's words and his face was now clouded with what looked like worry, his brow furrowed by lines, ugly lines that didn't really belong on someone so young. Adam stared helplessly back as though he'd just been told some devastating news and there was nothing he could do about it.

"Well?" said Smale, ignoring Adam and urging Bill to follow him to the bar as he got up from the table.

"Okay," he replied, rising too, while his friend sat, rooted and speechless.

"Drink, dear?" said Smale to his former lover, his voice dripping with hate.

"Bacardi Breezer, cranberry," he said, shrugging his shoulders morosely, like nothing mattered any more.

"Still got a sweet tooth, but it's the only sweetness left in that body," said Smale with real venom, turning to the bar like he didn't even expect a comeback such was the viciousness of the barb.

Bill again was left feeling like he was intruding on the messy denouement of a love affair, the final act, and was glad of some respite as they reached the bar. But the relief didn't last long because as the barman was pulling their pints, the Bacardi Breezer already sat on the counter garish against the rich wood, Smale licked his lips and turned towards him ominously.

"Mr Laws, I hear Adam's asked you to join him on his trip to HK," he said, voice at a whisper, even though Adam was around the corner and well out of earshot. "If you want to find out the truth about Sarah, go."

"What do you mean the truth?" spat Bill, grabbing Smale roughly by the lapels of his tweed jacket, rough cloth in his hands, whisky breath in his face. "What do you know?"

"I don't *know* anything," he replied and something in his steely eyes made Bill let go, back off, the barman hovering busily, waiting for his money. "Call it intuition, I don't know, just go to Hong Kong, it will help."

As he walked back to the table, Smale's words etched into his brain, he looked at Adam and wondered. He went over those words again and again in his head, haunting words that weren't going to go away.

CHAPTER NINETEEN

They arrived at The Peninsula and even the absurdity of its dated opulence seemed to mock him, make him feel totally undeserving. He was only staying a couple of nights, *he and Bill* were only staying a couple of nights, but Adam was desperate to take both their minds off what had become the ever-present memory of Sarah. He thought such a magnanimous gesture might just work its magic on his friend. He knew it would probably take more than a fancy hotel to get what he really wanted, but he hadn't completely lost hope, not having come so far.

Adam was also determined to experience the prelude to his capture, if it was to come to that, in style. He didn't want to feel like a fugitive, like he was being hunted. Even though Symons and Price, the spunky constable and the piggy-faced sergeant, hadn't visited the house again, he knew the truth would eventually out because people actually cared about Sarah, even if he didn't, and he knew how far that would work against him. But he didn't want to slink away from life the way the British had on the very ground he was standing on just a few weeks before. He'd watched as Tony Blair had grinned inanely through a highly stylised handover ceremony, 100 years of history reduced to a fireworks display, clammy handshakes and a few canapés.

Unlike Hong Kong's new Chinese masters, Adam wasn't looking to the future any more. He couldn't see past tomorrow because his thoughts were clouded with fear. He knew though as he looked at wide-eyed Bill that he had to enjoy the now. He'd already quit his job at Mars Bar, after having not turned up for several weeks and had made no plans for a second year at university because he knew there could be no going back, no going back to the way things were before, not now Sarah's body lay festering on an overused mattress in a lonely beach hut.

"Hey, what's bugging you?" said Bill, turning from the window of their hotel room where he'd been standing for several minutes. Yes, they were sharing, twin beds of course. "Just look at this fucking view. Isn't it amazing?" continued his friend, unable to keep the youthful enthusiasm out of his voice, turning back to whatever was out beyond the glass as though he couldn't believe anything could concern Adam when everything was so exhilarating and new.

Adam didn't even feel he could answer his friend, match his wonderment, he knew with a terrible resignation that he could never be so carefree and youthful again. Even if the body was never found there would be a grim penance to be paid. Finally he gave in and looked at the view over Bill's shoulders, his broad back invitingly close. In his warped mind he couldn't help but fantasise what was going on behind the windows of the gargantuan high-rises scattered all around glinting intimidatingly in the sunlight. He also wondered what possibilities could arise closer to home as he laid a hand on his friend's back.

"I want to talk to you about something," said Bill unusually softly, finally turning from the window, shrugging the hand from his back.

"Can't it wait?" Adam replied dismissively, not able to bear another emotional diatribe about how much he missed Sarah, like he'd bored him with almost continuously during the flight over. It was as though Bill didn't want to think about anything else, which was odd because when she was alive he'd spent most of his time trying to get away from her through his various dalliances, thought Adam. Besides he was hungry, which overrode everything else. "I'm going to eat downstairs in the lobby restaurant, we can talk there."

"I need a shower," Bill said quietly, brooding again. "I'll see you down there in ten. The lobby you say?"

"Yeah, you know, next to the entrance where everyone's sat around tables eating. Duh!" he said derisively over his shoulder, catching a glimpse of his friend stripping off his shirt as he left the room. He was captivated all over again and felt oddly comforted that his desire had endured despite everything.

On his way down to the lobby in the lift he wished he hadn't been so dismissive about what Bill wanted to say, maybe it was finally what he wanted to hear. Still, Adam thought, he'd waited this long, he could wait another 10 minutes.

Adam had only been gone a couple of minutes but Bill couldn't stand it any more. The doubt and curiosity planted in his head by Smale in the pub was taking him over, intruding on his every thought.

"If you want to find out the truth ..." he repeated under his breath again as though it offered some kind of legitimacy for what he was about to do. He dragged Adam's backpack onto the bed, feeling nervous as well as a bit stupid because he didn't actually know what he was looking for, apart from *the truth* of course.

He felt even more ridiculous unearthing the neatly folded shirts and trousers, so pristine compared to his own hotchpotch. It dawned on Bill that maybe Adam could be an innocent in all of this and that the professor was just being facetious. He'd sensed how turbulent their relationship had been. Their mutual hatred had poked ominously through the thin veneer of civility that afternoon in Hampstead. As he brought out a pair of socks he was beginning to wish he hadn't listened to Smale and his bitterness.

Bill was considering stuffing everything back, but beneath the inanity of underwear his hand touched something plastic and hard and he knew almost immediately it was the laptop. Surprised and thrilled all at once he drew it out as though he'd unearthed a big secret. Flipping up the screen he batted the "on" button. Battery powered it whirred into life but its efficient hum was drowned out by the shrill ringing of a telephone. Initially it made him jump, but his unease turned to annoyance as it took him a minute or so to locate it. Tentatively he picked up the receiver.

"Where the hell are you?" came Adam from the other end.

"Look, I've just had a shower," he lied. "I'll be down in a few minutes."

"Shall I order for you?"

"Just get me a cheeseburger or something," he replied impatiently.

"Bill, we're in China for fuck's sake and if you hadn't noticed, The Peninsula is not a cheeseburger kind of place."

"Oh yeah, sorry," he said but the line had already gone dead and he slammed the receiver back into its cradle, anxious to get back to the humming computer.

As he turned back to the screen it wasn't looking good, there was a box demanding a username and password. He clicked the right-click of the built-in mouse pad and Adam's name appeared in one field but his attempt to call up the password saw it remain an infuriating blank, the cursor blinking busily away in the empty space as though taunting him.

"Shit," he said.

In his frustration, for he was almost certain he'd never beat the password, Bill tried silly combinations like "*ABC123*". He also tried band names and lead singers he knew Adam was partial to. Then he had a thought, suspecting another of his obsessions could be the key, Adam's obsession with him, which had only become clearer and clearer since Sarah's disappearance. Once he'd gone into his friend's room and been disturbed to find an exercise book almost blackened by "*Billy Boy*", the nickname lovingly coined by Sarah but hijacked by Adam had been scrawled on every available space on the cover. He had opened the book with trepidation but found the pages were empty. He never saw the book again and was too embarrassed to mention it to Adam. He typed "*billyboy*" into the blank field, clicked "enter" and waited. His heart pounded because instead of "*invalid password*" flashing up on the screen it looked as though the computer was actually doing something. Finally, with a triumphant little beep, the black background disappeared to reveal a standard desktop with a number of icons. Through his fear and excitement it took him a few moments to focus, but his gaze eventually settled on a Microsoft Word logo labelled "*Diary*".

He double-clicked and found himself in a normal Word document as the phone rang again. His fingers jumped nervously across the keyboard, but he let it ring and ring this time. Panicking, sensing he was about to find something, Bill scrolled down frantically, not really paying attention to the pages of text, though he did notice dates clearly marked above each entry like it was a proper journal. As he scrolled further and further down, faster and faster, he realised he was only looking for one date, the day in June when Sarah had disappeared. Looking at the screen with unblinking eyes, the phone ringing urgently in the background, he zeroed in on that day and was shocked by the brevity of the entry, just a few lines in fact. Despite his rising anxiety, he forced himself to focus and read it: "*And then I pushed her down the stairs, I just couldn't take it any more, her any more, but I didn't mean for her to die. God how I wish she hadn't died, anything but that. It was an accident, only an accident ... Sarah's dead.*"

He read and reread it through his tears, hoping there was some kind of get-out clause, some mistake, but it was there in front of him, black text seared onto a blinding white screen. A few simple words strung together, that infused him with the anger to kill. Bill ripped the still ringing phone from its socket and sent it clattering against the wall where it exploded into splinters of plastic.

As he glided down to the lobby in the lift, calm descended again, a cold, calculating calm. He could see things more clearly. There was the need to avenge Sarah's death, *her murder*, and the need to cleanse himself of homosexual feelings. Now he was finally seeing it Dolores' way, the world really was only good or evil, black or white.

Adam looked across the candlelit table as Bill came towards him through the ridiculously lush lobby. A storm was raging outside, drops of rain exploding violently against the vast windows while the Palm Court orchestra played with such an urgency it suggested there may not even be a tomorrow.

"You look terrible," he said as his friend approached the table, shocked by Bill's dishevelled appearance. His downcast eyes so at odds with his bright appreciation of the harbour view less than an hour ago.

"I'm just jetlagged," he snapped, still not looking Adam in the eye, hovering over the table like he didn't want to sit, but he couldn't refuse when one of the waiters scurried across and elegantly pulled a chair out for him with a "sir" and a look that suggested colonialism wasn't dead.

Still gazing at Bill, his shoulders slumped, eyes ringed with a tiredness that he knew was more than just jetlag, Adam felt totally fraudulent for the first time, as fraudulent as the flunkies in starched white uniforms running around like it was the 1920s.

But he did what he did best and acted, acted as though what he'd done to get this far, to get Bill alone in a hotel room, was for a greater good, for *their* greater good. He tried to convince himself it had all been for the two of them, but Sarah's death had changed things, almost given him a conscience. Adam could feel his selfishness acidly eating away at him.

"I thought you had something to tell me?" he prompted his companion, still unwilling to give up, to finally admit defeat, sipping casually from his blackcurrant fizz, but feeling far from casual.

"Not now," Bill grunted, almost inaudible above the timely strains of *Strangers in the Night*, his tears clearly visible even though he stayed looking down at the tablecloth.

Adam wished they were joyful tears, relief that finally they could both be together. All the best films had fairytale endings, he reasoned, but Bill's lunge across the table shocked him out of months of delusion. He felt a rough hand around his shirt collar, and as he looked into the wildness of Bill's eyes he knew with horror that *he knew*.

"You killed her, didn't you?" Bill hissed, struggling to moderate his voice, rising from the table and dragging Adam towards him. "You fucking murdering faggot, I've seen the diary."

"Is everything all right, sir?" said a waiter pathetically, standing a few feet away, wary of getting too close.

The distraction was enough. Adam took advantage of the moment's hesitation in Bill's grip and wrestled free. He ran for the side entrance, people scattering as he went, knowing he was running for his life, the lies and deceit over. He exited the hotel and into the packed crowd of shoppers and tourists of Tsim Sha Tsui. The pavement was still slick from the earlier rainstorm but he kept running, sensing Bill was close, fear pulsing furiously through his veins. Tempted to look back, he saw his pursuer bearing down on him, just a few metres behind, words spilling grotesquely out of his mouth, but inaudible as yet.

He kept running. Such was the madness and intensity of his gait that the seething crowd seemed to miraculously part. He could hear Bill's relentless stream of taunts coming closer and closer. Desperate, he careered down the steps and into the bowels of an MTR station. He hurdled the ticket barrier athletically and people dispersed, but the following footsteps and the murderous diatribe, only got louder and louder, booming ominously in his ears along with his own heartbeat.

He awkwardly negotiated more stairs and finally arrived at a platform. He hoped to jump on a passing train but the station was at its fullest and he found it difficult to move along. Then with inevitability he felt an arm catch around his neck, and even though there were tens of people surrounding him, he didn't see anyone else but his pursuer. Bill's face an inch from his, like he was about to kiss him, but instead he breathlessly wheezed, "Why? Why did you do it?"

Adam was captivated by the face he loved but it was no longer love but fear that inflamed his every thought and he couldn't answer the question because there were no answers left, no justification.

The crowd parted again, like considerate guests at a wedding watching as two lovers entwine and they wrestled each other in that strange dance boxers do when they're both too spent to fight, neither wanting to let go. Suddenly the edge of the platform appeared, blackness just an inch or so away, yawning open, and a slight nudge was enough.

He fell, disappeared into the gloom that offered only concrete and metal. There was an ominous whoosh of air from the tunnel, a body framed in headlights, a sickening screech of brakes and then the cry that was horribly human.

CHAPTER TWENTY

Bill had fallen, like Sarah had, at his own hands, Adam thought, as he made his way roughly out of the crowded platform area. It had been so packed that only those directly next to him had seen the incident and they simply cowered from him as he used his murdering hands to exit. He elbowed people aside desperate to get above ground, get back to the hotel and get away.

Sprinting up the escalator it was a relief to feel the freshness of the air, signalling he was close to the mayhem of the street, closer to freedom. For a while Adam stood panting outside the exit, not really seeing the battalion of people marching by, noticing for the first time that he'd just come out of Tsim Sha Tsui station, a few minutes before it had just been a blur, a means of escape. He attempted to retrace his route back to the hotel but was confused, given the enormity of what had just happened and the fact that previously he'd only been focused on keeping a step ahead of Bill. The brashness of the neon, the roar of the traffic, the hum of the crowd had all been on the periphery, but walking now, desperate to avoid drawing more attention to himself, was almost worse than running. Running made it easier to avoid catching anyone's eye, which he was afraid of doing for fear it might reveal his guilt.

Finally arriving at the relative calm of the water's edge on his way back to the hotel, Adam took a snatched look across at Hong Kong Island, knowing that the clock was ticking on his freedom. The seemingly infinite towers that stretched across the skyline were lit up against the shadowy border of The Peak, but the awe-inspiring view meant nothing to him. He knew his vacuity would soon be replaced by pain and he was afraid of facing it as he took one final desperate glance across the water, his tears falling into the black vastness of Victoria Harbour.

Back in the hotel room he slung clothes first into one backpack then the other, so disorientated by panic he didn't even know which items were Bill's and which were his. He was intent on erasing all traces of both of them from the room, from ever having been there. A cacophony of thoughts were screaming in his head as he zipped up the last full backpack, contemplating his return to London to "face the music". He looked bitterly at the phone in pieces on the floor, where he guessed Bill had finally faced, if not the music, then at least the truth, the debris a frightening reminder of the intensity of his anger. Sitting on the edge of the bed he felt paralysed when he thought of where that energy could have been channelled, where that passion could have led.

The sweat was dripping from his forehead as he entered the reception, as if the guilt of what he'd done over the past few weeks was scored on his face. Adam wondered whether he could even manage the ritual of checking out when all he wanted to do was run.

He watched longingly as Bill's bag was wheeled away across the marble floor through swarms of guests to "left luggage" and emotion bit into him like he was watching a lover walking away, never to be seen again. Even in his delirium he pushed ahead of a queue of people and handed his credit card over to the harassed desk clerk almost without thinking at the presentation of what he took to be a bill. He hoped the receptionist wouldn't twig and hold to him account for the ruckus in the restaurant earlier, or worse, much worse.

"Leaving so soon?" said the receptionist, looking at him quizzically, the fact that he hadn't even been there a day only just registering with Adam, as it felt like weeks already. The sound of police sirens not far away shook him quickly back to reality.

"Erm ... I have to return home on urgent business and, my, er, friend has gone travelling," he stammered hopefully, praying he'd uttered the magic words. The clerk was too busy to care anyway, too distracted, swiping his card, a receipt thrust back into his sweaty palm.

"Excuse me, sir," came a voice as he was turning away from the reception desk. He knew instinctively he was being addressed. All his senses were on alert. He hesitated and contemplated running before turning back to his inquisitor.

"Yes?" asked Adam, prepared for anything, ready for the end.

"Forgive me, I almost forgot, you received a call when you were out, from a ... Professor Smale," said the receptionist reading from a slip of paper. "Or maybe it was for your friend, he asked to speak to a Mr William Laws."

"Yes, my friend's gone away for a couple of days, as I said. I'll let him know," snapped Adam through a thin smile, tears of relief springing to his eyes. He snatched up the slip of paper but let it crumple to the pavement as he exited the hotel, amazed he was still free. Meanwhile the wailing sirens seemed to be coming closer and closer and he quickened his stride to a trot, terrified the police were coming for him to cart him away and chuck him into some squalid black hole.

Despite the urge to run, the thought of Smale nagged at him, the fact that he'd called, as if he could offer some kind of solution to the whole problem. Although it was ridiculously early in the UK, he located the nearest payphone, looking around to check for pursuers as he did so, and dialled. He was peeved the professor had made the long-distance effort on Bill's behalf not his and was concerned at what he could want, what he had to say to Bill.

"Hello," came a croaky voice finally from the other end, apparently braced for bad news which calls in the middle of the night usually heralded.

"It's me, Adam," he said trying to sound breezy, squeezed into a phone-box outside the hotel, backpack at his feet, death on his mind.

"Do you know what bloody time it is?"

"Oh, I'm sorry, I guess I miscalculated the time, but the hotel informed me you called," said Adam, playing the innocent, which now, even he knew, was not even close to convincing.

"I was calling *Mr Laws*, questioning after his welfare. He seemed pretty down that day in the pub," Smale replied accusingly. "How is he?"

"We had a fight and he ran off," Adam blurted out, guilt and exhaustion not quite dulling his instinct for survival, his capacity to lie, but for him it was nearly a confession.

"Adam, dear, why are your friends always running away?"

"I'm cutting short my trip, I'm coming back," he said,

ignoring the professor's question because he knew he couldn't answer it.

"You should hold onto your friends, you never know when you might need us," said Smale, sounding as canny and calculating as ever despite the thousands of miles between them. "By the way, at our last meeting Bill told me he has gay feelings, that he wants you."

"Oh, my God," stuttered Adam, shocked into dropping the ironic inflection for once, replacing the phone with a crash as the impact of the words resonated.

On the way to the airport, still paranoid with the fear he could be stopped by the police at any time and immersed in the dread of returning to England, Bill's words and the matter-of-fact way they'd been delivered by the professor seemed to be the cruellest possible revenge on all of their parts: Smale's, Sarah's and Bill's. He wished now he'd said something earlier, been honest with his friend and with himself. He'd been so concerned about appearing cool, so worried about rejection and so terrified of finally getting what he wanted. Bill had become his whole reason for living, and he knew he couldn't have taken the devastation of that dream turning sour. But that's exactly what had happened, he thought, finding it painful to even look out of the window at the life continuing all around him.

Adam walked out of the airport, unsure of where he was going, unsure of himself. Then he felt someone touch his shoulder, about to make his decisions for him.

"I'll take you to the city, good price," said an old man with a crooked smile, looping a guiding arm through his. He had no choice but to follow the driver to his taxi, a garishly painted Toyota shimmering in the heat.

He had cancelled his flight to London at the last minute and flown instead to Bangkok. A perverse grin brightened his features as he realised, exhilarated, that he wasn't about to face the music after all.

CPSIA information can be obtained at www.ICGtesting.com
Printed in the USA
BVOW04s0004260214

346044BV00003B/161/P

9 781899 713134